# OLEG SAPPHIRE
# ALEXEY KOVTUNOV

# ME AND MY DEMONS

With our best wishe.

A. Kovtunov

Enjoy the adventure!

## Book One

Magic Dome Books

Me and My Demons
Book #1
Copyright © Alexey Kovtunov, Oleg Sapphire 2025
Cover Art © Vladimir Manyukhin 2025
English translation copyright © Liath Gleeson 2025
Published by Magic Dome Books, 2025
ISBN: 978-80-7702-266-8

# ALSO BY THE AUTHORS:

*The Healer's Way*
A portal progression fantasy series
by Oleg Sapphire & Alexey Kovtunov

*An Ideal World for a Sociopath*
A LitRPG series by Oleg Sapphire

*Ghost in the System*
An Apocalypse LitRPG series by Alexey Kovtunov

*The Order of Architects*
by Oleg Sapphire (with Yuri Vinokuroff)

*The Hunter's Code*
by Oleg Sapphire (with Yuri Vinokuroff)

*The Village*
by Alexey Kovtunov (with Dmitry Dornichev)

# TABLE OF CONTENTS:

# CHAPTER I

"ON YOUR KNEES, SLAVE!"

That was the first thing I heard when I opened my eyes.

"Did you hear me? ON YOUR KNEES, I SAID! I AM YOUR MASTER, AND YOU WILL OBEY MY COMMANDS!"

Trying to assert our authority, were we? I hadn't heard anything like it in a very long time... or, more accurately, I'd heard it plenty, but I wasn't usually the one being yelled at.

Damn... and it had all been going so well.

I looked around and took in the workroom around me. It was decently equipped, though probably only fit for the young apprentice of a rather inept master at best. There was no other way to describe it, and I was already putting it kindly. The state of the pentagram they'd used to summon me said it all.

"Are you deaf? On your knees, or I'll—" the figure in the grey, hooded robe waved his hands, losing his patience, and a dark pulse of energy flew at me. I felt a slight tingling sensation.

"Next time, it'll be even worse!" he leered menacingly.

I'd never understood these damn fanatics. I mean, you summon a demon, and the first thing you do is tell it to get on its knees? Didn't this moron know how proud demons were? Not to mention how powerful and partial to vengeance? If you wanted to get a demon on their knees, then you'd better have some serious authority. And this guy didn't have any... probably never had, either, or I would have smelled it on his soul.

And how had he even pictured this scene going, anyway? I was currently lying down, so what did he expect me to do? Hop up and then sink straight to my knees? Or just bend my legs from here?

"Messire, perhaps this demon is... defective?" suggested a second figure.

This one was significantly younger, but his voice betrayed no fear. His master's voice, in contrast, trembled occasionally, though whether from fear or anticipation, I couldn't tell.

"No, it's just stupid. Remember what I told you, novice? All demons are as dumb as rocks, but they're also rebellious, which is why you need to show them their place straight away," seizing the opportunity for a demonstration, the hooded figure turned back to me. "ON YOUR KNEES, BEAST!"

More yelling. This guy must have had mush for brains... Either that, or he hated his apprentice. I couldn't think of another reason why he'd be feeding him such nonsense. It was going to get the kid either devoured or torn limb from limb on his first summoning.

"Perhaps... I could try?" the novice's whisper was barely audible. After a moment's consideration, his master nodded.

I didn't need to use my eyes to see what was going on in this room. It was covered in pentagrams, along with symbols of both summoning and containment.

The novice thanked his master and stepped towards me.

"STOP!" the senior mage suddenly cried. "You can't step into the summoning circle."

"What?" the novice's eyes widened. "But how am I supposed to teach him to obey from here? You know my special techniques. Plus, my protective tattoos will keep me safe." The novice suddenly threw off his robes, revealing himself to be a boy of about twenty, every inch of his skin covered with ink. He looked like one of the convicts they shipped to the Order of Inscribers for the students there to practice on. And it wasn't always the most talented or experienced students, either... Sometimes, it was the worst students, working on punishment exercises.

The boy moved confidently towards me, totally confident that I couldn't hurt him. Could I, I wondered? I still wasn't exactly sure what I was actually working with. I'd been in this body for fifteen minutes at most, and I had to admit, I was having trouble getting my head around it. It would have been a different story in my own body, of course. In *my* body, I could have killed them both with barely the blink of an eye. But that wouldn't work here... or would it? I had to pull myself together. But I had no time...

The boy booted me hard in the stomach.

"On your knees, worm!" he cried, kicking me again and again. His enthusiasm was admirable, but he seemed to have neglected his physical training while studying all that magic. Even in this new body, I barely felt his blows. If the demon they'd actually been trying to summon had been here in my place, it would have just laughed. I could also have laughed, of course, but I didn't want him to go and get the crowbar again. Which reminded me — I was going to lodge a complaint about that crowbar to the appropriate authorities here, if they existed...

I had a rough picture of what had happened here. Hell, I'd done similar rituals myself, though not quite on this level. And I had a complaint: where was this body's memory? Why did I have only fragments of it? I knew everything there was to know about this world, but I hadn't a clue about who this body's owner was or the things they'd done. This wasn't exactly crucial information, but as an educated individual, I liked to learn — though it seemed there wasn't much to be learned inside this head. I concluded that the person must either be very stupid or still in the early stages of development. Seriously, how could a person have all this information about cars, but not understand how they work? How could you not care about something so important? Wouldn't it start eating at your soul while you were driving around? Shocking. Or take guns... *Insert the bullet into the chamber and pull the trigger.* That was all! Had this body ever even held one in its hands? Even with the scant knowledge I had, I was pretty sure a gun was more complex than that.

"Had enough, beast?" the boy asked, clearly pleased with himself. He also looked... tired. I just kept on lying there, thinking my thoughts. This body had sustained some soft tissue damage, but the organs were intact, which didn't say much for the novice's kicks. The kid needed to go lift something heavy. Exactly why he needed to lift something heavy, I wasn't sure... but my new memory seemed to think the phrase was appropriate, so I went with it.

"Messire! This demon is dumb," the boy turned his back on me to complain to his master.

"It happens," the senior mage stroked his beard. "Perhaps the ritual went wrong somewhere. Planting a demon inside a human body is a complex process, after all, and I haven't mastered every nuance."

"Damn the ancient bloodlines!" the boy's fists were clenched with rage. "If they didn't hoard their knowledge so greedily, then people like us could make the world a better place."

I had the urge to laugh, long and hard. Talentless amateurs talking crap about other people? I'd heard that one before. Losers with barely a few hundred years of experience under their belts, willing to spill the blood of others but never their own, complaining about life being unfair, about the big, bad secret societies who won't share their knowledge — even though the talentless losers deserve it more! Of course they do! Oh, yes, they could use that knowledge to... uh... get revenge on all their enemies! They know they could! They've been on the other end!

People like that always hide behind their lofty goals, but give them even a lick of the power *we* possess, and they lose their heads. All of a sudden, they're living it up: beautiful women, wealth, conquests and glory, the power to murder their enemies...

And the real trouble started when it came to women. I remembered one such case. The guy was a water mage. He attained some relatively impressive (though not mind-blowing) knowledge on account of his wife belonging to an ancient bloodline. As soon as he'd mastered a chunk of that knowledge, he dumped her. And then, he started killing... The man had a lot of enemies, so he killed a lot of people. The thing was, not all of those people knew they were his enemies; they might have jostled him in a crowd, or mocked him publicly, say. And his killing spree might have continued if he hadn't laid eyes on god's most perfect creation

— or that's how *he* saw Armanda, at least. He decided then and there that she would be his… *plaything*, so to speak, and kidnapped her. He got away with it, too. She was weak, brand new to the world, and didn't know him at all. But the Architects of the Order, of which Armanda was a member, knew the mage all too well.

They say that two thousand years have passed since the woman they now call Architect Armanda, Creator of the Twelve Terrors of Molfern, was kidnapped, and they say that the man who did it is still imprisoned, kept artificially alive through medical means.

It was a foolish tale — and a true one. I knew it was true, because the head of the Order himself had recounted it to me once when I visited on business.

"Damn," the novice looked crestfallen. "All those resources out the window."

"Boy!" the senior mage raised his voice. "What did I tell you? Nothing is ever in vain. This demon will still be of service to us. Get out of the circle, and I'll start summoning a *real* demon. Then, we'll watch how this one reacts."

"A real one? Do you think they're starting to suspect something? That's what I thought at first, but they turned out to be a lot… well… stupider than I'd assumed."

For the next six hours, I just lay there and chilled. If I moved, I'd have to avoid putting strain on my new body, and I was too lazy for that. My soul had only just landed in it, and you could say it needed time to adjust. Well, either that, or to kill the body, which happened in cases of incompatibility. It could also be more complicated than simple incompatibility. Sometimes, for example, a person would sign a contract when their body and soul already belonged to someone else, which then made inhabiting them difficult.

While I lay, I listened to what the senior mage and his apprentice were doing. The two of them thought I was a vegetable and were displaying absolutely no caution around me. Whenever they did get suspicious that I might be pretending, they'd hit me with some more blasts of dark energy from their artefacts, which were supposed to cause demons extreme pain. There was just one problem — these idiots hadn't realised that I wasn't a demon at all, but a human just like them, with a soul just as human as theirs.

I lay and listened to them arguing over what had gone wrong. They'd been trying to carry out a highly mystical, arcane ritual which summoned a demon into a human's body and bound it to serve.

Creating a 'demon' slave with no demon in, and one that can kick your ass to boot... wow. Their problem was they were nowhere near experienced enough to complete such a complex ritual. They had a single, charred spellbook, scavenged from the old estate of some demonology-inclined bloodline or other. The description it contained of the ritual in question was only partial, which was why they'd already killed more than a hundred people trying to make it work. I was actually their first success...

Hopeless! If only they actually understood what they'd done. They could have made good money off this experiment in more than one world. Well, that, or meet their deaths... at the hands of hunters, perhaps. Plenty of others would have a bone to pick with them, too, of course. After all, what could be more valuable than a human soul? What could be more important than the one thing a person carries with them from life to life?

I listened along calmly, not a worry in my mind. Why should I worry? There was magic in this body — the kind that suited me, even. The *demonic* kind... Plus, I was able to move already, which was an excellent sign. Naturally, that was the work of my own body rather than this one. I was also working on a highly sophisticated astral level to direct my new body's energy towards blocking the spots where necrosis was trying to set in.

"Ready! Let's begin," came the order from the most experienced demonologist in the room. Or so he thought...

"Should I call the others?" the novice asked.

"Yes — even Herman. I want him to see this."

The novice disappeared, and when he returned, he wasn't alone. Roughly twenty people entered the room. Only the one called Herman stood out among them; he was clearly of noble blood. His robes were finer, and he carried a blade at his hip, the hilt of which was adorned with a snake's head.

"My congratulations to the teacher," the noble-
man turned his attention immediately to the senior mage. "I imagine if you have succeeded here,
that you will soon be in a position to fulfil your
promise?"

This question seemed to make the other man
uncomfortable.

"It's not that simple. You see, this demon is
worthless — it isn't even functional. I'm afraid your
clan will have to wait a little longer for its army,"
the man cringed. "But we'll get there, I promise
you! We're on the right track!"

It was all clear to me now. The aristocrat was
here as an overseer for his clan. The demonologists
were probably investing in these two, hoping for a
return of demon-possessed soldiers who wouldn't
ask for a wage. Were the clan really that desperate? Or maybe they were prospering, if they had
money to waste on things like this...

These demonologists were nowhere near
strong enough to tame a demon this way. Demons
obeyed a strict hierarchy; the more power you had,
the more authority you possessed, and the strong
would never obey the weak. Sure, things like seals,
contracts, agreements and pentagrams could contain a demon, but for how long? Meanwhile, only
the very best demonologists could properly im-
plant a demon into a body, and even *they* needed
to be experienced with the ritual.

I studied Herman for a little while. He certainly
looked like he could afford all this. All the rituals,
experiments, sacrifices and whatever else they

were doing here. His only role was to sponsor the activities and occasionally observe, presumably on someone else's orders.

As far as I could glean from my current body's memories, this world's demonologists had been oppressed by the politicians, the aristocrats, the police — anyone and everyone, basically — for a long time. Because nobody liked them, these demonologists usually lived in hiding, making it practically impossible for anyone new to learn the craft. This was also why they trained and practised in dark basements, away from prying eyes. Even the previous owner of this body, however, knew that demonology manuals could be purchased at private black-market auctions, although how to actually find those auctions was unclear.

"Well? When are we getting started?" Herman snapped impatiently. "I hope this experiment will be a success? My uncle is expecting big things."

"It's going to work," the senior mage replied firmly. "You know I'm the best!" he added, puffing out his chest.

"I'm beginning to have my doubts," the aristocrat muttered.

"Hey! Remember who you're talking to, boy!" the demonologist, twenty years his senior, scowled.

It was entertaining watching the two idiots argue. I was starting to like this world... at least there was some fun to be had here. I looked at them standing there, thinking they were strong, thinking they knew anything about anything... In reality, they may as well have been speaking two different languages. One was talking about profit, while the other only cared about power — and neither would be getting either one.

"And remember that I need twenty more vagrants by this weekend!" the senior mage declared, distracting himself from the pentagram he was drawing yet again.

"*You* remember that we need results," Herman parried.

"You'll get your results," the old man snapped with a dismissive wave, turning back to the almost-complete pentagram. "I'm on the right track! We have the proof now!"

"I hope so," the aristocrat shot back, settling into an ancient, creaky armchair in the corner once he'd brushed off all the dust. "Don't forget — my uncle is expecting a report."

"Well, then watch and wonder. I'll give you something to report," the senior mage smiled as he took a few steps backwards. "Look at this!" he waved an arm to reveal me, still lying in the centre of the pentagram. I opened one eye just a crack (I couldn't resist) but shut it again immediately. I'd been curious to see what kind of ritual they'd come up with, but now, I wished I could scrub the image from my mind. A blind man could have done better! And why did they have to choose pentagrams? The pentagram was a very complex web of magical channels, subtly but powerfully imbued with demonic energy — but *these* pentagrams had been drawn by the idiot senior mage. Or worse, copied...

"Do I understand correctly that your—" Herman contemplated for a moment — "your *achievement* here is this person lying before us? Is he even alive?"

"It's not a person!" old mage cried. "It's a demon! A weak, fractured demon, yes, but still a demon, imprisoned inside this drifter's body."

"Fractured?" Herman frowned in confusion. The senior mage's irritation was palpable. Honestly, how could the man not know what that meant?

"Crippled, weakened — call it what you want. It's out of energy, and it would need years to recover. Until then, it's just going to lie there like a vegetable, unable to move a muscle," the senior mage began to lecture the aristocrat, displaying his deep demonological knowledge. I could see Herman receiving this education with great amusement, since the man in the robe was basically talking pure nonsense.

"So, it's broken, then," Herman murmured. "I want to look at it up close."

"Don't go into the circle!" the novice cried, but Herman only waved him away, already walking.

"You think this shabby little scribble can hurt me?" he scoffed. He stepped calmly into the circle and prodded me disdainfully in the shoulder with his boot. "Hey, idiot!"

My first instinct was to stand up and greet him, but I thought better of it. I was too curious to see how this interaction in the circle was going to go down, and if I gave myself away now, then the surprise would be ruined.

"Can it hear me?" Herman asked. The senior mage nodded firmly. "On the other hand, what could I possibly have to discuss with a sad sack of bones like this... It's so weak and powerless, I won't even bother reporting back to Uncle about it. What a useless piece of trash. It belongs back in the cesspool it came from!"

I couldn't resist anymore and let a faint smile play over my face. In a way, Herman was right; I doubted he'd be getting to tell his uncle anything.

"Hey, look! It smiled! That's the first time it's expressed emotion!" one of the students had spotted my smile.

"The demon must like to be insulted," another student smirked.

By now, I was dying for them to start their ritual. I was afraid I was going to lie there for eternity, but half an hour later, the senior mage collected his students, asked Herman to step back, and then began to work his magic — if you could call it that. The room was illuminated by a red flash of energy, which those assembled promptly began channelling between the various parts of the pentagram. Some of the students began to create more pentagrams out of thin air, which they then fixed in strategic locations. To the average observer, it would have been a fascinating sight. The red flares of energy, the glowing lines and patterns... it really *would* look good from the outside. But only if you didn't examine the details... The old man appeared to be drawing Inbular, the very simplest symbol in the demonic summoning repertoire. How could anyone screw Inbular up? All you had to do was draw three straight lines! And yet, he'd managed to make a mess of even that, drawing one of the lines slightly curved. The outside observer might point out it was only off by a millimetre, but a *whole* millimetre? That was as good as a million miles!

Anyway... I closed my eyes, lay there and observed. My hands were itching to correct the mistakes all around me, but I had to stay strong. Otherwise, I'd spoil all the fun...

The senior mage and his students struggled on for another twenty minutes or so, until eventually, a new pentagram was flaring at the centre of the original one. This new pentagram was considerably smaller. Suddenly, a burst of red flame subsided to reveal a little demon. It was a red-skinned creature with a single small horn — the second one looked to have been snapped clean off. In fact, the little demon seemed to be damaged all over. Its tail was tattered and bent, while one arm had been broken and then set incorrectly at some point in the past. But as banged-up as it looked, this demon could easily have murdered almost everyone in the room, despite being barely three feet tall.

"I think I overdid it," The senior mage sighed wearily. "The demon we've summoned is stronger than I intended."

"*Humans*?" the demon looked taken aback. "How dare you!"

It took a few steps forward and crashed into

the pentagram's protective barrier. Rather than being deterred, however, the demon just bared its teeth. "You!" it pointed a taloned finger at one of the students. "I'm going to devour you first, and then, I'll enslave your soul! You think this pentagram can hold me for long? I am Gargok the Flesh Eater!"

Smoke began to pour from the demon's jaw. "I fought in the battle of Valdaris! Mock me at your peril!"

This show was getting better and better. I slyly opened one eye again — I didn't want to miss a thing.

"Close your maw, demon!" cried the senior mage, the first to come to his senses. "Listen to my commands, or I will destroy you!" he yelled. He gathered a ball of demonic energy and hurled it at the one-horned creature.

"You missed! Puny human," the demon hissed with a mocking grin, dodging deftly. In response, the senior mage began to gather two swirling balls of energy, one in each hand.

"I can shoot again," the old man smiled. "I command you to devour your fellow demon. And I want to see it! Devour him, and you will be freed! And if you don't — I will make you suffer," the senior mage clenched his fist, and the red flames of the pentagram flickered. "You know I have the power to cause you pain."

The demon shuddered as this exact realisation washed over it. It would have to make some concessions.

"Devour, you say?" the demon mused. "Easy! They don't call me the Flesh Eater for nothing. But who am I supposed to devour?"

The creature still hadn't noticed that the two of us were sharing a pentagram. Now, finally, the senior mage pointed at me, and the demon turned around and began striding slowly towards me. "Nothing personal," it snarled softly. "I'm just hungry."

I opened my eyes and lifted my head. The demon froze, recalculated, and then turned around and ran headlong into the protective barrier. After that, it found the farthest possible corner from me, where it curled up into a ball.

"Hey!" the senior mage shouted indignantly "What's going on? Students, punish it!"

A few students pulled out shiny whips and began hitting the poor demon as hard as they could. Each blow seared its skin and must have been excruciatingly painful. But instead of screaming or writhing in pain, the demon only stared at me in terror, trembling from head to toe.

"Either you eat that demon right now," the senior mage gestured for the whipping to stop, "Or I'll order them to kill you!"

"H-huh?" the little demon now turned to the teacher with pleading eyes. "I can die? Really? Oh, thank you!" Smiling, the creature raised a claw and slit its own throat in one deft movement.

For a full minute, the silence in the room was deafening. The demon bled out peacefully, while the rest of the room just watched him die.

"...What just happened, Messire?" a student asked the question that was burning on everyone's tongues.

"I... don't know," the senior mage gulped.

"I think that possessed body spooked the demon!"

"Impossible! What a stupid notion!" the senior mage growled. "It was probably just infected with something. We must study it."

"But... how, Messire?" the student's eyes were wide.

"We must prepare a new experiment. I need that possessed body's hand... Mito!" the senior mage turned to the student with the protective tattoos. "Cut off its hand and bring it to the laboratory. We'll summon a new demon and observe whether they react this way to all the parts of the body. And if they do, we'll create artefacts from its flesh to ward the creatures off!"

Wow, what a genius! If only he weren't such an idiot... How did he even come up with this stuff?

"If this works, my uncle will be paying you handsomely," Herman grinned, immediately perking up. "Let me cut the hand off myself."

"No! Messire told *me* to do it!" the student huffed indignantly.

"How dare you speak to me like that!" Herman shot back with equal indignance. "Have you forgotten who I am?"

"I don't give a damn! The senior mage gave *me* the order, so *I'm* going to do it!"

"Enough!" the senior mage raised a hand. "You

can do it together.”

The two ceased their squabbling and both stepped boldly into the pentagram. I just kept on lying there, giving no sign of life — though I did pre-emptively pull my hands in closer to my body.

“Hold your hand out! That’s an order!” the student barked, but I didn’t react. “I don’t think it understands. Maybe we should hurt it?”

“Demon! I command you not to harm us under any circumstances!” the senior mage said, entering the circle and coming towards me. He was clearly getting impatient. “Stand up, demon!” he cried, and I decided that this time, I’d pretend to play along. I raised up slowly until I was standing before him. I saw the deep admiration on the students’ faces. As soon as I was standing, they started whispering about what a great man their teacher was. A man so powerful that demons obeyed him on command! “Put your hand out!” he ordered. Huh, orders from an idiot... Oh well, why not follow them for a laugh? Especially when Herman was standing right in front of me! The aristocrat didn’t even have time to scream before my hand smashed straight into his nose. I even poured a little extra energy into the hand to make sure it connected with a nice *crunch.*

“Command complete!” I reported, barely stifling my grin as I looked at Herman, who was lying crumpled in the far corner of the room.

“Cancel command!” the senior mage roared. I shrugged and dropped my hand.

Meanwhile, the students had been scrambling

to grab their artefacts and were preparing to fight me. Idiots... They should have run away instead.

"This demon is dangerous! It's tricked us!" the senior mage yelled, fleeing from the pentagram as the realisation dawned on him. He then drew some more containment symbols and set to work on a new summoning spell. "I'll summon my strongest demons! They're going to tear you apart!" he screamed. My little joke had obviously upset him. I just stood and watched as he activated the summoning spell, his arms waving.

"Are you trying to scare me?" I laughed. The summoning was almost complete. "I'd advise against it if you want to live."

"You're going to die, creature!" the old man bellowed, waving his arms even faster.

"Just you wait till I get up! I'm going to tear you apart myself!" croaked Herman, who was coming to his senses. No one was preventing him from getting up, though — he was just taking his time, waiting for the senior mage to take care of things.

Just as the old man was about to complete the spell, I poked my toe into the pentagram and scuffed out a couple of key symbols. Then, I lent the whole pentagram a little drop of my power. There was a flash, and two horned, muscular demons, each nearly two metres tall, rose up directly behind the senior mage. As a rule, these demons usually appeared *inside* a pentagram, giving the demonologist the power to contain and command them. And they *were* inside a pentagram... for now.

"Hmm," I screwed up my face. "This is awkward, isn't it?"

"You—" murmured the senior mage, bewildered at what had just happened, but whatever curse he was about to throw at me never left his lips. A set of long talons speared him in the back, and then, the demon sliced off his head.

What followed was a bona fide bloodbath. I sat myself in the centre of the pentagram and languidly observed the proceedings. Oh, and it had all started out so well... Still, I liked this world. If all the demonologists here were as painfully stupid as this guy, then this was going to be fun!

It took the two demons about a minute to take care of all the students and the aristocrat, who managed to land one blow with his sword before it was taken from him and then... given back to him, in a sense. Let's just say the sword got a new sheath...

Once they were done, the demons stopped and looked at me.

"There's one hiding inside the pentagram!" the first roared.

"He can't sit there forever," the second snarled. "Let's just wait for him and devour him when he comes out! Ahahah!"

I mentally corrected myself: the demonologists weren't the only idiots around here. These demons were also too confident for their own good, to the point that it seemed like they barely had two brain cells to rub together... I'd concealed the strength of my soul from them on purpose, making sure it wasn't visible in my eyes, to avoid scaring them away too soon.

"Doesn't it make any difference that I'm the one who brought you here?" I asked them.

"This human talks a lot," one of the demons scowled. "As soon as those protections fade, we're going to discover the taste of your flesh! You can't hide in there for long!" I didn't find this particularly funny, but the two demons burst out laughing again.

That was the last straw.

I got up, walked to the edge of the pentagram and erased the border with my foot, destroying the drawing completely. All the protections evaporated. The demons stared at me like I'd just expressed an urgent death wish.

"Well?" a smile spread across my face as my eyes flashed red. "Who wants the first bite?"

# CHAPTER 2

"I'LL SAY IT AGAIN," I looked the demons up and down and smiled again. "Who wants to devour me? Come on over — dinner is served!"

"What do you think you're doing?" one of the demons protested, its voice a little hesitant. "We're demons, not some kind of riff-raff! You can't speak to us like that!"

"Oh, really?" I cocked my head. "Why are your knees trembling, then?" I pointed with a smirk. "*You're* the great demon here, not me. Or perhaps you've noticed something in my eyes?"

"Uh," mumbled the demon, scratching between his horns.

"Oh, come on — attack me already!" I stepped out of the pentagram and took a few steps closer to them. "No? Alright, then," I waved them away dismissively and went over to one of the many clumsily-drawn summoning circles in the room. 'Incompetent idiots' was the only way I could describe these local demonologists. It took a heroic effort to keep calm every time I looked at one of their... *creations*. Carefully examining the circle, I dipped my boot into the blood of an unfortunate student lying nearby. At my touch, his body collapsed into pieces. Demons liked their kills to be... graphic.

"So... a line here... a line there..." I made my way around the pentagram. "A little circle here wouldn't go amiss... There, that's it. It'll do," I said with a nod, turning to face the demons, who were standing frozen at the other end of the room. "Well, what do you think? Did you follow that?" My question was met with silence. I decided to act like they weren't there.

I went over to the aristocrat's body. He was lying in a corner, hands clasped around his unmistakeably expensive sword. "I'm pretending not to see you, by the way, if you didn't notice," I said without turning around. "You know you could—" I raised my head to see the two demons sprinting towards my pentagram, jostling with each other to try and get there first. "Hmm..."

Two brief flashes later, I was easing myself wearily onto a stool. "What a pair of cowards." I shook my head. "Oh, well. At least I can rest now."

As I sat there, the aristocrat's sword caught my eye. I stood up again. "What am I sitting around here for? I'm hungry! And my throat is dry!" I grabbed the sword, hooked it onto my belt and strode out of the blood-soaked room. There was nothing more to see in there, and there was no point just sitting around in some dungeon. It was time to go and see how the local demonologists lived.

Based on the summoning room and the corridor outside, I doubted they were living the high life. When I reached their living quarters, however, I realised it was much, much worse than that.

"This is... wretched," I murmured aloud as I stepped inside. They all seemed to live in one big room, sleeping primarily on the floor. I surmised this from the dirty rags spread out here and there, as well as the other belongings scattered around. There was only one bed, which was partitioned off with a screen. I assumed this was for the dean.

I tracked down the kitchen by smell, sniffing my way along the corridors. I was rummaging through the meagre provisions, trying to find anything edible at all, when I spied... a bottle of wine! I searched the table, but found no corkscrew, so I had to gouge the cork out instead. Still, this would help me relax a little and gather my thoughts. Time for a little swig...

"Urrgh!" I spat out the liquid, tossing the bottle away. That home-brewed swill was *not* going to help me relax. As I was tossing the bottle, however, I spotted a plate of food that looked ready to eat. "Well, at least this will be safe," I muttered, sniffing a pile of fried potatoes peppered with chunks of ambiguous meat. I picked up a fork, wiped it, and carefully scooped up a little of the food... Ugh! I spat the horrible stuff out straight away. It was inedible!

Casting my eye around the kitchen once again, I assessed the state of the supplies, and then sighed wearily. Starving as I was, I couldn't call any of this muck food. Sitting on the grimy tables were basins full of withered vegetables, while the fridge contained a meagre store of meat that was far from fresh. In fact, the state of the room in general left a lot to be desired. It needed a thorough cleaning at the very least. My suggestion would have been plenty of flammable liquid and a match; nothing else could possibly get rid of all that grease and all those terrible smells.

I'd already resigned myself to my munchless fate when I happened to spy a forlorn chunk of bread lying on one of the tables. Surely, nothing could ruin a piece of bread! I grabbed the dried-out crust and sank my teeth into the slice...

... Ah, that was better. As I sat there chewing, I considered my next move. First things first, I needed to know what I was dealing with. Here I was, sitting on a table, swinging my legs and enjoying a chunk of stale bread. An unusual situation, but not unheard of.

But what now? I was in an unfamiliar world. Was that unusual? Yes. I hadn't planned to come here. My original plan had been to wait in my own world until the dome surrounding it ran out of power. I'd been trapped in a dead world by some nasty tricksters, and they'd made sure I wouldn't be getting off it anytime in the next few thousand years. And I hadn't *tried* to get off it, either. I'd just vacated my body to go and float around without one for a bit. But something had gone wrong, and I'd found myself forcibly summoned here. Then again, I wasn't complaining. This was way more interesting!

Okay, what next? We had a mountain of dismembered corpses in the basement, along with a bunch of poor, innocent, butchered pentagrams. If the inner workings of the pentagram were a mystery even to me (and I knew a lot), then the mages who'd drawn these ones had been hopelessly fumbling in the dark. Of the thirty-odd spells they'd encrypted, only ten of them had actually worked, and even that was an unbelievable coincidence. After all, pentagrams like these shouldn't have worked at all. I seemed to be at the centre of a rare and unusual occurrence... Then again, that was the universe's way; you couldn't always predict what it had in store. Maybe a comet had flown by and enchanted a random person ten thousand years ago, and a random spell was activated somewhere at just the same second, and a synergy arose, and bing-bang-boom — I appeared here! It sounded silly, but for whatever reason, that was how it worked. And the *why* didn't matter, anyway — you just had to work with the *what*. The only thing that counted was me sitting here now, chewing on a hunk of stale bread, trying to figure out the first thing about this world.

Well, not *quite* the first thing; I'd managed to glean some core details from the memory of the poor sap whose body my consciousness was currently implanted in. Because of this, the electric lights on the ceiling were no surprise to me. I knew this was normal, even if I hadn't the faintest idea how it all worked. All I could say was that there was no magic involved, but the system still ran. *That* was the most magical part for me.

This body would serve me nicely as a vessel for adventures for the next three thousand years or so, after which, it would be time to switch back. Time to destroy the defensive barriers around my dead prison planet and take revenge on those who'd imprisoned me... but until then, I was just going to live my life and get acquainted with my new reality.

I went on another hunt around the kitchen, trying to ignore my intense desire to burn the place to the ground. I grabbed a cup of water, and then headed off to take another look around the demonologists' living quarters. Before I had time to properly search the quarters, however, I heard hurried footsteps in the distance. A moment later, the door swung open to reveal three black-robed figures. They were the very same robes the novices in the summoning room had worn. One of the figures was holding a short wand, while the other two were clutching small blades. They burst into the room, looking all around, and saw me.

"Who are you?" the one with the wand barked.

"Good question," I mused. Who *was* I? Never mind, I could ponder that question later; right now, these three wanted an answer. "I'm not a local, that's all I can say," I answered honestly. "Who are *you*?"

"Tie him up!" the one with the wand told his companions. "We have to interrogate him!"

"Hold on a second," I put a hand up to stop them, quickly draining my cup. "Interrogate me? About what? Are you looking for information? Knowledge? Is it money? Or do you want to know what happened in the summoning room?"

The three stood blinking for a moment, and then looked at each other.

"Activate defence!" cried the wand boy, and a dome of magic sprang up around him. The other two hurried to activate their own defensive arte-facts. I could only smile as I watched on.

"It's good to have defences," I said, assessing their capabilities. "But do you know the most im-portant part of any defence?" The room was silent for several seconds. "No?" I sighed heavily. Why did I always end up being the teacher? "The most important part of any defence is the part where it *defends* you."

When they looked at each other again, I hurled my mug at them. They smirked at my chosen pro-jectile, not even bothering to duck. Then, my mug touched the defensive barrier of the boy closest to me, and something exploded. The room was in-stantly filled with roaring demonic flames as a powerful shock wave blasted the boys in all direc-tions. The reddish-black tongues of fire pierced straight through their barriers, inflicting horrible wounds and killing the two knife-wielders within seconds, while the mage was left lying on the ground, moaning in pain. Tut, tut, tut... Hadn't I just given them valuable advice? Shame they hadn't taken it... Your defences should defend you — was that so hard to understand? If only they'd listened to me, they could at least have gone down fighting.

In any case, I was glad I'd anticipated this. I didn't have enough energy to scan the area right now, but experience had taught me to always be ready for guests, and I didn't think that these three would be the last.

As I left the living quarters, I noticed a staircase at the end of a long corridor, leading up. The staircase was blocked by a gate of sturdy steel bars, which I decided I wouldn't even try opening. Why bother? So that I could get out there and end up face-to-face with a mob of fanatics even sooner? No, thank you. I was better off sitting here and nibbling on my bread crusts. In here, at least I'd be in familiar territory. I could draw all the pentagrams I liked here, which gave me a way to restore some of my strength and energy. Charging off blindly right now would be suicide for me, and I wasn't that desperate just yet.

"You'll... never... leave here... alive," gurgled the mage, who was, to my surprise, not quite dead. My spell had worked as normal, though... Hmm. He must have had some defences after all.

While it wasn't a problem just yet, I knew I was expending quite a lot of energy. I was able to do this thanks to a little trick of mine. I'd managed to

draw several energy-sucking glyphs in the summoning room. Through these, the two demons had
shared with me some of the power they'd absorbed
as they killed their victims. To the local demonologists, these glyphs had looked like the random
scratchings of a demon's tail, but the *real* demons
had recognised them straight away — and boy, did
it make them mad! Not mad enough to stop them
from trying to flee with their tails between their
legs, of course. And how hilarious they'd looked…

I heard something out in the corridor. It was
time for me to act. I knew that they were coming
for my head, and judging from the noise, they were
coming in force.

I sat down next to the bodies to plan my next
move. What were we working with, here? I couldn't
summon anyone from my personal demonic gri-
moire, which I'd written in a past life. That meant
I'd have to gather all my demons from scratch, a
process that would be both difficult and lengthy.
At the same time, I couldn't have rumours going
around that I'd been reborn on another planet into
the body of a weakling. The demons from the
planes I normally frequented would definitely pass
that gossip around, and after that, it would only
be a matter of time before the information reached
some very undesirable ears. No, I'd have to use
some totally different demonic planes — and I happened to have some up my sleeve for just such an
occasion. And in fact, doing so would also con-
sume less energy; every world had its own, local
demonic planes, and I'd be able to dip into those.

Back in the summoning room, I did a quick scan and found a portal to a plane that caught my attention. It was a plane I had christened the Plane of Demonic Chaos, and for good reason. Those demons were a lot of fun, but only the bravest demonologists dared to call on them. They were... *intense*, and that was putting it mildly.

"Hmm, who to summon," I murmured pensively, dipping the tip of my sword into a nearby pool of blood.

As I pondered, I drew a standard pentagram, calibrated it to my plane of choice and threw in a couple of protection spells as insurance. Demonology was an exceptionally dangerous profession, so you could never have too many protection spells. With that in mind, I added a few more.

All that was left was to add the last few details. The footsteps carrying through the open door were growing increasingly distinct, as were the threatening howls mixed in with them, so I had to hurry, which meant taking a couple of risks.

"For the parameters... let's try... these," I scribbled down a couple of symbols. "Lower-level demon... random summoning!"

The moment these last characteristics were in place, I filled the pentagram with energy. The circle was a little less than two metres across, and as soon as my power flowed through it, all the symbols burst synchronously into demonic flame. And from those flames emerged... a miniature horse with a horn on its forehead. Its fiery hooves glowed brightly, its body was covered with bony defensive knobs and sharp spikes protruded from its back. I didn't need a sign to know that this horse wasn't for riding.

"Congrats on the contract!" I said to the demonic creature by way of welcome. "Looking forward to working together?" In reply, the pony huffed out two small puffs of acidic steam and stamped its hoof. I'd found myself a genuine demonic argaster, albeit a small one. What a stroke of luck — although whether that luck was good or bad, I wasn't sure. Argasters were very hard to control, and there was no knowing what this one might do. I decided I'd better give it a glimpse of my strength. Otherwise, it might attack me, and that would end badly for the pony, not to mention waste my already limited energy.

"Hrr!" the argaster bent its head and took a step in my direction, stamping its hoof again.

"Hey!" I yelled. "I know you're not going to hurt me. I'm not one of these local morons — I drew that summoning circle right!"

The horse looked at me, gave the pentagram a quick appraising glance and blew some more clouds of steam from its nostrils.

"Alright then, if you insist," I sighed. I drew the curtain back on my power — just a fraction. The argaster suddenly froze. Its eyes bulged, and it forgot all about breathing its acid breaths. I heard a couple of *splat* sounds coming from behind it... Hmm, maybe I'd gone a little overboard. "Don't be so scared, I won't hurt you," I said, holding out my hand. I tried to lean in and pet it, but it scrambled away from me and then took off running.

"Hey! I summoned you for a reason!" I shouted after it, but it was too late. As the argaster was bolting for the door, another man in black robes, this time holding a gun, burst through it. The man was so busy trying to aim at me that he failed to notice the little pony galloping straight for him. Unfortunately for him, this resulted in the argaster running head first into his stomach — or *horn* first, to be more precise. The horse just kept on running, off into the bowels of the building. The man, firmly impaled on the horn, started scream-ing at the top of his lungs, but the argaster didn't even seem to notice. What the creature had seen was enough to drive it insane, and it just wanted to get far away and never look back.

I held back a little before stepping out into the corridor. Only once the panicked screaming, gun-shots and clatter of hooves had died down did I peek carefully around the door frame.

"Hmm, looks like the demon did its job, after all. In a very... *horsey* way, too," I mused, peering at the battered bodies scattered all over the corri-dor. There were six in all, and they clearly hadn't been expecting to meet a terrified, bloodthirsty beast in this narrow passage.

While I was pleased that these six were dead, the problem now was that the argaster had gal-loped off somewhere, most likely through that metal gate and out of the basement completely. By rights, I should have done the same, but I doubted they were going to let me get away that easily. I hated it when I accidentally summoned a horse… They were always too stupid to do the complex stuff.

Undoing the summons on the demonic equine with a wave of my hand, I went back into the summoning room. Wherever it had gotten to, it was about to disappear into a portal before it could cause any more mischief. It wasn't of any more use to me, and would only be a waste of energy to keep around.

I inspected the pentagram, made a few minor adjustments and then topped it up with a little more energy. Demonic flames flared up inside it, and from within them, I heard the familiar *splat* of something soft hitting the stone floor.

"Hey! You teenage-mutant pony!" I glared as the frightened argaster reappeared. "Isn't there anyone else on your plane?"

The poor creature backed away, but I called it back to me. I didn't like dealing with beings like this. If you couldn't make them understand the first time, there was no point trying a second time.

Meanwhile, I could hear noise again in the distance. This time, though, the crowd sounded a lot bigger. Currently, they were struggling with that gate, but very soon, enemies would come bursting into this room yet again, and who knew how many there'd be this time? Then again, they were only being this brave because they didn't know who I was.

In my world, every self-respecting demonologist had to be excellent with a sword. But I'd gone further than that... Over many hundreds of years, I'd honed my skills with the blade, training with the greatest masters and even taking lessons from high-level demons to truly perfect my abilities. I didn't have enough energy to carry out another summoning, so I only had one option left... Time to show'em all what a *real* demonologist looked like.

I pulled the aristocrat's sword from its scabbard and headed out into the corridor. I needed to warm up. It had been a long time since my last good sword fight, and even longer since I'd last fought with an energy deficit, something that rarely happened to someone like me.

"Hmm," I peered into the depths of the corridor before returning to my hidey-hole. Twelve people. That was a few too many. Next time, maybe, but right now, I wasn't feeling it.

Before they reached me, I used a table to bar the door to the summoning room. As fortification, I drew a few discreet pentagrams on it in blood. Thankfully, there was enough of *that* around to fulfil all of my magic-making needs.

As soon I saw them draw closer, I felt my energy rushing back. Talk about motivation! They weren't quite on my doorstep yet, though, which meant I still had time to make some improvements. First, I drew a couple of spells on the legs of the table that would make it immovable — or, in layman's terms, stick it to the floor. Then, I added some small but powerful pentagrams to the table itself, after which, I dipped the sword in blood again and drew a few extra circles under the table. Hmm, still a few seconds to spare... What other dirty tricks could I think up? I thought for a moment, and then dipped into my emergency energy reserves. Then, I sprinkled the table with toxic black demonic flames, which took hold instantly in the old, cracked wood.

Just at that moment, the first of my enemies appeared in the doorway, and I bolted away.

"You shall not pass!" I yelled as I sent a small arrow flying in his direction. It hit the guy's cloak, but the force of the impact sent him flying into the wall behind him. He fell to the ground, lifeless and crumpled, but two more attackers took his place.

"You want some more?" I yelled, two more arrows materialising in my open palms. I couldn't launch them, however, before one of the two raised his gun and fired two shots in a row. *Hah! You think your gun can stop me? I AM CONSTANTINE! Your bullets will shatter at the mere whisper of my name!*

... Or that's what I thought, at least. Reality had other ideas... The first bullet hit my armour and pierced it, biting into my shoulder. After that, I didn't wait around for the second bullet to reach me. I quickly dropped my attack spells and threw up a barrier of fire to protect myself as best I could against the gunfire. I wasn't sure if it could actually stop the bullets, but either way, no more came for me.

With my wall of demonic flame standing tall, I ducked behind the nearest pillar. What *was* that weapon? Thanks to my new body's memory, I had some idea of how it worked. You loaded the cartridge, and then the barrel would spit out a bullet — that much was clear. But how could the bullet move so fast? Why did these people bother with magic at all when they had weapons like that? Then again, these guys were hardly this world's strongest fighters, and I was pretty confident there was someone else out there with an even bigger, meaner gun than theirs...

I was glad I'd thought of the table. Without it, I would have been in a tight spot right around now. I had, admittedly, used the last of my strength setting it up, but I was very quickly getting a return on my investment. Maybe I shouldn't have let that horse go, though... I could think of some uses for it now. More specifically, I was thinking about how, given the right motivation, the argaster could conveniently have operated from directly under the table.

All too soon, my wall of demonic flame began to die down, and my enemies grew bolder. From my station behind the pillar, I watched them through a magic mirror. Spotting no viable alternative, I realised I was going to have to spend my energy once again.

"Don't take him alive!" I heard someone cry. "He's powerful!"

Aw, too bad. I loved the morons who thought they could capture me — they were always easier to deal with.

By now, my attackers had grown so brave that

one of them began clambering over the table. As soon as he reached the first pentagram, however, the symbol burst into flames and set the unfortunate boy alight. He howled and began to writhe in agony, but the flames only burned even brighter, until soon, he was nothing more than a skeleton.

The others, however, failed to learn from his mistake. They seemed to decide that I could only have boobytrapped the table once, and two more novices came vaulting over it, activated defensive artefacts in their hands. It didn't help. Both of them were also engulfed in flames, despite almost draining their artefacts dry. In the process, they also donated a lot of their energy to me. Needless to say, my traps weren't the standard type that would just kill a person. *These* traps would also suck strength from the body and transfer it to me along a delicate energetic channel, at least at short-range.

I sat and watched them in the mirror. I watched them trying to break the table, trying to move it, hitting it with their hands, chopping it with their swords, all to no avail. It was a job for an axe at the very least, and probably a job for multiple axes, because the table was only getting sturdier. I'd reinforced it with a spell from outside the discipline of demonology. It was basic knowledge, vital for mages of any element. Even this simple challenge proved to be beyond the novices, however, who just carried on trying to smash the piece of furniture up by everyday means — which only charged the reinforcement spell up even more. The only possible options were either to constantly reinforce it or not touch it at all, since hijacking it was impossible.

Meanwhile, the flames died out on the two new bodies and the table began to hiss, emitting an acrid, noxious smoke. One of the traps had malfunctioned, but no matter — I had more surprises up my sleeve. It had taken some ingenuity to set up such a warm welcome for my visitors using as little energy as possible, but, judging by their shouts, I'd managed it.

"He's out of energy!" I heard a voice ring out. "Forward, brothers! What are you waiting for? Get to it!"

That must have been their leader. For some reason, though, his subordinates weren't exactly clamouring to lead the charge. They'd seen what had happened to their comrades, and no one wanted to meet the same miserable fate as those three.

"Forwards, you bedwetters!" the commander bellowed, before grabbing the closest boy to him and shoving him forward. The boy fell onto the table, gave an odd shriek and started writhing in pain. Suddenly, he froze.

"Huh?" he gawped, eyes wide. "It doesn't hurt!" he cheered, proceeding to climb over the table and into the room.

"Forwards! The path is clear!" the commander shouted, and the next novice in line rushed at the table.

Seriously? You threw me a weakling like that

and you thought I wouldn't let him through? I wasn't going to waste my energy on magical traps just for small fry like him. Now, the *next* fighter looked a lot more interesting... The rifle in his hands and the glittering sword on his belt told me that this was an enemy who could cause some real trouble — so I didn't give him the chance. I snapped my fingers and a new pentagram flashed into life under the novice's nose, spawning a little pot-bellied demon. It was about a foot tall with stubby horns and a seriously nasty glint in its eye. As well as being nice and compact, these beasts were meaner than any other demon by a long shot.

The demon was holding a little knife, which it put straight to work. One swipe, and the novice's throat split open, a fountain of blood immediately gushing from it. Then, a shot rang out from beyond the door, and the demon's head exploded into pieces.

"Follow me, brothers!"

The novice I'd let through was now darting around with his sword out, trying to find me. He hadn't noticed what had happened to his comrade, which meant that he was still brimming with courage. The scene unfolding at the door, however, was pretty much nightmare fuel.

The captain was tossing one novice after another across the table, while the stream of demons spewing from my pentagrams just about kept pace. Here and there, the demons would manage to land a blow. While the kill shots were only occasional, it all began to add up, and the energy flowed into me in torrents.

What I didn't understand was why some of the novices had swords while others had firearms. Where was the logic in that? I also saw one kid holding a glowing sword. That marked him as a gifted one, albeit weakly gifted...

"Brothers! Advance! He's hiding!" the weakling continued to yell until finally, he turned and saw the bodies piling in the doorway, and behind them, the terrified faces of his comrades. "...Brothers?" At that moment, I leapt out from behind the pillar and ran my sword smoothly through his throat. Just the thing I needed... All those novices were tightly blocking the door, trapping me in here. I had to find a way out...

I hadn't expected there to be so many of them. I'd figured it was just a handful of idiots fooling around with pentagrams, but I couldn't have been more wrong — this was a whole *sect* of idiots! And their ineptitude, it turned out, wasn't due to a lack of resources. No, it was worse than that... they were just *useless*.

I grabbed the boy's limp body and ducked behind the nearest pillar. Out of the corner of my eye, I spotted some kind of metal sphere come flying through the door. My new body's memory prompted that this was a grenade, and that grenades could explode, so I shielded myself with my victim. The thing was, in fact, a grenade; several seconds later, there came a boom so loud, it made my ears ring, along with a blinding flash of light. Fortunately, the shockwave didn't reach me.

After that, the shooting started. The air was filled with shards of masonry flying in all directions, but I paid that no attention. I had something to work with, and I needed to get that work done as fast as possible. Scooping up a little more blood with my fingers, I started to inscribe more pentagrams on the pillar. My energy had been slightly replenished thanks to the pile of dead people on the table, so I could afford to spend a little, which I did.

Glancing through the doorway as I worked, I noticed that a new batch of novices had arrived. I could hear the original group trying to convince them that the door to the summoning room was perfectly safe, even though they were clearly in no rush to go through it themselves. Meanwhile, to my great amusement, new demons were still appearing. They were all getting at least one hit in. At one point, a fat, bald, imp appeared, and I could smell the fumes from the other end of the room. The imp knew its task, but it didn't have a weapon in its hands, so it looked around, scratched its belly and then punched one of the novices in the jaw. The novice passed out, and the imp disappeared in a flash of hellfire.

"Hey!" was all I could yell. Did that pudgy little beast think it could trick me? No way! I made some quick adjustments to the summoning spell. "I'm not paying you for that!" I yelled. I instantly felt some of the energy I'd spent on the imp return. The command was to *kill* the enemy, not just punch them!

I added a couple more pentagrams for good measure, and then stood back to wait while my energy replenished. There were two new bodies on the table, so I soon had enough strength to run to the next pillar. I darted out from my hiding place, lashing blindly at my enemies with a whip laced from tongues of fire. I was pretty sure I saw one kid get split in half, but after that, I got distracted by the hail of bullets flying at me. I was also being slowed down by the novice's body, which I had to drag behind me.

I wasn't just dragging the corpse around for fun — I needed the blood. Technically, I could have scratched pentagrams into the pillars with my fingernails, but that was less energy-efficient. Plus, spells cast in blood were a lot easier to activate, since they drew not only from the caster's energy, but also from the residual energy in the blood itself.

I raced from one pillar to the next, leaving a handful of tiny pentagrams on each. I kept on drawing until I saw the table finally shatter into pieces. Like I'd said, one hefty hit would be enough to take that line of defence down, a fact my enemies finally seemed to have cottoned on to. Naturally, they came pouring straight into the room, two guys with huge shields leading the charge. I guessed that these two were supposed to deflect my attacks and carve a safe path for the others to enter the room. The only problem was, their shields looked completely useless. Or was that the people holding them? Hmm. The two defenders took another step forward and slipped in unison on the droppings the argaster had left behind. The pony had been some use, after all... .

Seizing my chance, I leapt out from behind the pillar and started cracking my fiery whip with every ounce of strength I had left. Once the shield bearers fell, the stunned back rows were defence-less, and I took out six of them with one strike. Unfortunately for me, there were still about thirty left... I wasn't prepared for this. Why were there so *many* of them? What was I going to do if there were thousands more? I should really have done some reconnaissance first. Then again, who knew this place was going to be wall-to-wall with deadbeats looking for a fight? I'd thought it was just an ordi-nary basement in some regular old abandoned house! But hey — the more, the merrier, right? If this was how they welcomed their guests in this world, I dreaded to imagine the rest of my stay...

Anyway, I was only complaining out of habit. Demonologists were officially entitled to complain about life, after all. I thought it was only fair; you spent all your precious ingredients, time and effort crafting the most powerful pentagram possible, and in the end, you had as much chance of sum-moning some braindead demon who could barely string two sentences together as you did of sum-moning a strong one! And even a strong demon wasn't always it — not when you were after a de-monic drinking buddy, for example, or you just wanted to summon something you could have a heart-to-heart with.

Demonology was a complex science with a huge number of variables, and it was impossible to account for everything all of the time. Right now, however, just one thing was puzzling me. My summoning pentagram was absolutely perfect, and the demon I'd just summoned was clever, at least compared to other demons from its plane. But even being the wisest of idiots, it still made a foolish attempt to break free — not that it did the beast much good.

"Enough," I said softly, getting to my feet. As soon as the last of the novices had entered the room, I activated every single pentagram at once. The room lit up in a cacophony of flames as the pentagrams on each of the pillars came alive, spawning an army of small, but very nasty little demons. Each pentagram was about the size of my palm, and the summoned demons were not much bigger, but they were legion, each one winged and grasping a tiny trident in its fist.

Within a second, the room was thrown into utter pandemonium. The air was filled with gunshots, screaming, cackling and the flapping of demonic wings. Judging by the way things were unfolding, the people in the room had not been prepared for this, and the demons were getting the job done with ease. While they weren't particularly strong, these demons had a special feature; referred to as 'smoke demons', they would explode upon death, leaving behind a thick cloud of demonic smoke. The acrid smoke would cause a serious obstruction for most people, although I, as a demonologist, could see through it clearly.

Well, then... time to get my sword out and show these people just how dangerous a real demonologist could be. They may have met my demons, but they were about to meet the most terrifying monster of all... *me.*

* * *

"Mark, don't stand so close to it," one of the novices scolded another, taking a couple of steps back from the grated gate himself.

"Our brothers have taken care of it," the one called Mark nodded towards the door. "Can't you hear? It's all gone quiet!"

They'd been listening to the sounds of battle, demonic roars and human screams coming from the far end of the corridor for the past few minutes. All of a sudden, the noise had stopped, and the silence was now thickening around them. But not for long... Suddenly, the grinding, shrieking and clashing of steel picked back up again, and the two novices backed away from the door a little further.

"Mark! Stand your ground!" the first novice yelled, but his brother-in-arms, who'd thrown himself against the gate and was fumbling frantically for the key, didn't hear him.

"Someone's coming! Some of ours!" Mark cried out, still pulling at the gate, until the other novice yanked him away from it. They stared through the grating, and sure enough, two of their brothers soon appeared. One was carrying the other across his shoulders, and both of them were heavily smeared with blood.

"Let me through!" cried the one who was carrying his comrade. "Our brother is dying! It's hell in there! Let me through right now! There's been a demonic breach — we need urgent assistance! They're all dead!"

Mark reached for the key again, while the other novice ran to get help. They'd all been caught by surprise and hadn't had time to assemble a proper squad, so the novices had come in ones and twos.

"Faster!" the bloodied novice kept screaming, even starting to tug at the bars of the gate himself.

"I'm trying!" Mark's trembling hands tried one key after another in the lock, but in his panic, he couldn't find the right one. Suddenly, an officer came running, grabbed the keys out of Mark's hands and shoved him forcefully aside.

"Halt!" the officer roared. "Identify yourselves!"

"There's no time!" the novice cried. "He's dying! You have to save him!"

"But—"

"Please, I'm begging you!"

The officer, at a loss, hurriedly picked out the right key and opened the gate. The novice barrelled past him and up the spiral staircase, trying to get his dying friend to the sick bay before it was too late.

* * *

Up the stairs I went, lugging on my shoulders the body of the very first novice who'd attacked me. I really *was* planning to bring him to the sick bay. I wondered which direction it was in...

I'd been close to getting overwhelmed by their sheer numbers, so I'd had to think up a plan on the fly. I could have tried to use my remaining energy to summon something really powerful and have it slaughter them all, but that would have been an unnecessary gamble. The smoke demons had done an excellent job, and thanks to their efforts, I'd been able to finish off the rest of the novices. Unfortunately, only twenty of the thirty demons had survived.

The first thing I'd done was instruct the little demons to search the corpses for valuables, but they hadn't found a single coin! Were they really that dirt poor around here? Not even the officer's pockets turned up anything worth selling. So, I'd called off the search and decided on a radical change of plan. I'd smeared myself in blood, borrowed a set of robes from one of the bodies and threw another body over my shoulder. Then, I ordered the demons to holler and howl, break things, bang on the walls and generally make a ruckus.

"Halt!" a group of five novices had appeared. I rushed to them and clasped one by the hand.

"Please, hurry! Our brothers are dying down there!"

"What?" the novice stared at me, trying to free his hand from my grip.

"It's war down there! There's been a breach! It's chaos! Hurry!" I cried as I inched almost imperceptibly around them. They set off running down the stairs, but I couldn't resist playing a little trick and tripped the last one up just as he reached the staircase. He tumbled down head-over-heels, taking two of the others down with him. I could hear shouting and cursing, but I was already hurrying up and away, heading for the next door.

I regretted not taking my weapon with me. I'd left it downstairs so as not to attract unwanted attention, but things were so crazy up here that I doubted anyone would have noticed.

I yanked open the door and found myself in yet another long corridor. I immediately saw another group of novices and rushed over to them as before.

"What's taking so long!" their commander roared, but I completely ignored him, never pausing my incoherent stream of babble about the impending danger.

"My squad is dead!" I clutched the nearest novice. "Give me your weapon!" I grabbed his sword, but he shoved my hand away.

"Why?"

"Are you stupid?" I yelled, grabbing again with more force and taking his sword from him. "Come on! Run! Now! We need to gather more people!"

"B-but I..." the now-unarmed novice looked hesitantly at his commander.

"Didn't you hear the man? Run!" the commander roared again, and the little group disappeared out the door.

Once again, I'd forgotten to ask where the sick bay was, but I reckoned it was to the right. Probably. Maybe. You'd think they could at least have had a building plan displayed on every floor…

"Where are you going?" a man dressed in armour called out to me. He cut a much more serious figure than the others; he'd even ditched the robes, though his armour featured similar designs.

"To the sick bay! One of the prisoners escaped! He was a powerful fighter in disguise! My brother and I barely escaped!" I began to babble again.

"We need a medic over here!" yelled the man, to my pleasant surprise. "Hurry! Help him!" he grabbed his radio and started giving out orders. Soon, a medic arrived, and I handed the novice's body over. The medic passed his hand over the body and then gave his verdict.

"He's dead," the man shrugged.

"Nooooo!" I clutched my head in my hands and fell to my knees. "We've been through so much together! Our dream was to become real demonologists!" I whined. This last part might have been overkill, but it seemed to work, since a guard put a heavy hand on my shoulder.

"We will avenge him," the guard growled. "Don't you worry!" I staggered to my feet, clutching my side. "Medic! What are you waiting for? Help him!" he thundered, but I shook my head.

"No... I'll avenge him myself!" I drew my sword and turned back towards the stairs. "I can do it!"

Just at that moment, another wounded soldier entered the corridor. The medic gave the guard a questioning look.

"Go and help him!" I cried. "I will go and seek vengeance!"

"No, bring him to the sick bay!" the officer was shaking his head. "Your fight is over, brother. We will get revenge, trust me," he held a hand out to me. "We'll tear the creature limb from limb — you have my word! Once he's dead, you can view his body personally. And he'll be dead before sunset — we're gathering our forces already."

"You swear?" I looked him dead in the eye.

"I swear," he nodded, and we shook hands.

It was so hard not to laugh. Had he really not noticed the contract seal on my palm? Oh well, too late. The deal was already done, and a part of his energy would be flowing into me by sunset today. This was guaranteed, because the contract itself could never be fulfilled; how could I see my own body before sunset? Even if they killed me, the terms of the contract would remain unfulfilled.

"Take him to a safe place!" the officer ordered two novices. "The rest of you — with me! It's time for vengeance!"

# CHAPTER 3

WHERE *WAS* THIS GODDAMN sick bay? We'd been traipsing up and down the corridors and staircases for ten minutes now and *still* hadn't reached the elusive place. I had to say, these quarters had turned out to be a lot bigger than I'd expected. At first, I'd thought it was only the basement that was huge, but I could see now that the building itself was even bigger.

It was dark outside, so I couldn't see much through the window. All I could make out was a small amount of land surrounding the building, ringed by a low fence. Beyond that was only dense, dark forest.

After a few more gates and doors, we finally found ourselves in the sick bay. There was a spacious room with a number of small cots separated by screens, and another room with beds for patients to recover in. The doctors were too busy to see me, so I was sent straight over to one of the cots. Several of the others were already occupied.

"Hey! Did you come from the basement?" the room burst into life as soon as the two novices accompanying me had left, all the patients hopping out of bed to question me. "What happened? Tell us!"

"You don't know?" I groaned, acting like my whole body hurt.

"No! Tell us!" the injured men cried, crowding around me. I paused to think. What should I tell them? I'd tell them I was in the basement, yes. But what if they called it the 'secret summoning spot', or something? That would give me away instantly as an outsider, and I was currently clean out of energy. I was going to have to *get* some information before I *gave* any...

I clutched my chest and began to cough, my face contorted in unbearable agony.

"Vinny, leave him be!" barked someone at the far end of the room. "Can't you see he's in pain? You're here because you ate some gone-off soup, but this guy's fresh outta the basements! We all know the occultists finally managed to summon something they couldn't control — that much is clear. Just look at what this guy's been through!"

The other patients, muttering to themselves, began to disperse back to their own cots, and I breathed a sigh of relief. 'The basements', then. Thinking the interrogation was over, I started settling in to eavesdrop on the conversation around me, but no — this bunch was *very* curious about what was going on down there.

"Did you see anything?" the young man in the cot next to mine asked cautiously.

"Not really," I shook my head. "Some kind of monster or demon, I can't say what. I didn't get a good look at it. I was one of the first to go down... and when I woke up, my entire squad was already dead," I gave a deep sigh. "Can you imagine? All of them!"

"What group were you with?" the one called Vinny piped up again. It was a reasonable thing to ask, and it made me want to murder him right there on the spot. But it was okay — I knew how to handle tough questions.

"Why are you pestering him again?" one of the other patients called out sternly. "He must have been with Victor's group. They were the first ones sent down there."

A scrap of information. *Yes.* I started coughing even louder in a bid to hear more.

"Are you okay? Should we call the doctor?" my neighbour said, looking concerned. "Think you might have a broken rib."

Ok, fine. I wasn't stupid — I knew the coughing wasn't going to work forever. If I didn't change tack and try something more believable, I wouldn't be getting any information at all.

"To be honest," I said, wincing in pain as I turned onto my right side, "I hit my head against a wall and I'm having trouble remembering things. I remember Jonesy, Ivan, Peter... but I can't remember my own name."

"Definitely Victor's group," my neighbour nodded. "You must be one of the new recruits. And remembering your name's easy — just take a look at your tags!"

I'd figured those would come in handy... While I was examining the corpses to figure out who I was dealing with — humans or demi-humans — I'd noticed that each one had a dog tag around its neck. We had something similar in my world, so I understood what the tags were for. I'd yanked a set free from one of the corpses and stuffed just the chain into my pocket.

"But I don't have any," I murmured, touching my neck and pulling back my collar to highlight the lack of dog tags to all present. After that, I started patting down my pockets until I eventually produced the broken chain.

"Not to worry, they'll clean out the basements soon. I'm sure your tags will show up," my neighbour said, patting me on the shoulder. Soon? Unlikely. I still had a few more traps hidden away down there, and they wouldn't be done with *those* anytime soon.

Eventually, the fighters forgot about me and started chatting amongst themselves. I made myself comfortable and got down to eavesdropping. They'd pegged me as being from Victor's group because he'd had a lot of new recruits, and since none of the men here recognised my face, they reckoned I must be one of them.

"It's a shame about Ivan, of course," one of the

patients sighed. "He was a fool, but a brave fool."

"Why was he a fool?" I asked curiously.

"He really believed that demonology was the future, that the occultists would succeed," the man scoffed.

"You don't believe that?"

"Hah!" cries of laughter went up around the room. "Looks like you really *did* hit your head — you're braindead!"

Little did they know that *they* were the fools, but there was no point in arguing with them. At least I didn't have to work too hard to fake my suffering; I'd been roughed up pretty badly before the ritual, and my body really did need to recover.

"Hey, don't worry about it," said another of my neighbours, mistaking my pensive expression for one of sadness. "Maybe you didn't forget that — maybe you never knew it in the first place. We're not all occultists around here. There are normal people, too, like you and me," he smirked. The others made noises of agreement. "And anyway, you should be proud of yourself! You were in the *basements*. Not everyone gets to go down there," he said, coming closer and squatting down by my bed. "Say, what's it like down there? I bet those wasters just sit around getting fat."

"What do you mean, exactly?" I asked, confused.

"Oh, come on, think! You can't have forgotten *everything!*"

"You mean you haven't been to the basements yourself?" I frowned, pretending to be completely lost.

"Of course I haven't!" the man burst out. "We're not allowed down there! Not unless it's an emergency situation like today."

I was rescued from further questioning by the sound of footsteps approaching the door. The injured men leapt back into their beds and lay down, doing their best to look like they were suffering terribly. No one wanted to be declared healthy and sent to clean out the basements, especially since I was a walking advertisement for the horrors that awaited them down there.

The door swung open, and two guards were brought in to two of the empty cots. One was unconscious, while the other was burbling indistinctly about terrifying beasts with wings, which warmed my heart. All the attention in the room was now trained on these two, leaving me free to just lie back and listen. This chit-chat could teach me a lot about this unfamiliar place — and this unfamiliar world, for that matter. For example, I soon learned that the whole compound was owned and built by some aristocrat or other. It had been set up to look like a laboratory, but this was just a front. I also heard more about the 'occultists', as the men called them, who rarely appeared aboveground and practically lived in the basements. They also lived by their own strict rules, from which they never deviated. They followed a regimented diet on a rigid schedule, dedicated themselves to practising magic and had no contact with ordinary people, barring a handful from the upper echelons.

The laboratory was a cover for the aristocrat's real project. He was trying to summon demons for his own personal use, spending a lot of resources in the process. The locals, meanwhile, were obviously living in dread of how the whole thing might end. And now, one of the aristocrat's relatives had died down in the basements, which meant a serious inspection was on the horizon. By this stage, even the paper-pushers were wondering if it was time to jump ship. Their comfortable positions had suddenly become anything but. Not a single thing of note had happened in the two years most of them had worked here, and now, all of a sudden, fifty people had died at once, with twenty more injured.

I deduced that there were forty guards left in total, along with around fifteen occultists. That meant I'd already obliterated most of my attackers, which pleased me thoroughly.

A brief exchange with these men, and I could already tell that they were perfectly ordinary people. I wasn't blind, though — they clearly knew everything, and yet, they turned a blind eye to the horrors being perpetrated in this place. They couldn't care less that just below them, the occultists were torturing and abusing innocent people. They were getting paid, and that was all they cared about. They even cheerfully discussed how loud the screams from the basements had been earlier — right in front of me! They spoke of it with minor irritation, annoyed that it was disrupting their naps... They didn't seem to have an ounce of pity for the people being unjustly murdered.

And that was what sealed these men's fates. Once night had fallen and the whole sick bay was asleep, I snuck out for a stroll. By now, I'd gathered enough intel that if I happened to meet a patrol, I'd be able to get through the encounter without arousing suspicion.

When I found the kitchen, I stopped for a snack. I had to say, the guards ate a lot better than the demonologists. After that, I set off to explore the rest of the ramshackle building, and to cause as much trouble for its inhabitants as possible. Now and then, I stopped to look out a window and observe the goings-on outside. It was pandemonium out there. Trucks were pulling in, being loaded up with sacks full of corpses and then disappearing down the road into the forest beyond. And with all that activity, no one was paying any attention to me. So what if some poor guy wrapped in bandages was wandering the corridors? Let him wander...

Incidentally, they'd bandaged me almost from head to toe. The doctor who'd examined me had been a real piece of work. I couldn't understand how they let a person like him near sick people. In just the time I was there, he'd stitched up two different patients without any anaesthetic, even though the poor souls had begged him between their deafening screams. But the doctor didn't give a damn. Either he took pleasure in causing others pain, or he was just too lazy to go and fetch the drugs.

I, meanwhile, was perfectly healthy. By the time he'd examined me, even my bruises had started to fade. But I'd been prepared for this eventuality, and I'd poured a little energy into an unusual pentagram on the palm of my hand. This pentagram had been a bit of a gamble, you could say, since it wasn't certain I could find a capable provider in this world's demonic plane. In the end, however, the pentagram had flared into life, and when I'd opened my jacket, the doctor's jaw had dropped in shock.

He couldn't see the activated pentagram. All he could see were the horrific wounds all over my body — exactly what I'd wanted to show him, using the powers of a low-level demonic manipulator. After that, they'd even given me morphine! Plus, I got to watch the doctor scratching his head over how I could possibly be alive with such injuries.

At first glance, this spell seemed simple. It didn't cost much in terms of energy or resources. All you had to do was draw the pentagram, find your demon and give it your order. In reality, though, the technique was far from easy to master. You needed tonnes of experience in communicating with demons, and even then, finding the right one for the task was very tricky. The slightest mistake, and I'd be summoning a manipulator who could only work with sound — and what good would that be? The doctor could listen to my wheezing lungs, but he certainly wouldn't see any injuries on my body.

As I continued through the endless corridors, I had an unpleasant realisation. Those trucks weren't just taking bodies away; every now and then, they were carrying in reinforcements. That could be a problem before long. I'd have to do something about it. For the moment, though, my energy was so low that I'd had to resort to borrowing some. Wielding a sword in my current condition against so many enemies would be either stupid or suicidal, and possibly both. Not that I would actually *die*, of course... rather, my soul would fly free and return to my other body — the body still imprisoned in that dead world. But hanging around there for the next three thousand years or so wouldn't be much fun. I fancied staying here for now, thank you very much. To do that, though, I'd need to do things right. First, I had to repair this body, strengthen it and fine-tune it. Then, I'd need to perform a permanent summoning on a couple of creatures, pay a few demons for a few special skills... but it would all take lots of time and energy.

It was so much easier to think as I walked than stuck in that sick bay surrounded by patients. My head was bursting with exciting ideas, and soon, I was going to bring them all to life.

I found a cramped utility room littered with mops, buckets and assorted cleaning supplies. No one would be coming in here at night, so I could draw my pentagrams in peace. Tossing the filthy floor rug aside, I pricked my finger with a rusty tool lying nearby and began filling the floor with symbols. They weren't my prettiest work, of course, but they'd have to do. What mattered most was that they were drawn correctly; once those were in place, I could boost the symbols with energy later.

One after another, the pentagrams took shape. Each one was about fifteen centimetres across, but these were only the beginning. Once they were finished, I linked them together with a binding spell, which cost me a couple more drops of blood, and finally, I poured a little energy into them. I would have drawn more, but I was so low on resources that the blood outright refused to flow from my finger.

Ironically, my critical energy deficit was the only reason I was using blood in the first place... Blood was inconvenient, and you ran the risk of the wound getting infected. If that happened, you'd have to spend precious energy either killing the infection yourself or securing a demon's assistance. If you wanted to *restore* your energy, you needed to kill someone who deserved to die, and to do *that*, you needed to *spend* energy... The whole system was a tangle, and you had to find workarounds where you could.

As I mused over all this, the spell took shape, until finally, the three pentagrams burst into demonic flame. The guards here weren't stupid, and sooner or later, they were going to start suspecting that I wasn't the person I claimed to be. I definitely couldn't afford to relax. I was good, yes, but I also knew that no disguise was perfect. Plus, I was sure they had security cameras in here that I just hadn't spotted yet... and there was always the possibility that someone might simply recognise me from my very recent stint as a prisoner.

A few seconds later, a little gremlin appeared in the centre of each pentagram. They were bald, wrinkly, pot-bellied, bug-eyed creatures with short arms ending in stubby fingers. Every part of their appearance made them look utterly useless. They *were* useless, but my resources weren't exactly infinite, and desperate times called for desperate measures...

Gremlins were very low-level service demons, and they were some of the cheapest to summon. As soon as they appeared, they started looking around until they found me. Then, they dipped their heads in a slight bow. They were fairly dim, but also exceptionally obedient, which made them delightfully easy to control. They didn't argue or ask questions, just received their instructions in silence and then got down to the task, fulfilling their orders as best they understood them. They were actually most commonly used for heavy lifting; conveniently, despite their diminutive size, gremlins were strong enough to carry heavy bricks. They also had a respectable amount of stamina.

"Follow me, minions!" I said, and they filed in obediently behind me. I peeped out the utility room door and glanced up and down the corridor. Spotting no cameras or people, I stepped out into the corridor and moved to the nearest window.

The gremlins were great servants, alright, but when it came to fighting, they weren't much use unless you had thousands of them. In large numbers, they could be used on the battlefield to wear the enemy down. They could charge in a wave and attack with large sticks, provoking the enemy into wasting arrows and mass attack spells on them. And if they could handle a stick, I guessed they could handle some of this world's weapons... I opened the window, gave the gremlins clear instructions, waited for their affirmative nods, and then set off running as fast as possible in the other direction.

One by one, the three gremlins jumped out the window. One broke its leg hitting the ground, but it didn't make so much as a squeak and calmly set off crawling towards its target. The target was a stack of loaded machine guns. There was a group of sentries sitting nearby, deep in conversation. I just hoped the gremlins knew how to cock a gun and release the safety catch. As for me, I'd previously managed to examine one of these local weapons and had learned how to use it from my new body's memory. I wouldn't exactly have called my predecessor's knowledge extensive, but he'd picked up a few things from films and books, all of which I'd reinforced with some hands-on experience down in the basement.

I'd explained everything to the gremlins in great detail, but with intelligence as limited as theirs, it was anyone's guess what they'd actually do. What a shame there were no grenades lying around — that would have made everything easier. Just tell the creature to pull the pin and charge at the enemy...

It took the gremlins a couple of minutes to get to grips with the guns. All was going smoothly until one of them took its first shot... and managed to inhale and choke on the shell casing as it was ejected. The other two fared better, however, spraying the sentries with a hail of bullets at virtually point-blank range. A siren blared, alerting the other soldiers. They came running, and then the energy began to flow into me like a river. It was, of course, a shame that the gremlins were discovered and gunned down within seconds, but at least they took a couple of the locals down with them.

Admittedly, I didn't actually see this bit, since I'd gone off to get some sleep. I'd been forgotten for now. Everyone was running around, hunting for the demons, and judging from the conversations I overheard, a lot of them were convinced that the gremlins had somehow escaped from the basement.

As soon as the gremlins were taken care of, the soldiers began investigating the area. Some of the forces were sent down to guard the basements, while I was free to relax and unwind. I'd gained a little energy, and things were looking up.

I spent the next day sleeping and meditating. Maintaining my energy reserves was essential, but keeping my body and mind in good shape was just as important. While I recovered, I also gathered information. I listened out for topics of conversation, carefully studied the soldiers' behaviour, stole glances outside and considered possible escape routes.

Only once during this time was my peace disturbed. Into the sick bay arrived a soldier who'd been wounded in the stomach. He'd been shot by the gremlins and was determined not to share his energy with me. And once the initial shock wore off, he was even less agreeable...

"Oy, new recruit!" the man said to me once the doctors had left and we patients were alone. "Bring me something to drink!"

"Should I call a nurse?" I asked, my eyebrows raised.

"Don't you know how to follow a superior officer's order?" the man scowled. "Hop to it!"

I looked around at the other patients, but they were conspicuously ignoring us.

"Alright, then, I'll get it," I shrugged, heading for the kitchen.

I brought him water — *actual* water, rather than, say, demon's piss. I also made a mental note about him.

That night, the guy suffocated to death. The doctors, for some reason, decided he must have developed pulmonary edema, or perhaps a blood clot that had clogged his pulmonary artery. I was too busy revelling in the fresh stream of energy to really follow the conversation, though there *was* another explanation... This was just my personal opinion, of course, but perhaps the loud-mouthed asshole had been strangled in the dark by a skinny little fiend? My money was on this explanation, but the doctors didn't seem too interested in investigating, anyway.

And just like that, my third day in this place crept in. I had big plans for today. The aristocrat, the owner of this laboratory himself, was rumoured to be coming in a couple of hours. He would also be bringing his personal bodyguards with him in order to conduct a full debriefing.

Some of the soldiers had tried to flee in the night, but they'd been captured in the forest and thrown into the dungeons, so the whole compound was now on edge. As if trying to flee this madhouse was a crime... Last night, they'd captured two more vagrants and handed them over to what was left of the occultists. I hadn't been able to sleep for the awful screams coming from the basement. They may have been several floors below me, but those howls... Meanwhile, the men around me had slept peacefully, well used to the noise. I, a high demonologist, was horrified, but these people barely even noticed! I'd seen a lot in my time, but in *my* world, this kind of barbarism was already ancient history.

What set a demonologist like me apart from the under-educated ranks of two-bit demonologists out there? Simple. A two-bit demonologist would worship their demons and terrorise their own kind, while an advanced demonologist like myself was a demon's worst nightmare and would protect the ordinary people against them. This aristocrat and his retinue, though, were hardly ordinary people, and I had no desire to face them head-on. And so, when night fell, I went out for my usual evening stroll and headed for the utility room where I'd summoned the gremlins. I pulled back the carpet, inspected the dried-out pentagrams and got to work on some new ones. I drew so many, it was almost ridiculous, but it had to be done. I knew everything I needed to know about this place, and now, it was time to act.

Just drawing the pentagrams took me about four hours, after which, I had to distribute my energy out between them. The drawing was an interesting experience, too... I'd asked my neighbours in the sick bay where I could find some chalk or coal, but they'd wanted to know what I needed it for. I almost let the truth slip, but managed to cover it just in time by saying I needed to write a letter. That got me mocked for being an idiot again, but eventually, someone handed me a marker. I also got offered a pen and a pencil, but the marker was by far my favourite. I reckoned I'd be drawing with it from now on. It didn't seem to contain any magic, and yet, it was much more effective than any artefact... .

A little while later, energy began to flow into the pentagrams, triggering the irreversible summoning process. There were fifteen small circles in all, and a short black knife now materialised in each. Yes, I could have summoned more demons to wield these demonic weapons, but there was no guarantee they'd do a better job than I could. I was no weakling, and after the last few days, I'd also recovered some strength. Nonetheless, with my current energy reserves, it would have been tough to summon anything particularly strong.

I gathered up the knives and cracked open a small skylight window. Somehow, the ritual for summoning demonic weapons always seemed to be accompanied by a very... *pungent* smell of sulphur.

"Hey! What's that stink?"

The window hadn't helped. As soon as I stepped out of the utility room, I found myself face-to-face with a guard. He was pacing up and down the corridor, sniffing the air, searching for the source of the sulphurous smell. I'd seen him before — in fact, I'd made a mental note of his face. I'd watched this guard kick a stray dog while he was patrolling the perimeter of the compound.

"Oh, yeah, someone took a dump in the utility room," I said, pointing back at the door. The guard's nose wrinkled, but he went in to take a look anyway. He barely had time to glimpse what was left of the pentagrams before I buried a knife between his shoulder blades, catching him before he could turn around. There was a flash of red, and without a sound, the guard fell forward into a demonic portal.

"Good luck out there," I murmured, smirking. "Try kicking a dog." The demonic plane's residents were... well, *dangerous* was an understatement.

The red light vanished, along with any trace of the guard. Even the drops of blood that had splat-tered onto the floor were gone. This also meant that there were no pockets left behind for me to loot, but then again, that meant no evidence, either. Meanwhile, the man's energy had really boosted my reserves.

Not all demonologists were maniacs. In fact, many of us were perfectly sane. Take *me*, for example — perfectly sane. Well, relatively sane... probably... Anyway, I never usually shoved normal, sane individuals like myself into portals, because ending up in the demonic plane was not a pleasant fate, but...

I found my way to the kitchen and went about filling my belly, but all too soon, a rather hefty guard stuck his head in. I immediately put two and two together. After all, you couldn't get that big around here without a little nighttime raid on the pantry now and then...

Failing to notice me, he headed straight for the refrigerator and began rummaging around inside.

"Is this your knife, by any chance?" I said, and the guard jumped.

"N-n-no..." he replied, spooked.

"Oh, well," I shrugged, and then swiftly threw the black blade, hitting him dead in the eye. "It is now!"

The rest of the night turned out to be quite boring. I spent half the time wandering the corridors, sending any other lone wanderers I met straight to a date with the demons. My energy reserves grew and grew, and I started to think about calling something more powerful than the gremlins. Eventually, I came down to my last knife. I'd have to use this one on someone special...

I roamed around for another hour or so, crossing paths with ordinary guards. I didn't want to waste a gift like this on an enemy like that. Eventually, however, I found myself on the first floor, where I came across a man wearing black robes. His hood was completely shadowing his face, and he was moving towards me as if I weren't there, but I held my ground, and we bumped shoulders as he passed. The occultist turned and stared at me for some time with a bewildered frown. He was used to people making way for him, treating him with respect. If not respect, then he at least expected fear, although if the guards' talk was to be believed, the mere sight of an occultist filled them with nothing but pure disgust...

"Do you want to see some demons?" I smiled at him. This bewildered him even further, since we were strictly forbidden from speaking with each other. "I can show you whatever you wish!"

"Who are you?" the occultist burst out. "You worthless, insolent scum. What would you know about demons?"

"Quite a bit," I spread my arms out, taking a step towards him. "And *you* are about to learn more," I smiled, and the black knife slashed the pathetic occultist's throat open. I didn't feel a single twinge of conscience for this one. Not that I actually *had* a conscience — in my field, it tended to get in the way of one's professional obligations.

I'd managed to absorb a lot of energy tonight,

and more importantly, I'd left no trace behind me. I'd taken down fourteen guards and one satanist, and no one had even raised an alarm. That said, they were probably busy being hunted down out in the forest, since plenty of them had already tried to flee.

When the knives ran out, I went back to my utility room, drew a couple more pentagrams and summoned some more gremlins. It was a pleasure to work with such cooperative creatures, especially now that I knew they were more than competent with the local weaponry. And, as it happened, I'd recently picked up two pistols and a shotgun... I distributed the guns to my servants and ordered them to wait. Then, I headed back to the sick bay to get some sleep.

Two hours later, I was woken by the sound of chaotic gunfire and screaming. A couple of wounded guards were carried in to the cots, and I could hear sirens wailing and people running in every direction outside. All the while, I just lay there with a smile on my face, casually picking crumbling plaster off the wall.

* * *

*The chief of security's office*
*Sometime later*

Peter Gennady sat in his chair, staring at the young guard who was standing silent, his report complete. Looking hard at the boy, he sighed.

"You're certain?" Peter asked again, and again, the guard nodded firmly.

"Certain, sir!" the guard fired off crisply.

"Completely?"

"Yes. He's definitely not one of ours. I saw him among the prisoners not long ago. It's definitely him," the guard replied. "I wouldn't say so if I weren't one hundred per cent certain," he added.

"It's a serious accusation," the chief of security sighed again. "Do you really think we've been hoodwinked so easily?"

"I'm sure of it! I dragged him half-dead into the basement myself. I was with Gregory, he could have confirmed..." the boy trailed off. Gregory had died several days ago already, battling against some demonic beasts. "And now, that bastard is strolling around, eating our rations!" he clenched his fists, his jaw tight.

"I see," Peter murmured. "Some creature must have possessed him. We needed to mobilise and liquidate him as soon as possible!"

"But commander!" the guard declared. "Shouldn't we observe him? We need to know how he managed to escape and hide amongst us for so long. What if he has accomplices?

"It's too risky," the chief was shaking his head.

"But why?"

"Because I said so!" the chief roared, slamming his fist down on the table. "The Count's men will be here soon, and what do I have to show them? Let's at least show them this one! And invite the rest of the occultists — I mean *demonologists* —

too. They can join the fun."

The guard nodded silently and hurried out of the room to gather all the commanding officers, experienced soldiers and demonologists together. Raising the alarm wasn't an option. Instead, he went to speak to each individual personally; this operation would have to be carried out in secret.

The chief, meanwhile, stayed seated, a smile spreading across his face. This could be his ticket out of trouble... The Count had poured a lot of time and money into this laboratory, so he was expecting success. Now, at the very least, the chief would have some kind of result to show and might avoid punishment for his failures.

While the squad was assembling and preparing, the chief questioned some of the wounded soldiers in the sick bay. It seemed the escaped prisoner did nothing other than eat and sleep.

"He must be gathering his strength," the chief muttered thoughtfully to himself. "He's preparing to strike as soon as he gets the chance."

The chief was also aware that this person was likely responsible for those little beasts that had attacked earlier. And even if he wasn't, they could pin the blame on him anyway.

Night fell, and a squad of heavily armed soldiers made its way to the sick bay. The chief himself was among them. He was gifted, and with quite a strong gift at that. When they burst in, he saw the good-for-nothing creature with his own eyes, lying and sleeping peacefully in its cot.

"Go, go, go! Grab him!" the chief roared, and

the soldiers trained their weapons on the man...
who slowly opened a single, unbothered eye.

* * *

Honestly, capturing me in the night was just plain
rude. Couldn't they have come in the morning? I
was just lying there, not bothering anyone, minding my own business... Where was I supposed to
go in this world? Couldn't I just spend a few thousand years in peace without anybody spoiling my
fun? Admittedly, on that end, I'd come up with
plenty of ideas in the last three days. I could become a teacher, a philosopher, an artist... a new
world meant new opportunities! I hadn't quite
picked one yet, but not because I was slow; it was
just a big decision.

At that moment, the door flew off its hinges
and a dozen armed soldiers burst into the room
and swarmed around my cot. Bringing up the rear,
I could see a burly man with hair greying at the
temples. Ah, the chief. I'd seen him a couple of
times from the window, but the opportunity to finish him off hadn't presented itself. Not yet, anyway...

"Hi!" I gave them a wave as I sat up in the cot.
"What's up? You guys can't sleep either, huh?"

Forgetting their orders, the soldiers froze a
couple of metres from me, glancing at each other
in confusion. What, did they expect me to plead
and beg for mercy? That wasn't my style.

"Why so silent?" I looked at them. "Is something wrong? It's just that I'm pretty tired. You know, injuries and all that."

The soldiers didn't move.

"Hmm. Balthazar, take care of them, will you? I'm going back to sleep."

"My name's not Balthazar," said a big, beefy demon, crawling out from under the bed.

"It is today!" I grunted, throwing my hands up in frustration. "Come on, just take care of them!"

As I turned over, I heard the soldiers open fire behind me. The noise didn't last long, though; to a demon like that, this bunch of goons were barely even small fry.

# CHAPTER 4

ON I DROVE, PEACEFULLY MINDING my own business... To my credit, I'd tied up all my loose ends back there, so I could permit myself a little breather.

Every now and then, I'd meet armoured cars, gigantic off-roaders and assorted combat vehicles speeding the opposite way. Everyone was in a hurry to get somewhere, preparing to do battle with someone, and no one was paying any attention to the guy in civilian clothing heading for town on the rattling old moped. Choosing this hunk of junk as my mode of transport had been a pretty clever idea. Not that there hadn't been better options in the laboratory compound; I'd seen all kinds of armoured vehicles, including ones mounted with artillery guns and machine guns, as well as some fancy civilian vehicles. There was even a beautiful sports car, which I guessed belonged to the aristocrat I'd killed on the first day. But I'd taken the moped, and currently, I had no regrets. The only downside was that it was a little hard to steer in this cold weather, with the slush on the road constantly sending the wheels spinning in opposite directions. Still, I was drawing zero attention, which would have been difficult in a more noticeable vehicle.

The demon I'd summoned had made short work of most of the guards and occultists. Admittedly, he'd needed backup, but still... with the amount of energy he'd provided me, performing a few more summonings had really been no sweat.

The head of the guards was a seriously strong guy. Everything was relative, of course, but right now, I was relatively puny. And no, I wasn't trying to be hard on myself. It was more that, when I remembered how great my power had been before, it was hard to stomach the pathetic state I was currently in. But at least this state was only temporary... I knew I would recover my former strength soon. I just needed a little time.

Anyway, here I was, driving along on my moped. Yes, I knew it was a moped. My body's memory had returned by now, and I'd filled in the few remaining gaps with the assistance of my neighbours in the sick bay. I'd realised that I liked this world, in spite of all its strangeness. Just think — this ridiculous, clapped-out, two-wheeled piece of scrap was going faster than a horse! Not a magical horse, obviously — more like a lame, sick one — but still.

Mages tended to avoid technology in general, usually preferring to stick to what they knew. But that was only because they'd never had the chance to try out something like a bicycle or a scooter! That said, I'd tested out a bicycle back at the compound, but after a few laps of the main building, I'd realised it wasn't the right vehicle for me. As I saw it, the vehicle should be the one making *you* move, not the other way around.

While preparing for my escape, I'd planned out how to leave the compound as fast as possible once all the guards were dead. Once it was done, I'd grabbed my things quickly, taking only the most essential and valuable items, and packed everything into a sack. Then, I'd set the building on fire. I couldn't be sure of destroying *all* the evidence that way, but at least the archive and the chief of security's office would be destroyed, and those were my main targets. I couldn't risk leaving my picture lying around in there...

Another armoured car passed me, going in the same direction as the others. Well, they certainly weren't going to find anything of value back there... I'd taken most of the money, and I'd left the rest to burn in the flames. And there had, in fact, been quite a lot of money... as long as you didn't compare it to how much I used to make in my other world. I had about twenty-seven thousand dollars in all. The memories left over from my body's previous occupant informed me that the amount of money I had taken would be enough to buy a decent car or a cosy one-room apartment just outside town. Once I'd bought the apartment, I could then find myself a wife and start a family. Once we had kids, I'd get some demon puppies for them to play with, and then me and the wife would sit back and enjoy the quiet life. But sooner or later, that psychopath mage would show up and murder them all, and I'd be left to suffer, cursing myself over and over for prioritising happiness over strength... .

... Damn. How many times had it been now? I could name at least twenty people whose lives had turned out exactly like that. They'd been living in peace and comfort, only to have their family taken from them in the blink of an eye. After that, they would become consumed by their desire for revenge. One of them was a funny story, actually... He spent so long plotting his revenge, training and preparing to take his enemy down that in the end, his enemy died of old age.

The first things to appear on the deserted road were the lampposts. Then, more and more often, individual houses, and finally, whole apartment complexes. The closer I got to the city, the more people and cars I passed. The stream of military vehicles had dried up, however. The aristocrat must live outside of the city... either that, or he'd just run out of vehicles. It was strange, though... How could they just up and let me escape like this? Now, I was just going to disappear into the crowd and become untraceable forever...

The moped really was playing an important

role in all this. It was the last thing you'd expect an evil genius to be riding; powerful people had access to a whole other class of vehicle. I *was* an evil genius, though, just a more modest one flying very successfully under the radar. I'd even tied a bundle of firewood and a potato sack onto the back to make me look like a regular farm boy, and the fact that I happened to be heading in the direction of the nearest village also helped. I'd learned about the village in the sick bay. The guys had all been dreaming of making it there as soon as they could, with talk of getting set up and sorted out once they did.

The moped rattled on, and soon, I saw a sign for the city. Hello, Circle City! Circle City, the most beautiful place in the world!

I was taking in the sights so hard that I almost crashed into a car coming the other way. I stopped, got off and then looked around again. Huh... when they'd said this place was beautiful, it must have been a joke. I had to confess, it took a second to sink in. Then again, what had I been expecting? Everything was cold and grey, the roads covered in slush. But maybe it would be different when I entered the city proper — maybe it would be warm, pleasant and sunny there. Maybe. Things like that were possible in my world, but I knew better than to assume the same of this one.

I stood there on the side of the road for a while, observing the goings-on around me. I decided my first port of call should be somewhere to eat and sleep. I needed food first, and preferably, something tasty. My stomach had been rumbling for the whole journey; this body required fuel in order to sustain itself.

Once I felt rested, I shook the icy slush off my pant legs and headed straight for the centre of town. The traffic got much busier as I went, making it harder and harder to take in the city. At least I knew the rules of the road, even if I didn't have much experience behind the wheel yet. But hey, I could do this!

Fifteen minutes later, I was pushing the moped along the sidewalk. As it turned out, I couldn't do this. I'd gone crashing into a snowdrift once and tumbled off the bike twice, all in the space of five minutes. *I* knew the rules of the road, but the other drivers? Not so much!

I was now soaking wet, and honestly, a little flustered. But never mind — I'd save up a little, buy myself a great big car, and *then* we'd see who the king of the road was!

With the city being so much harder to navigate than I'd imagined, the first guest house that appeared seemed like a godsend. I felt like the universe had turned its gaze on me personally, finally guiding me to a soft bed and a hearty meal.

Just a few steps from the guest house door, I heard someone call out to me. I turned and saw two guys stepping out of a dark alley.

"Hey, you!" one of them called. "You wanna make some money?"

"No," I stalled, considering it. "Actually, yes I do!" I grabbed the keys out of the moped's ignition and strolled jauntily over to join them. We went down the alley, turned into a shadowy courtyard and stopped in front of a black car. There was barely any daylight, and no passersby at all. No one in their right mind would come down here voluntarily.

"Come on, then — get on with it!" I said to the two men.

"Get on with what?" one replied, sounding surprised.

"Attack me! Come on!" I threw my sack down and put my fists up, ready to fight. The two men just froze, staring at me in pure confusion. "Alright, you can drop the act — I know the score! You lure me in with the money, and then, I have to pay you not to kill me. Don't you think I've done this before?"

I'd drawn pentagrams on both my palms before I'd left the compound, so these two couldn't have hurt me even if they'd wanted to. On the contrary, I'd agreed to come with them because I could use the extra energy...

"Are you drunk, or something?" one of the men took off his hat and rubbed the back of his neck. "Help us push the car, will you? We'll give you two dollars!"

I lowered my arms. I looked at the car, which I could see now was stuck in a snowdrift. Well, this was awkward. But hey — two dollars was two dollars. It wasn't much, but it was honest pay. In fact, it would be the first money I'd earned in this world, so I could be proud of that.

A few minutes later, I emerged back out onto the well-lit street, parked my moped properly and headed into the guest house. It wasn't exactly luxurious. Actually, I wouldn't even have called it average. It had five floors, reasonably clean, and a small restaurant on the first floor which, in fact, looked more like a bar. The rates were low, and the clientele was mostly comprised of soldiers. It suited me just fine, although by this stage, I had to admit that I'd have settled for just about any place with food and a bed. Oh, and some heating, of course.

Remarkably, nobody asked me my name or wanted to see my identification. I just handed the price of a room to the man behind the bar and he handed me back a set of keys. No need for questions around here — you just paid on time and stayed until you decided to leave.

I ordered some food to my room and went to get settled in. The room was on the third floor, right at the end of the corridor. I went in, closed the door behind me and immediately dumped the contents of my sack out onto the bed. The way the bag looked, you'd never have guessed the riches it contained. Weapons, cash, silverware... Since I'd been in a hurry, I'd just grabbed all the valuables I could find, stuffed them into my sack and then filled the rest of the sack with potatoes.

In terms of weaponry, I'd nabbed a couple of pistols and one shotgun with half a magazine left. Then, there was some kind of gilded dagger I'd found lying in the desk drawer in the chief of security's office. After that were some occultist gadgets I'd grabbed by mistake. The copper discs featuring crudely drawn pentagrams were good for nothing but scrap, so I threw them out the window. Some poor down-and-out would probably be happy to find them. Naturally, I made sure to block the network of spells within the pentagrams before I tossed them; you never knew when someone might get the bright idea to reactivate them and end up getting themselves killed.

In the end, the most valuable thing I'd managed to grab was the cash. The rest might come in handy, but I was most likely going to end up selling it. I knew from my body's memories that weapons like these were by no means the best choice in this world, and anyway, I was much happier relying on my own magic and reflexes in a fight. And speaking of reflexes... Someone knocked on my door, and I fired all my trophies straight back into the sack. When I opened the door, however, it was just a kid wheeling a creaky trolley full of plates. I carried in the lot and sat down to feast. There were huge chunks of roast meat, a deep bowl piled high with vegetables — and a whole roast piglet with an apple in its mouth! Why *did* they put the apple in there, anyway? Just because they could, probably...

The chef here was no match for his demonic counterpart in my last world, but the food was at least edible. It was certainly miles above the slop the occultists were being fed back in the fake laboratory. The guards had been eating a little better than the occultists, but still, the leadership there definitely weren't investing in nutrition. I, on the other hand, was sparing no expense and had ordered all the most luxurious items on the menu. I knew there was a risk that doing so might attract unwanted attention, but right now, I didn't care. I was going to eat, and I was going to eat well.

Once I'd eaten my fill, I meditated for a while to accelerate my body's absorption of the nutrients. This was something healers and druids, having great control over their body and its functions, could do easily. I might not have been at their level, but I could still direct a little extra energy towards my intestines to support the digestive process.

After that, I wasn't sure what to do. I had no intention of lazing around in my room — I was ready to get out there and start exploring this new world! By now, my body's memory was functional, but I was still having some issues. At first, I'd thought that some fragments of memory must have been missing, buried somewhere in the mind, but over time, I began to see that the body's old owner had actually just been uneducated. The problem wasn't memory gaps so much as basic lack of experience. How and why did engines work? How did you maintain firearms? What was the correct way to shoot them? I knew, for example, that there were a lot of soldiers here in Circle City, but I had no idea why. I had a lot of superficial information in my head, but the moment I tried delving deeper, I'd run into huge gaps in my knowledge. My first order of business, then, was reconnaissance.

The warmth from the food had spread to every cell in my body, so I'd thrown my wet, worn, dirty pants and jacket in the trash. I regretted this very soon after leaving the guest house. A bone-chilling wind was still blowing through the city streets, sending tiny shards of ice digging into my skin. I realised that I hadn't thought to grow fur. I should have done that beforehand... Instead, here I was in my white t-shirt and light-weight pants... I must have looked ridiculous, to say the least. Everyone around me was wearing winter coats and warm jackets, and people kept turning to stare at me as they passed, twirling their fingers by their temples in the *crazy* gesture. Did I *look* like I was doing this on purpose?

I'd have to start by searching the city to find a good clothing store. For that, I was going to need a navigation system (a handy invention I'd recently learned about), and for *that*, I'd have to buy a cell phone...

It looked like I'd have to start off the old-fashioned way. Luckily, my head still held all my knowledge of demonology — I seriously doubted anyone could take *that* away.

I headed for the nearest alleyway, and once I was sure the coast was clear, I traced a small, faint pentagram about the size of my open palm in the dirty slush. It flared into life and a short, skinny demon sporting a tiny set of wings on its back shot out, landing head-first in a pile of snow.

"G-g-g-grah!" the demon righted itself in a flash and began shaking the snow from its short fur. "Seriously? You drag me from the nice warm depths of hell to *this*? Do you know what I could do to you for this?"

The demon met my eyes and its expression changed instantly. I'd decided not to beat around the bush with this one and was trying to look strong enough to be convincing.

"Well? What could you do to me?"

"I — could — complete the contract twice as fast!" the demon blurted, apparently clever enough to think on the spot. "It's either that, or freeze to death..."

"In that case, you can start by finding a shop that sells high-quality warm clothes," I nodded. "But be stealthy."

"Understood," the demon muttered. Then, buzzing like a bee, it launched itself into the air. With wings that small, the only thing keeping the demon airborne was how fast they could flap.

The flying demon disappeared over the rooftops, only to return a few minutes later with a detailed route to the nearest clothing store, which it transferred to me telepathically. Before it could buzz off back to its balmy home, I gave it a few more tasks; after the clothing store, I'd need to get myself a cell phone so I could find the shortest route back to the guest house. The bee-demon cursed at me, but I ignored it. I wasn't about to reveal my true power to some pipsqueak demon scout. Well... okay, I may have given it a *tiny* glimpse, but just enough to make it listen.

Back out on the street, people once more turned to stare at me as I passed, their faces puzzled. I didn't give a damn. No one knew where I was, and even if they were looking, I doubted they'd ever find me, so I didn't have to worry about blending in. That aristocrat might be powerful, but he had no sway in the city, he probably didn't even — my thoughts were interrupted by the sight of a group of patrolling police officers. Hmm, maybe blending in wasn't such a bad idea, after all... They glanced over at me, and when I saw one of them start to move in my direction, I ducked into a nearby store.

The first salesperson I crossed paths with scowled at me, and I saw him nod to security to kick me out.

"Please leave the store, sir!" said the security guard. He was the size of a gorilla, but his tone was polite, which was what saved him. I could have kicked up a fuss, butted heads with him and showed off my strength, but what would be the point? There was no need for that right now.

"You really want me to leave?" I smirked, pulling a large banknote out of my pocket. The guard glanced at the salesman.

"Please excuse this imbecile!" the salesman cooed, suddenly smiling from ear to ear. "Get out of my sight, you idiot!" he snapped at the guard, who rolled his eyes and stepped aside. I noted that the guard deigned not to grace the *real* idiot in the room with a reply.

As soon as the money appeared, the quality of the service shot from zero to five stars. The salesman flitted around me, taking measurements and presenting different items for my perusal. I was only in the market for one thing, however, and I quickly spotted it: a warm-looking down jacket. I paid, left the store and headed on to the next one.

The previous occupant of my body hadn't known a damn thing about phones. There were a few scant memories of some of the most expensive ones, but that was only because there were ads for them everywhere. Not to worry — I figured I'd get the hang of it fast. I chose a phone in the medium price range, making sure it was compatible with the thing they called the 'internet'. The internet was a kind of global information database that you could use at any time, from almost anywhere in the world, to get answers to any question you could think of. This was the description that had popped up in my memory, at least, but I still had some questions. Why, for example, had my body's old owner not bothered to *acquire* all that knowledge? After all, this cell phone was a fairly affordable, accessible item. Get yourself one, and you could spend every minute of the day absorbing information! It was that simple!

I headed straight back to the guest house, quickly got to grips with the phone and promptly disappeared down an information rabbit hole until dawn. Well, my memory certainly hadn't been lying about the vast amount of information on there. Not all of it was *true*, but you could easily separate fact from fiction by cross-checking multiple sources.

Time flew by. I could have sat there for days without ever tearing myself away from the screen. I ordered room service a couple of times during the night, and even as I ate, I just kept on scrolling through endless reams of information. I felt I was beginning to understand why people with access to this boundless database didn't actually become wise, all-knowing beings. It was because of the cat photos... oh yes, they were the *real* evil. You'd let yourself get distracted for a second, scroll through a photo or two, and then *bam* — a full two hours of your life, down the drain. Sure, I'd also spent four hours looking at cartoons, but I had no regrets there. My willpower could move mountains, yes, but it wasn't infinite.

All that said, the internet was incredibly useful, despite being fraught with danger and time-swallowing rabbit holes. By morning, I'd gleaned a decent understanding of the city, and now, as I sat on a bench by a lake throwing bread to the pigeons, I was contemplating my next move.

Incidentally, I wasn't feeding the pigeons out of the kindness of my heart. I'd had an... *altercation* with these birds in my old life. They may have seemed like brainless, useless creatures at first glance, but nothing in the world could make me cross them a second time. Better to give them a little bread here and there than to spend your whole life looking over your shoulder — or, more likely, over your head.

Just then, I saw something curious. I was just sitting there, throwing my bread and watching people as they passed by, absorbed in their daily lives and paying me no attention. But then, a woman in her thirties walked by. She looked perfectly fine on the outside, but I could see something remarkable happening to her astral body. There was a little horned devil clinging to her back, causing the woman constant back pain. *She* probably believed that she'd just strained a muscle, but that couldn't have been further from the truth. I knew that medicine would only do so much for her, and that eventually, the pain would always return, causing the woman constant suffering. The demon, meanwhile, was feeding on that pain, suffering and anger. But it wasn't strong enough to cause her any serious harm; instead, it was keeping her pain levels just low enough to prevent her from going to see a specialist.

It was only then that I realised the cultists back at the compound might have been some use after all. Everyone in the compound had been clean, in the sense that no one had had a demon clinging to their astral body. Here, on the other hand, almost everyone was carrying one or more demonic parasites on their back. And that could only mean one thing: the veil between this world and its demonic plane must be very, *very* thin. Something here was off.

Regarding being looked for, my suspicions proved to be correct. I learned online that there was a search operation underway in the city, and that the streets were filled with patrols hunting for some fugitive or other. However, none of them were taking any notice of the guy sitting and feeding the pigeons by the frozen lake. After all, a fugitive wouldn't be feeding pigeons, would he? Fugitives were supposed to flee, or at least hide out, not sit peacefully on a bench in the middle of town.

That said, I wasn't *just* feeding the pigeons. My demon-watching had briefly distracted me from my main task, which was planning my next step. Now was the time to decide my future, to choose my course for the next thirty years or more. My plans might come to nothing, of course, since I could easily die tomorrow, but if I was honest, I wasn't in the mood to die. It was fun here! It had variety. The world I'd left behind (for now) had nothing to offer but thousands of years of wandering through a lifeless wasteland, and that was *not* what I called a good time...

* * *

*Count Serpentine's mansion*
*Around the same time*

"What do you mean, there's no evidence?" the man in the severe suit slammed his fist down on the table. "Someone's going to pay for this! I told them to do whatever it took to bring me that bastard!"

The head of the Serpentine Family's personal guard said nothing, only nodded and left the room as fast as he could. The count was usually pretty even-tempered, but the loss of the laboratory had clearly angered him. And he wasn't the kind of guy you wanted to see angry... Even a small dose of Serpentine's energy could poison you for weeks, and that was if you were lucky enough to survive at all.

Alone in his office, the count leaned back in his chair and poured himself a little wine. How much effort, how many years had he poured into that place? How many laws had he broken? The number of people he'd had pointlessly tortured, on the other hand, didn't bother him much. He didn't even read the reports they sent him on the deaths down there in the basements — they were just an incidental cost, after all.

In any case, someone would be to blame for this. A couple of reports had already come in, and based on the intelligence gathered, it seemed that escaped demons were the culprits. They could say for certain that several charred demon bodies had been discovered inside the compound. But the investigation had only just begun... knowing his own forces wouldn't be able to dig up the truth alone, Serpentine had already called on the best of the best, specialists who'd be sure to turn up traces of the culprit. Assuming the culprit hadn't perished in the flames along with the rest, that was...

* * *

It was time to get moving, if for no other reason than because my situation was becoming precarious. I'd run out of bread, but the pigeons, judging by their expectant stares, were still hungry...

The problem was, I still hadn't come up with a solid plan for the next thirty years of my life. There was still so much I didn't know about this world, and I needed to fill in the gaps. I decided to head back to my room; at least I knew I'd have food there, and food was good. Plus, I could poke around on the internet in peace without anyone to distract me. Here, there was a constant stream of people passing by, and I couldn't ignore the demonic entities clinging to them.

As I walked along, keeping to myself, I took a moment to admire the local architecture. The buildings here had been built with durability in mind, and because of the harsh climate, the builders hadn't paid much attention to decoration. But even as simple as the buildings were, there was a beauty to them. If nothing else, they were a new sight for me, so I may as well admire them!

I came across a street sweeper clearing snow from the sidewalk. The man was cursing softly to himself, clearly aware that the snow was falling faster than he could clear it. Even so, he persisted, digging his shovel in again and again. Nearby, three men were tinkering with a broken-down car, although *car* was probably a generous word for it.

It looked more like a pile of rust held together with blue electrical tape. As I watched, they got the engine running, and the car even started moving, but as soon as they all jumped inside, the thing stalled again. All they could do was get back out and start pushing. It was like with the bicycle — *they* were moving the vehicle instead of the vehicle moving them.

Suddenly, my plans to head back to the guest house and relax were cut short by a highly abnormal event. I knew it was abnormal because I hadn't seen anything like it on the internet, and, well... an entire building flying into the air definitely wasn't normal. Right? It certainly didn't happen every day, I was sure of that much.

The mighty rumble made my eardrums shake, and I ducked behind the nearest car for cover, but my curiosity got the better of me and I peeked out again to watch the scene unfolding. And what a scene it was... The house seemed to have been hit by a bomb or a rocket and had practically collapsed from the force of the blast. Chunks of stone and shards of glass had gone flying in all directions, and several passersby had been hit by shrapnel. Others ran to tend to the wounded, and I would have joined them if it weren't for the very impressive flying machine that suddenly appeared suspended above the house as if out of thin air. It was as if a cloak of invisibility had suddenly been whisked away to reveal an aircraft where no aircraft had previously been. It had a pair of short wings, each with a powerful turbine attached, and a grey, pot-bellied body adorned with a selection of cannons and rocket launchers. If my body's memories were to be believed, it was a pretty high-tech contraption.

A hatch opened in the belly of the machine, and dozens of soldiers in white armour began to descend on thick ropes.

"That one's gifted... that one's ungifted... those two are gifted," I murmured to myself, carefully studying each of the soldiers from my spot behind the car. I had to admit that even from here, their gear looked seriously expensive. The armour was perfectly fitted with virtually no weak spots, the helmets fully enclosed the head and the vital organs were protected with reinforced plates of a material I couldn't identify.

But what were these soldiers *doing* here? A quick scan of my surroundings soon gave me my answer. Lying on the ground not far from me was a small, twisted sign that had recently hung inside the ruined building. Judging by the few fragments that were still legible, it had been some kind of government building, possibly a city archive of some kind.

By now, the soldiers had hit the ground, unhooked themselves from the ropes and started shooting. As I watched them fan out, I tried to identify a pattern to their targets but couldn't see one. I wasn't sure what to do. Should I stay here and quietly observe, or should I just hightail it as far away as possible? One thing I *shouldn't* do was overestimate my abilities; these were trained soldiers, and going up against them would be tough. Maybe if I just sat here, they'd go away on their own... Or should I engage them in combat? No, that would be stupid — I didn't even know if they were the good guys or the bad guys. I needed more information.

Then again... maybe I already knew enough. I could see plenty of other civilians hiding behind other cars all around me. By now, the soldiers were firing indiscriminately, and it looked like anyone was a target, including unarmed civilians. I had to find a way out of here. I decided to start by putting some distance between myself and the soldiers through a combination of crawling and sprinting in short bursts. In two bounds, I made it behind a small van parked nearby, but then, everything went wrong. A rope dropped down on me from above, and a second later, a soldier clad in high-tech white armour was standing in front of me. Wow... the armour looked even better from up close! I could see the servo motors on it now — they probably boosted the fighter's strength, and possibly even improved their aim and accuracy.

I looked around. There was nowhere for me to run. The soldier saw me and took aim, ready to shoot. It was pointless to try and flee, so instead, I stood my ground and prepared for battle. I wasn't going to give up that easy. That said, there were a lot of them... I counted at least a dozen white-armoured figures, all armed with sophisticated weapons. They appeared to be emptying the ruined building, carrying boxes out onto a special platform that had been lowered down from the aircraft.

"What's taking so long?" another soldier appeared behind the one with his weapon trained on me. This one had a gold stripe on his armour, suggesting a higher rank.

"He was just sitting here alone, sir. I thought it might be wise to shoot him..."

Woah! *Shoot* me? I thought he hadn't pulled the trigger yet because he was going to take me prisoner! Were these guys really going to make me summon without pentagrams? In this state, that might kill me. Then again, the rifle pointed straight at my forehead might kill me, too... In fact, I'd say the likelihood of the latter was a whole lot higher.

Time was ticking. I swiftly tapped into my reserves of strength and focused on opening the internal floodgates that would release my energy, but I was just a little too short on power.

"Wait," the officer stepped forward to take a closer look at me. "He was hiding, you said? Not running?" The soldier only shrugged in reply — so far as it was possible to shrug inside his suit, at least. "He might be from the building. Take him to the plane," the officer said, waving a hand. It seemed I wouldn't need to use my energy just yet. The pentagram-free summoning could wait — phew!

The soldier grabbed me roughly by the collar, tearing my jacket slightly, and started dragging me in the direction of the square, where everything of value from the bombed-out building was being collected. Other soldiers were hurriedly piling up boxes and wrangling people in lab coats, preparing everything to be taken away as soon as possible. I could hear sirens in the distance, which I guessed meant that things were just about to kick off.

"Who's that?" boomed a voice as we stepped onto the platform. Based on the number of golden stripes on his armour, I reckoned this guy was the head honcho. As the soldier opened his mouth to answer, the platform shuddered and began to ascend slowly towards the aircraft.

"Not sure, sir," the soldier shrugged. "He might be one of them."

"Are you an imbecile?" the commander glared at the soldier. "Do you see him wearing a lab coat?" The man turned to address the lab-coated captives: "Is he one of yours?"

"Never seen him before," an old man shook his head. "You should just let him go. He doesn't know anything."

"Hah!" the commander suddenly burst into riotous laughter, the rest of the soldiers snickering along at the man's suggestion. "Oh, well, if he doesn't know anything, then of course we should let him go, shouldn't we? And compensate him for the inconvenience — ahahah! That's what we *always* do with Imperial scum, isn't it, boys?"

They all thought this was funny, did they? Fine. Another ten seconds, and I'd be finished scratching this pentagram into my palm with my fingernail. Then, I'd be laughing along with them...

"What do you think, Imperial?" the commander came towards me. "I'm afraid I don't have any cash, but since this was our mistake, let me give you—" — a knife suddenly flashed in his hand — "a gift!" In one swift movement, he stabbed the blade deep into my thigh, piercing it straight through. Still laughing, he sent me flying with a powerful kick.

I just kept my cool. I could have fought them hand-to-hand, but the platform was a little small, plus, the hostages might have gotten hurt. My airborne condition made things much easier, especially considering the platform was still only about four metres off the ground.

My short flight ended with a relatively soft landing in a pile of mushy snow. I lay there for a moment, enjoying the feeling of cool wetness and the clear blue winter sky. I wouldn't forget this... Naturally, I was pleased to have the knife (I could get a good price for it later), but the rest of this experience wasn't exactly going to make a cherished memory.

I heard a burst of gunfire. Two white-clad soldiers plummeted down from the sky. There was return fire, and then a couple of explosions. I just lay there, staring at the sky until someone grabbed me under the armpits and dragged me away.

"Can't you just let me lie in peace," I muttered wearily.

"We've got an injured civilian! Stab wound to the thigh! Possible internal injuries! I need an ambulance! And a medic!" the soldier shouted into his radio, still dragging me away from the battlefield.

Soon, I was on a stretcher, and people in blue uniforms were carrying me to a van filled with medical equipment.

Once inside, the two young guys who'd been carrying me got straight down to treating my wounds. One of them appeared to be a doctor while the other was a medic. They had the knife out of my leg in no time, after which, they stuck a needle in my arm and installed the thing they called an 'intravenous drip'. All the while, I just watched them work in amazement. What a stroke of luck that I'd crossed paths with those soldiers in the white armour... This was *fun*.

"Give me back my knife!" I held my hand out. They weren't going to steal my weapon!

"You... what?" the medic stammered, but I was already grabbing the handle.

"It was a gift!" I yelled, yanking the knife towards me. "Listen, I'm sure you're both great guys, but I can't let you have it." After a moment's thought, I fished around in my pockets and pulled out two dollars. "Here," I said, "take these instead."

In my world, the custom was to pay healers straight away, and it was a good idea to be generous. That always worked out cheaper in the long run... I rarely had need of their services, though, since there were plenty of demons out there with similar abilities. It was always simpler for me to have a demon do the job than to haggle with a human. The two who'd just treated me, however, refused the money point-blank, and they even handed me back the knife, no questions asked.

Just then, the door of the van swung open and a man appeared. He was modestly dressed in plain clothes. For several moments, he stared in confusion at me, the money and the knife, before raising a questioning eyebrow at the medics.

"Everything's fine," the doctor, just now realising how the scene must look, smiled.

"Phew," the man exhaled. "So, it's alright if I question him, then?" he nodded at me. The two men gave affirmative nods, and the third man stepped into the van and closed the door behind him. "Sir, could you please describe briefly what you saw today? You are one of the few people to witness the events up close and survive."

"Well, I don't know... I guess the building exploded, and then that big plane appeared and a whole task force of soldiers came out of it," I shrugged. "They started shooting, and then they flew away. Something like that."

"Right... maybe you could explain in a *little* more detail?" the man said, a note of exasperation in his voice. Well, why not? I retold the story in excruciating detail, even describing my personal audience with the enemy commander on the platform.

"I see," the man nodded, scribbling something down in his notebook. "Thank you for the information. We'll look into it," he said, getting up and heading for the door. "I won't disturb you any further."

"Can I ask you something?" I called out. The man stopped, and then nodded. "Who were those soldiers?"

"*Who were they*?" he looked at me, gob-smacked. "They were the New Imperials, of course!"

Aha! I'd guessed right! I'd read something about these New Imperials online. It seemed I'd finally figured out which side I was going to choose...

Previously, I'd felt I needed more information before I formed any opinions about the New Imperials. Now, I was firmly of the opinion that everything the internet said about them was absolutely true.

Right now, I was on the territory of the Empire. Recently, a breakaway state — the New Empire — had formed within the Empire's territory, and Circle City happened to sit almost on the border between the two. The article I'd read had described the situation as 'tense'. As far as I could tell, it was more than tense — it was an all-out war. I must have been reading the wrong articles...

I thought again about what a stroke of luck it had been to end up here. I was learning more and more, and as soon as the wound in my leg was fully healed, I'd be off to enlist in the army. I'd considered becoming an aristocrat, but instead, we were going to work our way up through the ranks, wreaking vengeance in our path!

I chuckled softly to myself as I gazed out the window...

Meanwhile, the Imperial forces had stopped shooting after the disappearing plane and were yelling into their radios. They were insisting that the aircraft was already out of reach, demanding that air forces be sent out to capture it and complaining that the enemy had activated some kind of impenetrable shield. The only message they got back was that capture was impossible due to their close proximity to the border. Sending their own costly aircraft into enemy territory would be too risky, and successful capture of the enemy would not be guaranteed.

They needn't have worried. While the medics went about their business, I reached down and pushed a finger into my wound, releasing a little energy, and then closed it off with a magic knot. With this, I also activated the magic mark I'd planted on the platform. Seen by no one, a flash of light went up inside the enemy plane, and the hulking vessel began to fill with a blood-red mist.

"I'll find you now, you bastards, no matter where you hide," I murmured to myself. "And better than that — so will the demons."

# CHAPTER 5

"AND YOU CAME STRAIGHT HERE to enlist?" the rather large, moustachioed man in the green army fatigues asked once more, looking me up and down yet again. "And you're sure?"

"Why would I come here if I wasn't sure?" I replied, throwing my hands up. "Yes, I want to serve, defend my country, get paid, change my name... Listen, do you need recruits? Or should I go somewhere else?"

"No, no, don't leave!" the man replied, suddenly animated. "It's just... aren't you a little scrawny for the army?"

"There's nothing wrong with me," I replied, settling more comfortably into my creaky chair. "So? Will you take me, or not?"

The man let out a heavy sigh and looked over at his colleague. The colleague only shrugged, as if to say, *do we have a choice*? After all, people weren't exactly queueing around the block to sign up.

If I was honest, that part surprised me. I'd been expecting at least *some* kind of crowd, especially after what had just happened in town. Instead, there were about fifteen people in the room, ten of whom were already serving in the Imperial Army and were here to process paperwork or encourage potential recruits to enlist. They clearly weren't doing a very good job of the latter.

"Alright, fine," the moustachioed man opened his desk drawer and pulled out several sheets of paper, which he then held out to me. "Read these carefully, and choose wisely!"

With that final instruction, he left me alone to read the documents. They outlined the terms and conditions for army service in comprehensive detail. Every page bore a seal, and each seal was a different shape and colour. There was blue, yellow, green... but it was a different colour that grabbed my attention. As it happened, the words on that page grabbed my attention, too...

As I studied the contracts, the two men at the desk chatted casually.

"Can you believe what happened?" moustache-man said, sounding indignant. "An attack, right in the middle of the city! Those Newies are already so brazen!"

"Yeah, and we only have *these* hopeless cases signing up to fight them," the other man sighed, glancing my way.

According to the news articles I'd read while waiting for my leg to heal, the situation really was bleak, and, by all accounts, the New Empire was growing bolder by the day. Still, attacks on Circle City itself were a rarity, an extremely brazen act that the New Empire had only dared to carry out a handful of times, and all within the past month. Before that, the New Imperials had been too scared to even step foot across the border.

"Alright, I've chosen," I said, signing the piece of paper and holding it out to moustache-man. He looked at the paper, then at me, and then back to the paper again.

"Who do you think you are, kid? You might want to read those terms again," he said eventually, his jaw hanging slightly open. "That's a black contract! Maybe you haven't heard, but around here, we call those guys suicide soldiers. And believe me, we call them that for a reason!"

"Relax," I smiled, waving him off. "No need to worry about me."

They tried to talk me out of it for quite a while, but I stood firm. Finally, the moustachioed man shook his head and stamped my papers, cementing my contract with the Imperial Army and adding me to the ranks of suicide soldiers.

"Well, it's your life, kid," the man sighed, regarding me with pity. "Anyway, we'll finish your registration here, and then, you need to report straight to your unit's location."

"When do they give me my new identity?" I asked.

"Soon as you're fully registered, just be patient. There's just one more thing I need to ask you... Are you sure you're not crazy?" he squinted at me.

"I don't know," I shrugged. "It's been a while since I checked."

Okay, okay, that was a joke — the truth was, I'd never checked. My world *did* have healers who worked with mental issues (similar to the psychologists and psychiatrists here), but for some reason, they didn't take on demonologists as patients. Admittedly, there had been a few unfortunate cases... One healer, for example, had promised to cleanse a demonologist of all his inner demons. The demonologist had reassured the healer that he was quite content to have the demons, and to prove it, had decided to show them to the man... After that, it was the poor healer who needed treatment.

"And you're sure you want a new identity?" the moustachioed man asked.

"I'm sure," was all I replied. I wasn't going to explain myself to him, and anyway, I was fully entitled to request an identity change.

"Ok, then," he shrugged. "Your unit will handle that, in any case. Truly an interesting contract you chose... You surprised me, if I'm honest."

I'd actually read up about this so-called 'black contract' back at the hospital. They'd practically dragged me there after I was injured. I'd spent the night there, and by morning, I'd figured out that I had the right to refuse treatment and be discharged early. Once I'd done that, I headed straight back to the guest house, where I'd poured energy into the wound to continue the healing process.

By now, there was hardly any pain at all, and soon, there wouldn't be a single trace of the wound left. I wasn't a healer, of course, but the injury hadn't been serious enough to require asking for help, and anyway, any mage above a certain level could harness healing energy. That was true of the mages *I* was used to, at any rate... I was yet to meet one of those here.

Anyway, the healing had given me enough downtime to think and do some research on the army. I'd also entertained thoughts of joining the aristocracy, becoming a merchant, or even opening a clinic. The piles of information I sifted through convinced me to drop the aristocrat idea as too dull. I'd held a title in my old life, and quite a major one, at that. It was possible I might return to that life someday in the distant future, but while I was here, I intended to live an action-packed existence full of excitement and adventure! I wanted to try something new, to have a fresh experience getting to know this world.

Plus, if I wanted excitement and adventure, then I was going to need a lot of energy. That was my main reason for choosing the army, though there were certainly others. As far as I could tell, the military in this world was roughly equal to the aristocracy in power and status. A decorated major could easily brush shoulders with barons and dukes without turning any heads. However, this privilege would not be extended to, say, a major who'd spent his entire career pushing papers in a stuffy office and only received his rank through length of service. Respect was only bestowed on those who'd earned their rank through their hero-ism on the battlefield.

Meanwhile, those in the upper ranks of the army had practically the same privileges as aristo-crats; both could find themselves in control of troops, land and even property. As respected fig-ures, soldiers would also be invited to balls and parties. The only difference between them and the aristocrats was that they got into fights more of-ten, but that part didn't scare me. Quite the oppo-site — that was the part I liked.

Beyond that, it started to get ridiculous. Under the Empire's duelling code, soldiers had exactly the same rights as aristocrats. This meant that the second I was enlisted, I could go and challenge a baron to a fair fight, and the baron would be una-ble to refuse.

All of this was because the Empire was perpet-ually at war, and while its forces were mighty, it had plenty of jealous enemies abroad with mighty forces of their own.

Soldiers hadn't always had these privileges. In fact, they'd been introduced during a coup d'etat. The emperor's brother, taking advantage of the fact that the Empire was weakened by a drawn-out war, incited a riot and stabbed the ruler in the back. It was the military who'd come to the ruling regime's defence and kept the country from falling apart. The New Empire had been formed within the old one, with borders that happened to fall just short of Circle City.

In essence, the die was cast: we were fated to fight the New Empire, and fight them we would.

"Hey — you need a medical exam first!" the moustachioed man called out as I turned to leave. "They need to asses you and assign you a fitness rating."

Oh, what the hell, why not? I went back to my seat with a shrug and sat down to wait.

Soon after, a woman came in, gestured to me to follow her and led me into a different office, where a bunch of doctors were already waiting.

The first doctor was supposed to check my general physical condition. As soon as he laid eyes on me, the large man in the white coat let out a long sigh. Signing my document, he dismissed me with a shake of the head and a "please move on."

The dentist looked in my mouth, added his signature to the document and then passed me along to the psychiatrist.

"I've been wanting to visit you for a long time," I said, taking a seat, and the elderly man smiled. He was about to say something when he caught sight of the black stamp on my contract and slammed my file shut.

"Get out!" the smile vanished from his face. "I know everything I need to know about you."

How rude! If I couldn't share my inner demons *here*, then where *could* I? Only kidding, I was going to share them, alright... but not yet. Right now, I had to do what I was told and move on to the eye doctor.

"God, you're frail," muttered the broad-shouldered woman. She was wearing a pair of enormous glasses. I wanted to retort that at least I had good eyesight, unlike her, but I didn't. Instead, I just waited for her to sign the document and hand me back my file, after which, I headed back to my moustache-sporting friend.

In the end, I got my fitness rating. My piece of paper had a nice new stamp — two whole points! I knew for sure that two was greater than one, so I reckoned I could be very proud of my result.

"Lord, you're as weak as a kitten!" said moustache-man, echoing the eye doctor's sentiments as he leafed through my file. "You couldn't even carry a case of ammunition without help."

"I won't need to," I shrugged. It was the truth. Why would I need to carry anything when I could just summon a demon to do it?

The man shook his head. "Still, two out of ten."

Out of ten? Oh... I'd figured it was out of three. Two was still more than one, though, wasn't it? And it was *way* better than getting a zero. All the same, this was going to give me a certain reputation, at least to start with, even though my true strength lay elsewhere.

"Alright, skin-and-bones, sit down," the moustachioed man sighed. "Saman will come and finish up your documents now."

I didn't mind sitting down. I'd had a hearty

breakfast, with all the tea I could drink, before leaving the guest house, so I wasn't in a hurry to go anywhere.

Soon enough, the man named Saman arrived. He was also moustachioed, but was older than anyone else present and was completely grey. He didn't even try to hide the pity in his gaze when he looked at me, and I actually heard him swear quietly under his breath when he saw my contract.

"Your results indicate the presence of a gift," he began. "I am responsible for recording all of the army's gifted soldiers, so this is a necessary procedure." The old man took a seat next to me and his assistant handed him my file. "Well? Talk," he said, looking at me, pen in hand.

"I'm a demonologist," I shrugged. The old man only stared at me, blinking once or twice. Meanwhile, the rest of the room had fallen silent, all eyes trained in our direction.

"You're a... what?" the old man frowned.

"A demonologist," I repeated. The old man tensed.

"Are you sure?" he asked, squinting.

Right now, I *wasn't* so sure... Had I messed up somewhere? I thought I'd read that they had demonologists here, and that it was a perfectly legal gift. I knew that there weren't many around, but that was hardly a crime...

"Ahahah!" the old man burst out laughing and slapped me on the shoulder. "Well, you're doomed then, my boy. My sympathies. Why did you join the army with a gift like that? I mean, you're doomed in the Black Squad *anyway* — they don't call them suicide soldiers for nothing, you know. But with that gift? You're truly a suicidal soldier — looking to go out with a bang! So to speak! Ahahah!" the man shook his head, wiping tears from his eyes. "You'd be more use if you were a weather mage. At least that way, you could give yourself some nice clear skies to die under!"

"Let me get this straight — you think a weather mage is worth more than a demonologist?" I scowled.

"Of course! Not that we get much rain here, I admit, but it *is* always cold. Just imagine the things you could do! Picture it," he leaned in, barely suppressing his laughter, and went on, "You and your squad go out on a mission at night, and the moon is shining up above you. We can't have that. You wave your hands, and hey presto, the moon is covered by clouds! The enemy can't see you, and your mission is a success!"

"You're giving me goosebumps," I said dryly, and the old man burst out laughing again.

With that, my registration was complete. I was given an address to report to the following morning. They'd certainly given me a lot of time to relax — the whole day, in fact. Oh well, all the better.

I left the recruitment centre and decided to take a walk. I had some thinking to do.

I was thinking over my decision. There was a reason they'd all been so shocked when I'd ticket the black box. There were other, easier army positions out there — ones where they trained you for a couple of years first, and then sent you out on relatively safe postings. In one of *those* positions, I could easily be posted deep within Empire territory for years, only being sent into action in the case of all-out war. But I'd chosen the Black Squad for a reason. The preparation time before deployment was just one week, and I'd read that only soldiers with heavy combat experience joined up.

One drawback was that you had to agree to serve for no less than seventy years. However, the Imperial Forces were also in possession of a highly advanced technological device — one that I would be sticking my hand into tomorrow. They called it the black box, and the name pretty much said it all. It looked just like a regular black box, and in fact, it functioned in a similar way. It located every possible scrap of information on you from every possible source, gathered it all and then simply destroyed the lot. And just like that, your life was a blank page again, and the army could give you your new identity. It didn't matter if you were a wanted murderer; get to the black box, and no one would be hunting you for your old sins ever again.

The catch was that the rules for Black Squad soldiers were exceptionally strict. For the first five years of service, you couldn't leave the base without permission from your superior officer. That meant no strolls, no interaction with civilians and no taking time off. You did your service, went on your never-ending combat assignments and that was that. *After* five years, you were entitled to short leaves and infrequent free time. After fifteen, you could assemble your own combat team, or you could go on military leave for six months. You also had the opportunity to purchase your own estate, house or apartment. Plus, you were finally allowed to start a family.

While it was wiping your identity, the black box would make a small mark on your wrist. This was a magical tattoo and would stay with you forever. From what I knew, the black, demonic face it depicted looked slightly different for each soldier, depending on their rank and how decorated they were.

Far from branding the person, this tattoo was a badge of honour. It marked the bearer out as more than just an ordinary soldier. This person was prepared to wade into the thick of it on the battlefield, sworn to take on every fight that came their way. And when the person bearing that mark was elderly, it meant they'd completed their service, a feat that inspired profound respect in others.

I'd get to choose my own name and surname, and I could even pick my new date of birth. My record would be completely clean, my past destroyed, and I, impossible to trace. Whoever the old occupant of my body had been, it would be like he'd never existed.

If a soldier of the Black Squad did complete their service, the world was their oyster. They could join the Imperial Guard, command an aristocrat's personal retinue or any other force their heart desired. Wherever they went, they'd be welcomed with open arms. Incredibly few made it to this stage, however; black contracts were known as 'death sentences' for a reason.

By this stage, my head was swimming with information. This was a very rare occurrence for me, since intellectual processing was usually one of my strong suits. But hey — while I might not understand the finer points of military service just yet, I was sure I'd figure it out along the way. The main thing was that the terms of the contract suited me just fine. Once my seventy years were served, I'd be able to keep fighting as a gun for hire — and I probably wouldn't even have to wait the full seventy.

I'd learned that the army had its own way of calculating length of service and pay level. If you were stationed in Circle City itself, every year you served was counted twice. That was because this post consistently sent you on two combat missions a week, if not more. On top of that, you could sometimes earn bonuses for especially dangerous operations. Depending on how complex the mission was, you could sometimes cut two, three or even six months off your service in the span of just a few days. To top it off, you'd still get paid for the time cut.

With the way I operated, I knew I was going to coast through this. I planned to fight every second I could, so my seventy years would be flying by in double time.

So, it was settled. My main mission now was this: join the army, learn the ropes and get five years of service under my belt as fast as I could. Why I'd chosen five years as my goal, I wasn't sure. Maybe I wasn't ready to give up my dream of someday opening a demon-staffed massage parlour...

A car sped past me, dousing me from head to toe in grimy, freezing slush. Just in time, I activated the faint pentagram on my palm and watched the spray bounce harmlessly off my clothes. Hah! I was starting to get the hang of this world. I wouldn't be splashed a second time!

I wondered again if there could really be so few decent demonologists in this world. I remembered Saman's reaction when I'd told him about my gift. I'd wanted to ask him to explain, but hadn't wanted to arouse suspicion. But he'd said that a good demonologist would never join the army here... Of course, the strong demonologists usually came from the powerful clans, who had the resources to train their offspring. That would seem a much more inviting position than serving in the Imperial Army...

Well, that was just fine. Let them underestimate me for now.

My next task was to check out a certain curious spot. After that, I'd head back to the guest house and collect my things, and tomorrow, I'd begin my new life. Whatever was coming, I had a feeling it was going to be fun — and wasn't that the most important part?

"Good afternoon, sir," said the old man behind the counter as I stepped through the door. The store was somehow cramped and sparse at the same time. It looked like the man must store his actual wares elsewhere. In the corner stood a low table piled high with catalogues. Personally, I thought selecting goods out of a catalogue was a pain, but apparently, that was the way they did it here.

"Can I help you?" the old man asked, snapping me out of my thoughts.

"I need artefacts," I said firmly as I approached the desk.

"Oh? Any particular kind?" he replied, putting on his glasses. He looked at me carefully.

"I'm not sure yet," I shrugged. Then, I laid practically every penny I had down on the table. "But I'm going to need a lot of them." I smiled as I watched the man's eyes take in the stack of bills and pile of coins.

"I see," he mused. "Well, young man, we'll certainly have something for you! I think this should be enough for..." — he assessed the cash again — "several artefacts! Small ones, that is..."

# CHAPTER 6

"I MEAN, I KNEW this wouldn't be easy," the soldier's voice was pensive, "but who knew it would be like *this*?"

As it happened, I completely agreed with him. The rest of the squad, to a man, nodded, all thinking the very same thing.

I hadn't gotten my tattoo yet, nor had my identity been scrubbed. They'd said it was to give me one last chance to back out of the contract. We were just a few days in, and already, we were out here in the middle of the forest trying to complete some kind of group trial. Our task was to capture a polar bear that had recently attacked a checkpoint and eaten a soldier. In between his jokes and jibes, the commander had given us some parting advice, his tone so serious that his words had sunk in with everyone. He said we couldn't afford to lose more than ten people. We would need at least twenty soldiers to take down this bear — not a man less.

"Movement on the left!" a soldier cried, and a split-second later, a shot rang out.

"There's no movement over there, you idiot!" growled a man with a scar on his face. "If it spots us now, we're dead!"

"But I saw it! I know I did!" the younger soldier squealed. "Look, there it is! In the bushes!"

"That's a squirrel, imbecile!"

Sat in a nearby snowdrift, I just shook my head and watched the farce unfold. I could see a few other guys close by also descending into a deep gloom as they realised just what kind of squad they'd been lumped into.

And it had all started so well... I'd made my way to the assembly point, met the rest of the Black Squad sign-ups and then been transported in a truck to the base, which was just outside of town. We'd gotten to know each other on the way, and were also made to sign yet another mountain of paperwork.

Next, they'd given us uniforms, lined us up on the parade ground and told us that we were all great — but that only the best could be suicide soldiers, and therefore, they were giving us one more chance to reconsider. They'd said the Imperial Army leaders believed in fairness and wanted to be sure each one of us fully understood what a black contract meant. To ensure this, they were going to give us a taste of what a suicide soldier's life was like — *once* all our papers were signed.

For three days, they'd tortured us with a training program so intense, it made death look like the easy option. They shot over our heads, forced us to crawl, made us dig trenches in the frozen ground and fight each other. Then again, that was pretty standard army stuff, and I'd actually kind of enjoyed it. I hadn't had such a good warmup in a long time...

After that, they'd handed each of us a combat uniform and a weapon and brought us all out on the hunt. The commander had spent some time describing how dangerous this bear was, emphasising its great magical power, how many people it had killed and how urgently it needed to be stopped. Then, they'd abandoned us in the forest with a "good luck!" as they drove away.

The forest itself was also a challenge. In fact, the terrain was arguably more dangerous than the bear. Not only was it freakishly cold, but it was... *strange* in many ways. For example, the background energy of the place was so volatile that I'd been struggling to tune into it for some time. On top of that, we kept coming across all kinds of animals I'd never seen before, neither online nor in my old life.

Amongst all of these threats, however, the single biggest one was still the bear. And now, some idiot had fired into the bushes and revealed our location to the predator. All we could do was sit and wait for our imminent deaths. Another idiot lost his cool, and then another, and soon, they were seeing movement everywhere and shooting at the breeze.

But we also had some seasoned fighters in the group. They looked calm and collected, only shaking their heads every now and then. They understood the importance of the task; the commander had clearly stated that no one would be putting their hand in the black box unless we completed the mission and brought that bear back to base.

One small mercy was that we could take as long as we wanted. What mattered was the result, not how long it took or what we did to get there. But the commander had made it clear that if we failed, our contracts would be torn up. Though I had a feeling the bear might devour us first...

I wasn't complaining, though. This was fun! Plus, I had all these cool weapons... As for my gun, I'd been told in no uncertain terms to guard it like the family jewels. I wasn't quite sure what that meant, but I understood the instructions well enough. I'd wrapped the gun safely up in a rag and tied it to my back. I wasn't used to firearms, but I had no plans to work on that just yet — not when using a blade was so much more convenient.

In any case, I couldn't summon any demons for now. While I still hadn't adjusted to the anomalous flow of energy in this forest, I *could* have performed some minor manipulations, but I decided against even that. I wanted to watch and learn how people worked in this world, and for that, I needed to avoid drawing too much attention to myself. I was willing to bet that this trial was easier than the commanders had made it out to be... it was designed for newbies, after all.

There was a rustling sound, and they all raised their machine guns sharply.

"Don't shoot!" the soldier with the scar on his face roared. "It might be one of us!" His battle experience was clear, and I could see that he wasn't succumbing to panic like the others.

As I looked around, I noticed more unusual details about the forest. It was cold, and the snow lay waist-deep, but yet, there were berries and thick foliage on the bushes. Meanwhile, some of the trees were completely bare. I wondered if there were mushrooms hidden beneath the snow...

But the strangest part of this forest was the magic. It was so highly concentrated that with a few special rituals, you could bury yourself in the ground and easily stay there safe and sound for a decade or more. The energy in the earth would be enough to keep you alive — assuming the bear didn't dig you up early.

I was beginning to consider that maybe bears *weren't* the biggest threat out here... I hadn't seen a single bear so far, but I *could* see the tiny white bird that had been watching us for half an hour now. It may not have looked like a threat, but those eyes... They were bloodthirsty, predatory. One look, and I could tell that bird yearned for murder and destruction with every fibre of its being.

And then, there was the squirrel. It was small, fluffy and quite sweet at first glance. But *only* at first glance... It ran right out in front of us, stared at me and then switched its gaze to the guy next to me. It gave a snort, and then crushed two nuts between its paws with such force that the shell violently exploded. It then pointed a paw at the poor guy, whose face was now white, as if to indicate that *his* nuts would be next.

After that squirrel, I started scanning my surroundings a lot more frequently, and I kept a tight grip on my machine gun. The demonstration with the nuts had made quite an impression on me...

The one thing that united us all was that every one of us had joined the Black Squad in order to change our name and erase our old identity forever. This, however, had its drawbacks. One of these was that we could only refer to each other as 'Hey, you!'...

There *were* a couple of military guys among us who must have screwed up bad on their former assignments. Those guys had quickly grouped together, assigned themselves numbers and were now using those as names. Lucky for me, I *had* no previous name, so I didn't have to worry either way. Since my past could be said to be non-existent, I didn't have anything to hide.

We stood and listened to the rustling for a long time. After an hour, we were so cold that we just had to move. And since our commanders weren't here, that meant we'd have to organise ourselves. In the end, we decided to split into groups of five and head out in different directions to find this lazy bear ourselves. We all knew one thing: the first group to find that bear would be dinner. After that, the rest could come storming in, roaring and shouting, take down the bear and complete the task.

Catch and kill... it seemed... *silly* to me. And the funniest part was that the drop-off point was only an hour's walk from here, even less without the heavy snow. We were so close to civilisation, and yet, crazy stuff like this was going on... I was starting to understand why every year of service in Circle City counted twice.

Our first skirmish went down very differently to how I'd pictured it. I heard a distant scream, a howl, and then a series of gunshots. I raced towards the sounds, and when I reached them, I saw... a soldier holding his machine gun tight across his neck, with a wolf trying to bite the gun in half to reach the man's throat. I was the first to reach them, so I quickly slashed the wolf across the back. The beast's hide instantly began to ripple as it activated its natural defences. But that wasn't going to stop me — I could activate some defences of my own. Like this little pentagram of demonic power drawn on my hand... My next strike sliced smoothly through the wolf's defences, splitting the beast into two perfectly equal halves.

I could have sworn it was still looking at me, sizing me up. I had a feeling I'd be seeing more wolfish grins before this adventure was out...

"Thanks for the help... that could have been... well... yeah," said the kid, gasping for breath as he lay in the snow.

"Don't worry about it," I replied, helping him up. He stuck out a hand.

"Let me introduce myself. I'm..." the kid suddenly froze, his voice trailing off.

"...Yes?" I asked, amused.

"Uh — no one. I guess I'll have to owe you an introduction," he gave me a sheepish smile.

We stood and looked at the carved-up wolf for a while as I waited for the rest of my group to come running. But no one was coming... I had a bad feeling about this. What if the bear had found them? After all, we'd all agreed to come running the second we heard a gunshot...

"Why were you alone, by the way?" I asked, the thought suddenly hitting me.

"They kicked me out," the kid shrugged.

"What? Who? I thought we all agreed to stick together."

"I don't know," he sighed. "They just told me to scram, and that was all."

"I see," I said, realising as I spoke that *my* group had also decided to abandon *me*. "You can come with me, then."

If only I'd known what a misguided idea that was, or that I should never have saved him from the wolf...

It only took me ten minutes to realise that the poor old wolf had been trying to do the world a favour before I cut it in half. The thing was, the kid just *would not shut up*. He just kept on talking and talking — pointing out unusual trees, trying to discuss the weather, telling me about different types of berries, anything and everything you could think of. He talked about the life cycle of a bear, about its behaviours, migration patterns, reproduction, feeding and food preferences, average life expectancy, how fast it could climb a tree, how thick a layer of ice it would take to support an adult specimen, and so on and so on, until I was practically drowning in information.

"Stop!" I exploded, coming to a sharp halt.

"What is it? Did you see something?" the kid asked, grabbing his gun and glancing around.

"No, I realised something. I see now why they kicked you out," I replied, looking at him gravely. "Could you please shut up? Just for a little while?" The kid clearly knew a lot, and his bear facts were interesting, but his talking was masking the sound of any creatures potentially stalking us.

"Why did you enlist, anyway?" I asked, my curiosity getting the better of me. I prayed the question wouldn't set him off again.

"I have my reasons," he sighed again, and I nodded to show I understood. If I was honest, I'd been expecting a more expansive answer from a motormouth like him, but I wasn't going to torture him for the details... or *was* I? No — just kidding!

Before long, night crept up on us. Out of thirty soldiers, only five now remained. The rest had lost the battle against exhaustion and their own lack of backbone, simply heading back to base once they realised that the bear was most likely no longer traceable. But although we were only five now, our food was quickly running out, and by morning, only one of us would be left standing... And who would that be? Yours truly, of course. It was going to be me, because Constantine was not the kind of guy to back down. Plus, I was now free to use my powers fully — interference from the magical forest notwithstanding, of course.

By now, I was getting tired. We hadn't found a single bear, nor even a trace of one... The only thing stopping me from turning around and going home was my own stubbornness. I'd been told to find a bear, and that meant I was going to find a bear — come hell or high water! Now that I was alone, however, I could finally fall back on my own tried and tested techniques to do so.

I'd managed to get the lay of the forest over-night and had located some unusually stagnant spots in the area's magical plane. I felt confident I could draw summoning circles in those spots, al-beit basic ones.

Sitting in one such spot, I traced a summoning circle in the snow. The only thing I had to work with was energy, so I used that to begin my penta-gram. It was hard work; while this spot was less highly charged than others, its energy still kept in-vading my work, constantly erasing my lines and symbols and forcing me to redo them.

Suddenly, I heard a faint whistling sound. I in-stinctively engaged my powers and threw up an energetic shield. Not a second later, something connected with my skull so hard that I flew into the air and landed with a bone-shaking thud six feet away.

"You?" I gasped. The squirrel was perched on a nearby branch, looking perfectly innocent. "You..." I narrowed my eyes at it as it turned to leave. "I knew it!"

* * *

Drawing pentagrams in blood was a whole lot easier. My only regret was not having more of it, but at least I'd collected enough for four summoning circles. I poured a little energy into each and then took a few steps back so as to give my demons an appropriate welcome. Four bright flashes of flame illuminated the forest, and a small, winged demon, quite plump and completely naked, appeared inside each circle.

"...*You* called us, human? You must be kidding."

With the summoning ceremony complete, the circle dissolved, depositing the demons unceremoniously into a snowdrift.

"Ah! It's cold! What kind of a jerk would summon us *here*?" the demons cried, floundering around in the snow. Once they'd finally found their way out, they turned to look at me. "Uh, oh," one of them murmured. "Please excuse us, the cold — uh — scrambled our brains. Yes..."

Well, what did I expect? With my powers so severely restricted, I couldn't summon anything better. I ended up spending half an hour — yes, half an hour — trying to explain to those little degenerates what a bear looked like! And of that half an hour, I actually spent twenty minutes explaining that I didn't want to hear any whining about the cold, because I was hardly warm and toasty myself!

Anyway, if those creatures couldn't find the bear, then the bear could go to hell, and I could go get warm. They couldn't kick us *all* out, could they? Well, I guessed it was possible — the army tended not to joke around. Plus, this particular army seemed to be extremely keen on following procedure, but that was no surprise. There was a reason why people liked to compare the army and the aristocracy...

Something I liked about this country was that a count or a lord couldn't receive the title of general just for having aristocratic blood. Want the job? Then you had to go and enlist. You could have the title, alright, but only if you earned it. Frankly, I was deeply impressed.

The demons set out on their reconnaissance, and I found myself alone in the forest once again. All I could do now was wait. To make the wait a little more comfortable, I drew one more pentagram and summoned another small demon. I set it to work building a snow shelter around me. It sniffled miserably as it bustled about; even the coldest part of the demonic plane was much warmer than this forest. The demonic plane's cold regions were also inhabited by a completely different kind of being to this one, but I'd executed the easiest summoning possible. That was why the little imps had shown up naked and unprepared for these temperatures.

"Oy! No lollygagging!" I yelled at the little beast, who'd decided to take a break. "Don't think I don't see you! You want your energy or not?"

"I'm sorry, but my hooves are frozen solid," it whined pitifully.

"Well, then work faster. That'll warm you up!"

It really did start building faster, and soon, my roof was almost finished. All that was left was a small opening, just big enough for the little demon to fit through. But just then, the four winged demons returned. They pushed their way in, widening the opening until they could squeeze through.

"We found it! Give us our energy and we're even!" they screeched.

"Where is it?"

"Fifteen kilometres from here! Come on, release us! We're freezing!" they pleaded, their teeth chattering pathetically as they hopped from one hoof to the other. Fifteen kilometres... What the hell? They'd told us the bear would be within a kilometre radius of this location, and now it was *fifteen kilometres* away? Either they were morons, or that was the fastest bear alive...

Oh well, there was only one option. If the order was to catch a bear, then I had to catch a bear, even if things weren't exactly going to plan. But it was going to take me another day...

"Want to earn some extra energy?" I smiled.

"No!" they shrieked in unison.

"I appreciate your enthusiasm," I said, ignoring their answer. "Bring me to the bear."

* * *

*Base*
*Sometime later*

The Black Squad's commanding officers entered the barracks, where the new recruits were already lined up and waiting. They inspected the remnants of the company, their expressions amused as they strode up and down the rows in silence.

"Well, soldiers?" said the general eventually, putting on a scowl. "Did you complete your important task?"

The silence was deafening...

The major was the first to break. He clutched his stomach and burst into hysterical laughter, which soon spread to every member of the command. For the next few minutes, all they could do was laugh at the terrified faces of the green recruits.

"Alright, that's enough," the general croaked, wiping tears from his eyes. "They tried their best! Good for them!"

"It works every year!" the major gasped, still in hysterics. "How? How do they always fall for it? And five of them were so spooked, they even broke their contracts!"

"Only five?" the general asked, eyebrows raised. "I was expecting more," he mused, stroking his beard.

"Well, they came back quickly this time. They

had enough and realised this wasn't the job for them," the major shrugged. "But then again, that's exactly why we invented the bear story."

"Oh, yes, that was a good one!" the general chuckled. "Anyway, please present the results."

"Three wounded and—" the sergeant major began, but the general cut him off.

"What do you mean, three wounded? *How*?" he cried. "Did they meet an actual bear out there?"

"No. One of them was accidentally shot in the leg by his own group. They carried him back here, though... The second one also injured his leg, this time, by falling into a hole, and the third one got caught in a trap," the sergeant major explained.

"A trap? Where did it come from?" the general's eyebrows shot up again.

"Poachers, sir," the sergeant major shrugged. "They're fond of the area."

"How can people be so careless with their lives? Sneaking into such a dangerous place for the sake of a few pennies. They could end up getting shot by us, or by the Newies, or eaten by an animal."

"On the subject of animals," the sergeant major interjected, "we also have one missing person."

"Where did you *find* these idiots?" the general bellowed. "Wounded are one thing, but how could you lose someone? How is that *possible*? They were just supposed to look for a non-existent bear!"

"Permission to speak!" a soldier cried, stepping forward. The general nodded. "He said he was going to find the bear."

"Where would he find a *bear*? They live on the other side of the *border*, for god's sake!" the general roared.

"There was one recruit who was quite," — the major sighed — "strong-willed."

"What do you mean, *was*?" the general's face darkened.

"Well, the squirrels may have gotten him. Or, perhaps he froze to death," the major replied pensively.

"Oh, damn those squirrels!" the general cursed, his jaw clenching as he recalled his own encounters with the little beasts.

The squirrels were, in fact, practically the most dangerous thing in the forest. They liked to gang together, circling like vultures, and then pounce on anything that moved. They knew no fear and were extremely bloodthirsty. They also hunted their prey to the bitter end, such as, for example, the veteran who sustained irreparable damage from a devastating nut to the groin. Once that veteran had finished his service, however, he'd dedicated himself to a life of poaching and had gone out into the forest, intent on wreaking vengeance on the little red critters...

"Assemble a search party. We need to bring that one back. Maybe we can make a real soldier out of him," the general rumbled.

"Should I send some of the new recruits?" the major queried.

"Absolutely not! Lock those morons away before they accidentally kill themselves!" the general roared. "Send some of the regular troops!"

The senior officers got to work, rushing straight off to find some experienced trackers. Not five minutes later, a group was assembled, but just as the general began to brief them, the duty officer came running in.

"Sir! We have a situation, sir!" the young man quavered. "The new recruit is back!"

"Don't interrupt me, you little milk drinker! Anyway, as I was saying, your mission is... Wait. What?" he looked at the young officer. "What do you mean by 'back'?"

"Well... he's *back*, sir! But sir, that's not why I'm here! We have an *emergency* situation, sir!" the duty officer was now waving his arms wildly.

"Fine, let's go and take a look at this situation of yours," the general sighed.

"But I can give you a report, sir..."

"I said, let's GO!" the general thundered as he, his retinue and the search party headed for the door. As soon as they reached the threshold, however, they all froze. There was an enormous bear, far too big for one person to drag all the way back from the forest, lying in the middle of the parade ground. "What? How?"

"Sir!" one of the new recruits was waving at the general. "The order was to capture a bear, sir! I've fulfilled the order... sir!"

"But why the hell did you drag it back here? Actually, forget about why — *how?* How on *earth* did you drag it back here?"

"The squirrels helped," the new recruit said with a shrug.

The general was frozen in shock. He goggled at the bear. There weren't supposed to be any bears out in that forest. They didn't like the area's unstable magical field, so they didn't go there — he knew they didn't!

The general was snapped out of his stupor when a grey-haired ensign by the name of Birch, approaching the new recruit, exclaimed in astonishment:

"He hasn't even fired a single shot!"

"Well, you told us to protect our weapons and use our bullets sparingly," the new recruit said with another shrug. "So, I protected it. I even kept it wrapped up in this rag. There's not a scratch on it — look."

"But you were given two magazines of ammunition... Why have you come back with three?" Birch asked in wonder.

"Oh, I found it while I was hunting the bear."

"...My god!" Birch suddenly gushed, pulling the new recruit into a hug. "I've found the perfect soldier! I've found him! Do you want some tea, son?"

"Tea? Well, I'd prefer something harder, but I won't say no!"

"Perfect! Just perfect!" the man exclaimed again as he grabbed the newbie's gun and headed off to the armoury with it. "I'll be waiting for you in my office!"

The general surveyed the scene for a few moments longer and then turned around and walked directly back into the command centre. He needed some time to digest these developments, and he wanted to hear what his specialists had to say on the matter.

Some brave recruits dragged the bear away into the base, where it was examined and dissected. Fifteen minutes later, a soldier came to deliver the initial report.

"Speak!" the general barked.

"General Rester, sir! Reports indicate that the new recruit couldn't have defeated the bear alone! Marks on the body suggest that the bear was attacked by squirrels, and that the recruit then happened across it in a weakened state. But even so, he couldn't have killed the bear by himself! Or if it *was* him, then he's hiding something..."

"Every soldier in this squad is hiding something," General Rester mused.

"Possibly, general!" the soldier hastily agreed.

"All the same, he's certainly made himself stand out. You know what?" the general smiled. "Why don't we call him in here and ask him a few questions?"

"Not possible, sir!" the soldier replied, standing up extra straight.

"Why not?"

"He's currently in Birch's office drinking tea, sir!"

"Hmm, if he's with Birch, then I suppose I can't disturb them," he stroked his beard. General Rester was much more senior in rank than the ensign, but everybody knew that Birch was a legend. He'd completed his service years ago, but had volunteered to come back and make himself useful on the base, which he'd been doing ever since. Everyone respected him for that, including the general himself.

*   *   *

"Did you see what he did? He found a dead bear and dragged it all the way back here! The guy's a beast!"

The three soldiers were chatting before lights out. Their topic of conversation was a certain new recruit. They didn't like to see some try-hard upstart showing off like that, no they did not...

"I agree, though — we need to teach him his place. Did you see that look he gave us? Looked at us like we were trash!" one of them spat.

"What should we do? We gotta think of something," another replied.

"Why don't we wait a bit? Do we really need to go looking for trouble?" the third one, outraged as he was, wasn't keen to take any risks.

"No, it has to be now," replied the first one, who was the most confident. "He's already sipping tea with the top dogs! I know the ensign is a nobody, but he's just the beginning! The kid has broken away from the group, and that deserves to be punished. We're going to make an example of him!" he crowed, a wicked grin spreading across his face.

"But... *we're* new recruits, too. This is going to cause trouble for us, Baz," said the second one, also getting cold feet.

"Oh, relax! Listen, I'll fill a bucket from the sewage tank, dump it on him when he's sleeping and then sprint back to my own bed. And you two can say that I was asleep the whole time," said the first one, laying out his plan.

"Hey, that sounds... doable!" nodded the other two, finally swayed, and the little band dispersed. Not one of them noticed the tiny demon perched in the corner, scribbling quietly into a notebook.

Surprisingly, the night passed without event. Morning, however, was a very different story. Everyone started getting out of bed — everyone, that was, except for Baz. For a while, no one could figure out where the stench was coming from, until finally, they pulled back Baz's blanket and found their answer.

"He's pissed himself!" one of the new recruits exclaimed. He was staring at the bed, eyes wide. "What the hell? Did you drink thirty litres of water last night?"

A few minutes later, the entire barracks was standing outside in formation while General Rester glowered at them.

"Which one of you *pissed* on a fellow soldier?" the general bellowed. You could have heard a pin drop on the far side of the parade ground. "Judging by the looks of things, every one of you deviants must have joined in! Do you think this is *funny*?" the man was now red in the face.

"Maybe I... did it myself?" Baz said in a small voice.

"Don't be a damn idiot! That was at least thirty litres!" Rester roared. "I repeat! This is your last chance to own up! Our investigators will be finished reviewing the security camera footage any minute, and then, we'll know everything!"

No one owned up. A minute later, a small man appeared and whispered something in the general's ear. Whatever it was, it made the general glower even harder.

"Our specialists have assessed the footage. You can all relax — the soldier pissed himself," he boomed, before turning to the wretched Baz. "So, you really drank thirty litres of liquid? How is that possible?"

"I'm s-s-sorry, but — could I please break my contract?" tremored Baz. "If it's not too late."

"Actually, it *is* a little late... but fine, you can break your contract," Rester sighed. "Better now than later, I suppose."

# CHAPTER 7

"TELL US, HOW DID YOU kill it, anyway?" we were sitting in the steam room of the bathhouse, and my fellow soldiers were hitting me with their favourite question. I'd heard it a dozen times by now, and I always gave them exactly the same answer.

"Well... I went into the forest..."

The room suddenly fell silent as they all leaned in to catch every word of my enthralling story. "I saw — a bear! I went up to it, and I killed it! And that was that!"

"But was it injured, or something? The way you describe it, it sounds so *easy*. I don't understand," the guy with the scar on his face said, scratching the back of his head. He was clearly a former career soldier, though he hadn't yet said it himself.

"How should I know?"

"How should you *know*?" the scarred soldier repeated incredulously. "If it's got wounds, you can see them!"

"It didn't have any visible wounds. It may have had some spiritual wounds, but I had no way to tell," I shrugged. "I'm not a hunter, I can't read souls."

Just kidding — of course I could read souls.

Take, for example, the glum-looking kid sitting in the corner. One look at him, and I could tell he was here because of a broken heart. I wasn't an expert soul-reader, but some people wore their souls on their sleeves, so to speak, and you could tell a lot about them in a single glance. I didn't like to mess around with soul reading, though, since it required energy. Trading souls was much more my style, but that was a totally different business. Everyone saw demonologists as scumbags and scoundrels just because they traded in souls… but soul-selling was a very different process than most people imagined, and being a soul-seller wasn't anything to be ashamed of. And there was no point trading the souls of morons, in any case.

The new recruits decided that grilling me about the bear was a waste of time, and the conversation segued naturally on to something else. It was clear to everyone that I wasn't giving anything away.

Watching them all trying to get to know each other was fascinating. How could you get to know someone without exchanging names? A basic hello was about as far as you could go.

"You're a demonologist, right?" the room turned to look at me again.

"Something like that," I shrugged.

"What can you do?"

"I can summon demons. I could get one to come in here and kill you all!" I said, telling the truth. They all burst out laughing.

"Yeah, sure... Seems like your sense of humour is in working order, anyway."

"Why are you here?" asked the guy with the scar. "You're young, and your odds of survival here are slim. I guess you'll rake in the rewards if you make it ten years, though."

"Rewards?" I asked, suddenly intrigued.

"Yeah — you get to die ten years older!" the guy chuckled. For some reason, the others didn't seem to find this funny. "Listen, I've been a soldier a long time — I'm used to this life. But I was framed for something on duty and they forced me to enlist here. It was either this or a court martial. But I guess I've only got myself to blame," he sighed. "I shouldn't have been so trusting."

Bathhouses had a way of making people open up. After the scarred soldier, some of the others began to share details of their old lives and their reasons for joining the Black Squad. After all, there weren't many army positions that let you erase all trace of your past and start a new life. A short, dangerous life, but a life, nonetheless.

"So, what brought you here?" the room's attention returned to me.

"My story's not that interesting," I replied, trying to brush off the question, but all eyes remained fixed curiously on me. "I don't even remember most of my life, if I'm honest. I woke up in a basement someplace, surrounded by flames. Demons were roaring, and there was blood, guts and fighting all around. Someone attacked me, so I killed them."

"What happened then?" a soldier cut in impatiently.

"I ran away," I shrugged. "I didn't know where to go — didn't even know who I was. I had no papers, no connections. So, I came to the recruiting office. What else could I do?"

"You're telling us tales!" one of the other recruits burst out, making everyone laugh. "Where did all this even happen?"

"Oh, just out in the forest, not far from here," I smiled. This only made them all laugh even harder. All except for one scruffy-looking guy who was staring at me suspiciously.

In any case, they still didn't believe me, even though I was telling them the honest truth. Not the *whole* truth, though...

Sooner or later, they were going to find out the truth about me, so I didn't see any point in hiding it. Still, I wanted all these probing idiots looking for payback to know that I wouldn't be easily cornered. Even the aristocrats were no threat to me now. That said, they might still try to target me. The army offered a certain level of protection in this empire, but the high command could still be bribed to send me on a guaranteed suicide mission. That was nothing new — it happened in every world. But what they *didn't* know was that I was actively seeking danger, and that I was afraid of nothing.

Even if you'd murdered an aristocrat, as soon as you joined the Black Squad, your ill-wishers could kiss their plans for vengeance goodbye. And I'd killed an aristocrat as soon as I got here... There was a reason why so many aristocrats had a problem with our unit. Get yourself recruited and sign that contract, and you could practically consider yourself untouchable. Admittedly, you now had an endless onslaught of *new* threats to worry about, but that was a different story.

We finished up in the bathhouse and got dressed. Before long, we were summoned back to the parade ground.

"You worthless pieces of shit!" Rester roared. "You failed to complete your task!" I raised my hand, and the general sighed audibly. "Alright, yes, *you* completed it. You got lucky, congratulations. But the rest of you! This exercise was supposed to teach you that serving in the army is not a walk in the park! It is fear! It is pain! Anyway, it's time for your initiation. The even *more* worthless pieces of shit than you have already been weeded out — but *you*, you mistakes of nature, are here not because you are brave, because you are dumb! Now, go and get your new names — they're fit for idiots like you!"

The man spoke well. I could tell that he was a masterful orator. He knew exactly how to bring his entire audience to its knees. In fact, he would have made a decent demonologist!

It was clear to me that demonology and the military were comparable on many levels. In both fields, it was very important to be precise. Orders had to be given with crystal clarity, leaving no room for one's subordinates to misinterpret them. Tell an idiot not to fire, and you knew they wouldn't fire. Order them only to fire at trees with yellow leaves, and you knew they'd only fire at trees with yellow leaves. It was the same way with demons; if you weren't able to draw the Argonus Lufus pentagram, then it was better to skip the amateur art session altogether and just draw something else. You needed to lay out your conditions so clearly and precisely that even the infernal plane's most moronic imp could grasp them. I was going to have some demon servants very soon, and if a demon sensed weakness off you, it was only a matter of time before they would rebel and, ultimately, devour you whole.

"Approach the box one by one and put your hand inside. Your documents will then be sent to the Imperial registry, where you will be officially assigned your new names and surnames. In the meantime, you will be referred to by your call signs," Rester said, concluding his oration. "Who wants to go first?"

I raised my hand. To my surprise, no other hands went up. I shrugged and stepped up to the black box.

Suddenly, a squadron of combat helicopters

soared overhead and disappeared behind the treetops. An icy gust of wind hit me. It sent big flurries of snow twirling the air, as well as into the faces of a passing unit in full combat gear, who responded with some impressive obscenities. They were heading for combat, which meant that they'd be out in the freezing cold for a long time to come, so I couldn't really blame them.

While the initiation might have seemed momentous to the new recruits, in reality, life was marching on around us, and no one was paying us much attention. Just the latest round of rookies, mostly of whom would barely last the year — it was nothing special.

Still, we were about to become official suicide soldiers — or, as I'd just learned we were casually called, the War Demons. I wasn't sure how the others felt about the nickname, but it suited me down to the ground.

I inserted my hand into the special slot in the box and glanced down quizzically. The box was interfering with my body's magical structure — I could sense it loud and clear. At some point, I began to wonder if I should stop the interference, but as I observed the process further, I realised it was only affecting my outer layers, which meant that it was safe. I was also curious to see what would happen next.

"Don't worry, kid," Birch said encouragingly, shuffling papers at a nearby desk. "If you want to cry, go ahead. Happens all the time."

Oh, right! This was supposed to be painful —

*very* painful, even. I needed to act natural. I had to at least *look* like I was suffering... The thing was, demonologists weren't afraid of a little pain. For us, pain was second nature, something you just got used to over time.

After a couple of minutes, the box chirped, and I was told to remove my hand. There, just above my wrist, was a little demon tattooed in black ink. The tattoo was small, clumsy and vaguely pathetic.

"What the hell is this?" I asked, holding out my wrist.

"It's a demon tattoo," Rester said, walking up to me. "Wear it with pride!"

"A demon?" I wrinkled my nose. "Has it been stepped on by a bigger demon?"

"Hey, watch your mouth," the general growled, shoving me. "Move along and stop holding up the line."

I went over to Birch's desk. He happened to have my file already in his hands.

"Your documents will be submitted shortly," he smiled, and then started taking pictures of me; first, my face, then, my tattoo, and finally, a full body shot. "I'm not really supposed to do this... " he said slyly, "but to my knowledge, you're the only one who cleared the initiation task, so I'm going to do you a little favour. Any wishes regarding what name you'd like?"

"Constantine," I shrugged. "More precisely—"

"Yes, good, noted," he cut me off briskly.

"Can I ask a question?"

"Go ahead, kid," the man nodded.

"Why don't the others get to choose? I don't see why they shouldn't... and what if someone doesn't like their new name?"

"We took that option away on account of all the numbskulls abusing it. You'd think people would be sensible, but when they started calling themselves things like Vintorious, Tentacle and Eduardo Pimpernelle the Second, well, we had to change the rules." He shook his head, shuddering at the memory of names he'd been forced to register in the past. Good thing I hadn't had the chance to request my full name — I'd been planning on titles and everything. He probably would have run out of paper!

"Since you went first," Birch spoke again, not looking up from his notes, "your call sign will be One, at least for now. It may change again in the future."

Just then, the next recruit came to Birch's desk, and I was sent back to rejoin the rest.

The ceremony lasted around an hour. By then, darkness had fallen, and we returned to the barracks. Now, I was lying on my bunk, musing. Life was strange... I was now completely untraceable, my body's former inhabitant wiped permanently from every database in the world. I hadn't seen my former name or surname, but I *had* managed to catch a glimpse of something in the ensign's records — one of the few things that wasn't crossed out or inked over.

My body's former owner had been a petty aristocrat, the last of a penniless line. He'd owed someone money and had ended up losing his estate, but had never gotten himself into any major trouble. According to the notes, my body-buddy had had a vicious temper but had never been convicted of any serious crimes.

The remark I was most excited to see, however, was this: 'Will not be missed.' This was precious, since my biggest fear here early on had been that I would have to play the role of a beloved son, brother or whoever. Life was going to be simpler from here on out. I'd made the right choice, and I didn't feel an ounce of regret about choosing the army over the aristocracy for this life. I might still end up with a title at some point, but I didn't care much either way; I'd had my fill of all that in my last life, and that was enough for me.

Aristocracy was more of an elf thing, anyway. Those damn snobs... We had a joke in my old world that rang absolutely true: if you wanted to talk to an elf, you'd better make sure you were five times stronger than him first. That was because, in the space of one conversation, you'd probably breach at least five rules of arcane aristocratic etiquette, and an elf would want to kill you once for every breach. But those rules were a mystery to all but the elves themselves! How was *I* supposed to know that I shouldn't swear at someone when greeting them? Or that elves didn't like being called big-ears? Come on — their ears *were* big!

While we waited for our names, we had a lot of questions about our call signs. How were we supposed to talk to each other now? With my excellent memory, I could identify everyone, from Two through to Twenty, but I wasn't so sure that they could do the same... For example, a woman from my squad had approached me just now and said: "Seven, do you want to come eat with me?" I would have gone, except that I wasn't number seven! Basically, we now had no idea how to communicate without getting ourselves all mixed up.

We got our answer soon enough. Our training regime began, and for the whole next week, all we did was train, train and train, with just three hours' sleep every night. We were too exhausted to communicate, which meant that the confusion with the call signals ceased to be a problem. They made us drink restorative tea, gave us healing potions and then sent us right back out for more gruelling training, on and on in a continuous loop. We went to bed in the dark, got out of bed in the dark, and for the last three days, we didn't sleep at all. That was on account of the alarms; practice drills the first two nights, and on the last night, an assembly to witness a grenadier infantry unit returning from the depths of hell. While they weren't quite mercenaries, around here, grenadiers were considered almost as elite.

Some of those men were in soaring spirits, but just as many weren't, and lots of them were missing an arm or a leg. Strange... they were leaving such a thick trail of blood in their wake that a demon could easily have caught their scent, tracked them down and finished off the entire squad. It could only mean one thing: there were no demonologists in the enemy ranks.

The training was tough, even for me. I had to feed my body a constant stream of energy, carefully monitoring my physical state. There were actually a few other recruits who were also gifted, and they were also using their abilities to try and avoid dying from exertion. It was hardest for the ungifted ones, but it was starting to look like they wouldn't last long, anyway. That said, I was the one getting most of the sideways glances, given how frail and weak I looked.

As if all this wasn't enough, they'd saved the best for last. At the end of the week, our training was complete, and we could consider ourselves human... or so the instructors said, at least, erupting mysteriously into laughter as they did so.

After our final training session, they let us catch five hours' sleep. Then, it was out to the parade ground again, where we lined up with the new recruits from other units. There must have been a thousand of us, give or take.

I was so sick of these endless lineups. I wanted to fight, but all we did was train, get lectured by the commanding officers and then train some more. I was seriously considering summoning a demon doppelganger to stand in for me at these things.

"Today, you are no longer useless losers!" Rester roared. "Now, you're just *regular* losers!" he chortled at his own joke. "Not one of you has any combat experience, which means..." he trailed off.

My hand was in the air. "Oh, here we go again... One!" Another five or so hands went up. What did the general expect? All the units had been given the same call signs. "No, not you! *That* One! Put your hands down!" he barked. "And *you* — wrestling a bear is not the same thing as going into battle!"

"But it was big and scary!" I pouted. "It roared at me and everything!"

"Enough! Drop and give me four hundred push-ups!" Rester screamed, beside himself with rage.

"Yoohoo! Thank you!" I cried, diving to the floor. "My legs were going numb from all that standing around!"

"And after that, I want seventy laps!"

"Great!"

"You insolent prick!" the poor man's head looked like it was about to explode. "You keep your damn mouth shut when I'm speaking!"

"Got it! Thanks!"

"Damn you to hell! You're going on night duty! I'll have you sorting dusty crates in the warehouse!"

"Thank you! Happy to be of service!" I called back cheerfully.

"You son of a bitch! Are you looking to get punished for the rest of your contract? I'll make you dig trenches! For the next *week*!" by now, the general looked like he might pass out at any second.

"Even the biggest digger in the world is no match for a soldier with a shovel!"

"The perfect soldier!" Birch whispered, wiping a small tear from his eye.

From there, Rester returned to his speech, while I merrily did my push-ups. A mage ought to stay in shape, after all. That said, it was important not to overdo it; we weren't aiming to become body-builders. As with everything else, balance was key.

Most of the strongest guys here weren't much to look at physically. There was, however, one notable exception: Atilla. But Atilla was notable for more than just his physique; he also possessed the fascinating gift of levitation. It was one of the most out-there gifts I'd ever come across. Atilla hadn't even been able to find a teacher, on account of there simply being no one else like him. But Atilla, not deterred, had honed his gift alone. He'd also managed not to die in the process, which was even more awe-inspiring than the gift itself.

"The unit commanders will now assemble you into your units. Stand and wait! Do not move!" Naturally, I froze. If the order was to stay still, then I was going to stay still. "One! Move! Push-ups, now!" Again, five other recruits hit the floor and started doing push-ups. "Not *you*, you dolts!" Rester spluttered. "Where do we find these morons?"

"Oh... we thought—" the other five began to mumble, but the general, about to snap, moved his hand to the holster on his belt. "Yes, yes, understood!"

I just kept doing my push-ups, feeling fine and dandy, the thin crust of ice on the ground gradually melting beneath me. I saw a pair of feet approaching. Well, tough — I hadn't gotten the order to stop, so I wasn't going to stop. Then, another pair of feet approached, and then another. Well, well, well... I was suddenly mister popular! Apparently, three different commanders had all decided they wanted me in their unit... until suddenly, all those feet disappeared in unison. I thought my popularity had disappeared along with them, but soon enough, another pair of feet arrived. The feet stood awhile, discussing something with Rester, and then disappeared like the others.

I'd only caught the briefest glimpse of the person standing above me. He was a bald man of stocky build. If you didn't count the web of scars covering his head, he looked like a perfectly ordinary person. But I'd realised then why the other commanders had scattered so fast; in my short time here, I'd already heard plenty about this guy. The only question was how much of it was true.

Once the commanders had chosen their soldiers, we were each handed an envelope and dismissed. The ensign had kept his word — I really was Constantine now! My surname, Princely, wasn't bad, either...

"Finally, I can introduce myself," the scar-faced soldier was walking towards me with his hand outstretched. "Val Bunner!"

"Bunner?" I repeated. "I bet my boots your call sign will be Hot Cross!"

"Hey!" Val frowned. "No way! In this division, call signs are only given as a combat distinction."

"And *yours* will be Hot Cross! I know it," I chuckled, shaking my head. Thankfully, Val chuckled too, not taking offence. He probably knew as well as I did that he was fated to become Hot Cross, and that there was no point in fighting it.

"Let me introduce myself back," I held my hand out. "Constantine Princely."

"Shit, you must have bribed the ensign!" Val exclaimed. "Anyway, I came over because... well, I wanted to get to know you before it's too late."

"Why, are you dying?" I raised my eyebrows at him, and he chuckled again.

"No, I'm talking about you. You were doing your push-ups, so you didn't see who chose you. The Bird is legendary around here, and every one of those legends is worse than the last."

Captain Victor Cardinal, nicknamed the Bird, had earned his call sign, Joy, for a reason. He'd signed a twenty-year contract, but had completed it in just ten years, winning enough distinctions in combat to have the remaining ten struck off. He loved the military life, and this was an enthusiasm he liked to share with his troops. Unfortunately for the troops, what Captain Cardinal loved most were things like being shot at — and the greater the number of bullets and projectiles coming at him, the better. Choosing the most dangerous missions, plunging himself and his squad into the fray without hesitation — that was what brought the man joy.

"It's a rough deal, but there's no way to transfer," Val sighed. "Sorry, buddy, but you drew the short straw."

"What's the problem? If he's made it home from every single mission in ten years of service, doesn't that mean I'm in safe hands?" I retorted.

"Yeah, *he* made it home, but what about the others?" Val slapped me on the shoulder, and then turned and headed back to his unit.

"Ah," as I stood with one finger raised after him, it finally hit me. "Aha... I get it!"

Presently, I and fourteen other short-straw soldiers were escorted to a new barracks. It was very clean inside — sparkling, even. Soldiers didn't actually do their own cleaning here; instead, it was done by paid staff. I was of the opinion that soldiers should be free to focus on fighting, and the Empire's government obviously felt the same. It was nice to see that those in service were taken care of here.

We were shown to a large room lined with bunk beds and informed that this would be our new home. There were other, much more comfortable bunk rooms in the building, and even some private rooms. These, however, were for soldiers who'd served a long time and had earned the privilege of a private living space. Rookies like us were confined to the common dorm for a while.

"Line up!" Cardinal barked, marching swiftly into the room. All fifteen of us new recruits filed into a neat row and stood to attention. The only thing wrong with us was that everyone looked utterly miserable. "I like this kid," Cardinal pointed straight at me. "He's smiling, he's happy. What are the rest of you so down in the dumps for?" Someone further down the line burst into tears. "That's right! Get your tears out now, because you won't have time for'em later!"

"Because... I'll b-b-be — dead?" the poor kid raised his tear-stained face.

"How should I know?" Cardinal scoffed "None of us knows when our time will come! Just enjoy your life!"

"Yes, s-sir..." the kid sniffled, letting out a miserable sigh.

"That's what I like to hear! And you have exactly fifteen minutes of enjoyment left! No more after that!"

"Why?"

"Because you're new recruits! Which means you need a baptism of fire," the captain was beaming with delight. "And you are in luck! You can't imagine how much wrangling it took to snatch this mission for my squad. But for now, gentlemen — relax!"

"Are we relaxing, or going on a mission? Which is it?" a guy asked, puzzled.

"Relaxing, of course! But not for long. We'll meet here in fifteen minutes, get you equipped and then you'll receive your first combat mission." With that, he turned smartly on his heel and made for the door.

"Nice knowing you, boys," someone muttered.

"Oh, I almost forgot!" the captain stopped in the doorway and spun around. "Anyone here already have combat experience?"

"I served twelve years in the infantry and have more than fifty combat missions under my belt!" a rather large man announced proudly, taking a step forwards.

"Hmm, that's not much," Cardinal sighed. "Then again, I'm not exactly spoiled for choice. You're the commander!"

"Yes, sir!" the man beamed, though his pink cheeks betrayed his embarrassment at being put in his place. I wondered if I should speak up about my combat experience, too... No, better to stay quiet for now. My time would come.

"Any other questions?" the captain asked. Another soldier raised his hand. "Go ahead, son."

"Does this building have a shower?"

"It does. But I warn you, you won't find any rope in there!" he laughed loudly. "Oh, don't look so surprised — there have been incidents before. And yes, the shower has excellent sound insulation and no one will hear you cry, boy."

"I'm forty-two years old," the soldier mumbled.

"Oh really, that young?"

What had I gotten myself into? Oh well, it was entertaining, if nothing else. I wasn't about to start complaining.

The Bird went about his business, and I went off to relax. My relaxation plan consisted of finding a quiet corner and getting as comfortable as I could. There happened to be a neat green-painted nook nearby with a bookshelf and some comfortable armchairs, so I settled in there.

Finally, a moment alone! I began tracing pentagrams on my skin. I added a couple of summoning runes, too, but I drew those using energy lines to keep them invisible. I also used a little of my blood, though I then had to layer a concealment spell over it. The red lines sank beneath my skin, ready to be activated with a single mental command.

Ten minutes later, our rested band of soldiers had already gathered in anticipation of their captain's arrival. A conversation about our terrible situation and awful luck was also in full swing.

"Well, what did you expect?" scoffed our newly-appointed commander. "Where do you think you are?"

"In the army," a soldier huffed.

"All those other divisions — *that's* the army. But *you* signed a black contract! You sign up to *this* division because you need a second chance and a new identity, and *this* division works differently. Only ten in a thousand will survive, but those ten will be the best of the best!" the big man guffawed, looking around at their dejected faces. "We're going to be staring death in the face, so you'd better brace yourselves!

"Hey, what's your name, commander?" another soldier asked.

"My name doesn't matter. To you, I'm Twelve," he replied, his voice hard.

"Why won't you tell me your name? I mean, you just got it," the other soldier shot back indignantly.

"You clearly don't know how it works around here. I did my research before I came. For the first year here, your name is irrelevant, a worthless piece of information. Out of the hundreds of names given today, *all* of them will be irrelevant a year from now save for two, three, or maybe ten, if we're lucky."

Suddenly, the commander shut his mouth and leapt to his feet. The Bird had entered the room.

"Nice and relaxed? Good on you!" Cardinal grinned. "Now, then. Your task couldn't be simpler," he said, unfolding a map as he came closer. "There's an old, abandoned mineshaft located here," he pointed. "They used to mine magical ore there, until it got too dangerous to dig any deeper and the whole thing had to be abandoned," he looked around, noted that this information was of absolutely no interest to us, and moved on. "Some of our scouts were returning from a mission and noticed suspicious activity in the area. There might be illegal mining going on, and those miners might not be alone down there. There could be enemy soldiers hiding in the mine, which is why we need to do a more thorough reconnaissance." He looked around at the group of soldiers once again and smiled in satisfaction, noting the looks of despair now spreading across their faces.

"On to the task at hand! Your job will be to scout the area, and if the enemies are few, eliminate them. If they are many, complete your reconnaissance and get out of there — we'll send a more experienced unit in after you. Your main task is just to confirm the presence of enemy troops, but if there's only a handful of them, then you are to take them out yourselves."

"And if there's as many of them as there are of us, can I make the call on whether or not to attack?" Commander Twelve asked.

"You can make any damn call you like, so long as it's in the best interests of the Empire. Understood, soldier?" Cardinal said, giving the guy a look.

"Understood," Twelve nodded quickly.

"Now, for the best part," the captain said, a fresh grin spreading across his face. "There are fifteen of you here. This mission requires seven souls. Decide amongst yourselves who's going." Twelve raised a hand, and Cardinal swiftly added: "Your commander has to be one of the seven!"

On his way out, the captain once again paused in the doorway.

"Oh, by the way! To help you complete the task, you will be provided with three silent snowmobiles. Count your blessings — we could have made you walk, but old Joy here was looking out for you," he chuckled.

"Silent snowmobiles? Are they magical?" a soldier asked, his face lighting up.

"They're electric, you moron. You think we'd let milk drinkers like you near the magical ones?"

No sooner had the captain left than the room burst into a cacophony of squabbling voices. Soldiers suddenly started coming down with sore legs, back injuries and various other afflictions.

"I'll take the next mission," one soldier said, stretching lazily. "This one's too easy for me. Plus, reconnaissance isn't really my thing."

"I can't hold a gun — I dislocated my finger in training!" another said hurriedly.

"You look like a melee fighter," a third soldier frowned. "Why would you need to hold a gun?"

I just stood and watched the circus unfold. I didn't understand — hadn't they read their contracts? It was spelled it out in black and white: the War Demons were the best of the best, but your chances of surviving were slim. And they'd spelled it out for a reason; there was no room for weaklings here.

By now, the room had descended into total chaos. The reality was that this was all just another training exercise — the rest of them just didn't know it yet. It was a very clever tactic from the captain.

The idea was for us to identify and assemble the ideal group for the mission. The group should have a technician, a shield fighter, a sniper, and so on until all the necessary skills were covered. Instead, the whole room had just ended up trying to weasel their way out of going, spouting excuses for why they couldn't join the mission. Only Twelve sat alone in the corner, looking defeated.

Finally, I'd had enough. I walked over to the commander. He smiled and called out to the others:

"Oho, we've got a clever one! While the rest of you are whining to each other, he's decided to come straight to teacher! Go on, soldier, let's hear you beg. What's wrong with you, hm? Got an itchy foot? Kids waiting for you at home?" he chuckled.

"No. I just wanted to report for duty," I shrugged.

"Huh," Twelve murmured with genuine surprise. "That's a curve ball, but hey, by this stage, I've seen everything." He turned to face the rest. "Alright, guys, five spots left! Let's go!"

The group was silent for a few seconds, and then the squabbling broke out even more fiercely than before. Ten minutes passed, and still not a single other candidate had been selected.

The captain popped his head in the door.

"The names, please?"

"We can't choose. We just can't agree," Twelve shrugged helplessly.

"Oh no? Alright, is Seven here?" One of the soldiers raised a hand. "Excellent! You're on the team! I'll be back again in two minutes, boys!"

In the end, it was the captain who chose the rest of the team. This confirmed my suspicions. Though he made it seem like he was choosing numbers at random, Cardinal was, in fact, assembling a team that was well-balanced and perfectly optimised from a tactical perspective. Once the group was complete, we were led to a warehouse, where we received our gear, vehicles and weapons. I tried to skip the weapon, since I knew it would only get in my way, but I was told the gun wasn't optional, and that I was going to need it.

The thing was, I wasn't a great shot. I'd had a

go a few times in training and figured out that firearms really weren't my strong suit. But in my defence, I wasn't an all-rounder — I was a demonologist! In a pinch, I could just summon a demon
marksman and let it off on a shooting spree.

Next, we jumped onto the snowmobiles. The
compound's main gates swung open before us and
we set off for our location. Twelve and I raced
ahead on our snowmobile, leading the way, with
the other two following in our wake. The last snowmobile had a sledge tied to it, upon which our
technician and signalman were proudly installed,
sitting shoulder to shoulder.

I observed with interest the way Twelve navi-
gated using the compass, cross-checked with the
snowmobile's digital navigation system and took
notes. The technology seemed decent, though I
still trusted my magic far more.

Suddenly, a strange feeling interrupted my
thoughts. I peered into the distance, confirmed the
feeling with my senses, and then tapped Twelve on
the shoulder.

"Take a left in twenty metres," I told him. He
slowed down and turned to look at me.

"Why?"

"Just do what I say if you want to avoid trouble."

We slowed down even more.

"Can you sense something?"

"No, it's just a hunch," I replied, telling him the
near-truth.

"A hunch can make or break a situation like

this," Twelve nodded, and then swerved left. Good job, commander!

We sped away from the magical trap that lay waiting for us on the main route. I hurriedly noted its location on the tablet strapped to my left arm. We'd all been issued one, complete with personal login accounts and everything. I marked the spot as booby-trapped and made a mental note to pass the information on to headquarters later.

Then again, how could I possibly explain how I knew? I couldn't. I reconsidered my plan. I'd have to take care of the trap myself...

Around two hours later, we came to a stop at the edge of the forest. Everyone jumped off the snowmobiles. One idiot actually suggested we stop and build a fire already, which earned him a smack across the head from his comrades and a reprimand from his commander.

"Enough yakking!" Twelve barked. "Spread out!"

The group scattered, everyone rushing off to assess the area. We'd certainly chosen an interesting place to park... How were we supposed to cover our backs here if necessary? Stand in a circle? And what about the bear I could sense sleeping directly below us, fifteen metres under the surface?

I wondered if I was just some kind of bear magnet, or if they really *were* everywhere in this world. Either way, this one was hibernating, so we had nothing to worry about. But there was one niggling little thought I couldn't shake... What if, say, a little imp was to give that bear a kick? Would it wake up? I tried to put the idea out of my head, but my desire to summon an imp was growing stronger by the second...

"Our target is five kilometres south-west!" Commander Twelve announced. "Camouflage the vehicles and let's get moving." Special white tarps were produced from the equipment trunks and spread over the snowmobiles, and we set off briskly for the mine.

We covered the first three kilometres swiftly and in silence. Suddenly, Twelve raised a hand, and the entire squad dropped to the ground.

"I'm checking our comms," he said. "There doesn't seem to be any interference. Our connection is clear."

"How do you know that?" one of the soldiers asked.

"I'll explain later," Twelve brushed the question off curtly. "Right now, I just want to make sure we *have* a later."

Meanwhile, I was wondering what we were even doing here. Looking around at these people, I realised it would have been quicker to just shoot us back at base. The end result would have been the same...

"I need a volunteer to get closer to the mine and report back on the situation," Twelve said, scanning the group. "Any takers?"

"I'll go," I shrugged.

"Fantastic!" Twelve said. A whisper rose up amongst the others, and I picked out the word *moron* a couple of times. So what if I was? I was going to die of boredom sitting around here.

The others escorted me to my departure point as if they were walking me to my death. Then, under the incredulous gazes of my fellow soldiers, I carefully swaddled my rifle in a soft cloth I'd brought for the purpose. Only once this was done did I set off for the mine. The thing was, the rifles we'd been issued were costly, high-quality weapons — at least as far as I could tell. Each one was fitted with a silencer, a scope and special camouflage paint. I was actually quite curious to shoot mine, but strictly for fun, and somewhere safer than here.

Once I was a good distance from my comrades, I hid behind a bush. I could work in peace here without having to shield myself from prying eyes. I pricked my finger and got to work inscribing a summoning circle directly into the snow. Soon, there was a flash of light, and a short, skinny demon with small wings appeared in front of me. No more than four feet tall, the bald creature was holding a curved, sickle-like blade in its hands.

"Who dares summon me! I'll cut you into cubes!" the demon roared. It turned and locked eyes with me. Suddenly, it seemed to fall speechless.

"Are you done?"

"All done, Master! I'll shut up now," the demon bowed courteously.

"You're ready to work, then?"

"Always ready when a great mage such as yourself summons, Master. I listen and obey. I even have my own sword," it raised the sickle thing and began waving it around.

"Give me that!" I grabbed the sword. "You're going to cut yourself, you idiot!"

"Oh... I bought that with my first pay check," it murmured, looking crestfallen.

"Fine, put it away, then," I tossed the sword back. "I have a different kind of task for you, anyway. Activate your camouflage." The demon smiled, and then slowly faded out until it was translucent... all but the wings, which were flapping hard. "The wings, too!" I commanded. "Everything!"

"The wings cost more energy, though," the demon whined.

"I pay — you obey!" I scowled, and the beast's wings faded out to match its body.

"By the way, could I interest you in a discount?" the demon suddenly perked up. "If you become a regular client, you see, then—"

"Investigate the area and report back to me on what you find," I interrupted. "The search radius is no less than five and no more than six kilometres from the site." At this, the demon gave a whistle. "Hey!" I snapped.

"Oh! No whistling, or no payment, understood. My lips are sealed!" said the demon, raising its hands in apology.

I gave the creature my final instructions, listed its responsibilities, and then sent the little demon on its way.

I wasn't fond of lower-level demons. Yes, they were cheap, but they were also dumb as rocks.

You needed to formulate your orders extremely carefully when working with them. Imagine, for example, that I'd told my demon to search everything within roughly a five-kilometre radius around the site. The demon could easily have flown off for the rest of the day, searching everything within a *thirty*-kilometre radius and only returning when the intel was no longer useful. In that scenario, I'd also be obliged to pay the thing an hourly wage. Instead, I'd clearly instructed my demon not to go further than six kilometres, and lo and behold, it returned less than two hours later with a detailed report on the activity in the area.

"There are six wimpy-looking guys a few kilometres from here. They're sitting on a log," the demon puffed, catching its breath. "I reckon I could kill two of them right now, and leave the rest for you, Master," it bowed. "If you're in the mood for a little fun, I mean."

"Forget about them!" I waved a hand impatiently. "Anyone else?"

"I didn't go near the mineshaft... I could sense some kind of defensive power encircling it, radiating outwards. But you did tell me to stay away from any defences I came across," it shrugged, and I nodded. No one would set up defences like that without a good reason... Someone important was down in that mine. "Anyway, there's more. Roughly three kilometres north of here is a camouflaged hideout. There are three people there dressed exactly like you, with the same colour patches on their shirts and everything."

Now *that* was interesting. According to the demon, we had three tough-looking soldiers apparently lying in ambush. It hadn't dared attack them by itself — each one was probably ten times more deadly than all six of the wimpy log-sitters combined.

The two men and one woman had dug a small hollow in the snow and covered themselves with a camouflage net. They were carefully observing activity around the mine through a pair of binoculars. They were well hidden, and they'd also set up traps around their shelter, preventing the demon from even getting close to them. There were two possible explanations. Option one, they were enemy fighters disguised as Imperial soldiers... .no, that sounded stupid. Why would the enemy bother? Which pointed to the much tamer option two, namely, that this mission was not as improvised as it seemed. Everything had been planned out in advance, and we hadn't been sent out here alone. The energetic defences around the mine suggested that the mission might still be real — complete with hostile enemies — but that the camouflaged group were not only watching over us, but were also ready to cover us in case of attack.

Ultimately, this didn't change anything. We still had our orders, and our job was to carry them out: stick our heads into the mine, count the enemies, and either attack them, or head on home with new intelligence. And now, we had three guardian angels to see us through...

"Fly in close and observe them," the demon

nodded. "And report back with any new details. Got it!" The creature fluttered away, and I set off towards the mineshaft once more.

Twenty minutes later, the demon touched down next to me, a sly grin on its face.

"I've got *information,*" it said in a conspiratorial whisper. "It'll cost you, though." It stretched its hand out, a small, bright flame bursting into life on its palm.

"Where do I put the cash?" I asked.

"Woah, hold your horses!" the demonic messenger cried. "I'm an altruist, see! I was just kidding! Listen, those people are tuned into your radio frequency. They know about your every move!"

"I see. Good work," I shot the demon a little flame, which it accidentally caught, letting out a shriek of pain.

"Aah!"

"Absorb it, you idiot!"

The demon slapped a hand to its face, finally cottoning on, and began greedily soaking up the flame's energy.

"Mmm... what power... what strength!" it crooned, its body going slack. "You can summon me anytime, Master! I'm yours forever!"

"Can you just shut up for five minutes?" I sighed wearily, and the little creature pulled two fingers across its lips in a zipping gesture.

I now understood why we'd been ordered to conduct all our communication across internal comms systems only... The three-person admissions committee lying in the camouflaged dugout were going to use those conversations to assess us. Well, that was wise. I'd been wondering what high command's selection process was; after all, it stood to reason that they wouldn't let just anyone join the ranks of the War Demons. We'd all be sent on missions like this one, and only then would they decide who to keep and where to assign them.

As soon as I reached the entrance to the mineshaft, I ducked behind a tree. Occasionally, I braved a quick glance into the black abyss of the tunnel. From the outside, you'd never guess there were people down there, but the disturbances in the magical plane around it screamed that the mine was occupied.

"I'm here," I said into my radio.

"Good work!" Twelve responded immediately. "What can you see?"

"Nothing," I admitted.

"Can you sense anything? Is anyone there?"

"I think so, yeah," I shrugged. Come to think of it, though, I couldn't see any footprints in the snow... Could they be camouflaging them some-how? Or maybe they were transporting the mined ore by air... I suddenly remembered the plane I'd seen in Circle City not long ago. The New Imperials certainly had the resources for something like this. "Awaiting further instruction, commander."

"Hey, One!" someone else butted in. "Mosey on down there and check if anyone's home, why don't you?"

"Listen, why don't you take a hike into the for-est and get eaten by a—"

"Who do you think you are, taking that tone with me!" the angry interceptor cut me off.

"Maybe I should come back there and we can discuss this face-to-face?" I retorted, savouring the thought.

"Enough!" Twelve hissed, cutting our altercation short. "One, we're not coming to your location. There could an ambush nearby, you see. We'll take the long way round and hit the enemy from behind!"

Yeah, right. If that was the plan, then why were you all hiding up a tree?

"No worries," I replied coolly. "Anything else I should do?"

"Let's see, give me a second," I heard radio static, and then the connection cut off.

"Come in! Do you copy?" I said into the radio. I tried again and again, but all I got in reply was blank static. "This is One! Come in!"

*   *   *

*At the top of a very tall tree somewhere in the forest Around the same time*

"Hey, techie! Why did you cut the connection?" Commander Twelve scowled.

"Don't you guys think this whole thing is starting to stink?" the technician narrowed his eyes. "Command made it clear that not all of us would make it back from this mission, and that they'll only select the best of us, right?" he looked around at the others, who averted their gaze. "Listen, I know how it sounds, but I propose we send One down the mineshaft to investigate. If no one's there, he comes back out, and we're golden! And if someone *is* there, why send the rest of the squad in to be slaughtered? We can always just say there were more than three of them and we had to fall back. We can add in a shootout, tell them we lost One, and hey presto — we've carried out our orders, completed the mission and can all head on back to base."

"He's right," another soldier chimed in. "We can complete the mission without putting anyone else at risk. If we try it the other way, all of us could wind up dead and we'll fail the mission to boot. What do you say?"

"I say it's a bad idea and we should all go in together," Twelve said, shaking his head.

"What's the point in all of us croaking it, huh?" the technician burst out. "He *chose* to go in there, and personally, *I'd* like to stay alive a little longer. The Bird knew perfectly well that some of these recruits were green, and yet, he sent us on this suicide mission! We've only had a week of training, and before that, three of the guys had never held a weapon in their lives!

"...Reestablish the connection," the commander finally growled. The technician had no choice but to comply with the order. "One, do you copy?"

"Loud and clear! Was there a problem with the connection?"

"Not sure. Here are your orders!" Twelve declared, scanning the faces of the others. "Your task is to go into the mineshaft and conduct reconnaissance. Do not engage with the enemy. Just get in, get out and report back. Are we clear?"

The commander knew what he was doing was wrong, but he had big plans for his career... He may have been dishonourably discharged once, but he wasn't going to let it happen again. To make sure of that, he'd need to rack up lots of successful missions with minimal casualties. And anyway, no one even *liked* Constantine. Not that Twelve liked anyone here; they were all just a bunch of low-lives running from one thing or another. He felt his own reasons for being here were *much* more noble. He'd been expelled from the army for looting, which was a blatant injustice; as he saw it, looting was a soldier's well-deserved reward. What was the harm? It wasn't like lifting the valuables off a freshly-dead soldier (or civilian, for that matter) was going to hurt anyone.

"One, is that clear?" Commander Twelve repeated.

"Yes, clear, of course," One sighed. "I just have one question."

"Go ahead, soldier!"

"Are you guys out of your minds?"

Twelve gritted his teeth.

"One, I could report you for failing to comply with orders!"

"You know what?" Constantine said, a smirk in his voice. "I'll comply with your orders. But you and I are going to talk about this later!"

"Like hell we are!" Twelve sneered. He realised then that he really didn't want Constantine to make it back.

The squad shimmied its way down the tree and, on their commander's orders, headed for the snowmobiles. On their way, the radio crackled into life again.

"I'm five minutes from the mineshaft entrance. Do you copy?" Constantine's voice carried over the static.

"We copy," an evil grin suddenly spread cross Twelve's face. "Fire up the vehicles," he ordered the rest. We're going to follow his tracks and head for the mine."

"But—" one of the soldiers said hesitantly.

"I could shoot you on the spot, you know." Twelve's jaw was clenched. "You have your orders!"

They sped away, and soon, they were spread out in position a few hundred metres from the mineshaft entrance. Five minutes passed, then ten...

"Do you think it's really empty down there?" the technician said, puzzled.

"We'll find out soon enough," Twelve snickered, unscrewing the silencer from his rifle. Then, he fired a series of shots into the air.

For a few seconds, nothing happened. Then, they heard return fire from the mine entrance. The sound of gunshots grew and grew, building into what sounded like repeated bursts of heavy artillery fire. By the time the grenades started flying, Twelve and his squad had already fled back to the snowmobiles and were flooring the gas.

"That was more than three people!" Twelve shrieked. "The captain ordered us to retreat!" He turned and cocked his head at the technician. "Can you wipe the last half hour of communications?"

"Sure thing!" the technician shot him a toothy grin. "I used to be pretty high-ranking, you know. Just give me five!"

*　*　*

The admissions committee, lying in the dugout from which they'd been covering the new recruits, were silent for a while as they tried to contain their rage.

"Buffalo," the man holding the sniper rifle murmured. "Did you hear all that?"

"Yup," the large man next to him sighed.

"You think they're gonna follow regulations?"

"Yeah," Buffalo's brow furrowed. "No way around regulations. In the case of treason or desertion, the entire group must be eliminated."

"Maybe we can start by helping the poor kid in the mine?" the woman said. "He might still be alive!"

"We take the traitors out first, and handle the rest after. We follow procedure," Buffalo replied, shaking his head.

"They're already on their way back. I don't see

the point in wasting bullets on them," the woman muttered.

"That's the point — they shouldn't make it back. Doesn't matter what or where you came from — once you join the War Demons, the rules are clear, and treason is a no-go." Buffalo would have been happy to repeat this last part all day long. "Now, let's go down there, clean up the mine and recover the kid's body. He deserves to be buried with honours — he fought nobly to the bitter end, after all. Even when they stabbed him in the back...

# CHAPTER 8

"TARGETS SIGHTED! Permission to open fire, Buffalo!" the man with the sniper rifle said urgently into his radio.

"Permission granted Falcon!" the group's commander responded immediately. He heard three silenced gunshots. The electric snowmobiles suddenly veered and came skidding to a halt. The three remaining enemies scrambled off into the bushes or hid behind trees, but they needn't have bothered; Buffalo and his faithful companion Cobra were already lying in wait for them. They closed in on the cowering traitors from behind, ready to finish them off.

Cobra was a fan of close combat. She blasted the recruits with a powerful wave of energy that toppled them onto their backs in the snow, even knocking one soldier's gun clean out of his grip.

Meanwhile, Buffalo — who was at least six-foot-five — was fond of his machine gun. He didn't wade in straight away, as he knew the sound of the gun would carry all the way into the mineshaft. Still, he kept his weapon at the ready, although he was well aware that he could kill these worms with his bare hands if he had to.

"Hey, we're on your side! Are you stupid, or something?" the one with the call sign 'Twelve' roared. "ON. YOUR. SIDE!"

"We don't side with traitors," Buffalo growled, aiming his machine gun at the man's chest.

But Twelve really was an experienced soldier. He was nowhere near the level of *these* three elites, but he'd still managed to divert their attention, and was now slyly pointing his pistol at Cobra. He fired once, then twice, but the bullets only bounced off some kind of invisible shield surrounding the woman.

"Where the hell did you get an artefact like that?" Twelve cursed.

"We're not all bottom-feeders like you," Cobra hissed, and in one swift movement, she was standing over the prone commander. She plunged her two long daggers into his chest and twisted. This struck fear into the hearts of the remaining soldiers who, in a desperate attempt to save themselves, started shooting wildly in all directions. In the midst of all the chaos, Cobra shot rapidly from place to place, her movements almost a blur.

"But we executed the mission optimally!" the technician whimpered, a knife sticking out of his leg. "We haven't betrayed anyone!"

"You abandoned one of your own!" Buffalo snarled. "That's treason!" the big man loomed over the bewildered soldier, his arm raised to strike the finishing blow.

"What the hell? We're the War Demons! Of *course* we're willing to sacrifice our own!" the kid's voice was getting high.

"No, the War Demons do not sacrifice their own. They perish together on the deadliest of missions, defending each other as brothers to the very end!" Buffalo sneered, disgusted by the soldier's words. They were an utter perversion of everything the black contract stood for...

With that, Buffalo struck, and the woods fell silent. Yes, they'd had to make a bit of a racket, and the enemy would surely have heard all those gunshots, but that didn't matter right now. He ordered the others to gather up the dead soldiers' things, and then they fired up the snowmobiles and headed for the mine.

When they got there, they carefully scanned their surroundings, keeping their eyes peeled for any potential ambushes.

"Something's off about this," Cobra whispered.

"I agree," Buffalo nodded, "but our orders are clear. If the new recruits fail, we go in. We're the best of the best for a reason!" he clapped the woman on the shoulder, and she chuckled.

They advanced in short bursts, sprinting from cover to cover. Cobra had drained one of her defensive artefacts during their altercation with the traitors, so Falcon had given her a spare. He himself planned to keep as far away from the enemy as possible — as far as the range of his gun would allow, in fact. As it happened, Falcon very rarely found himself in close-range combat, thanks to his masterful ability to conceal himself during even the fiercest of fights.

Their precautions turned out to be unnecessary, however. At the entrance to the mine, the fighters noticed several spots where magical traps had been wiped. It was standard practice to bypass or deactivate traps you came across on the battlefield, but to actually wipe them? That was unheard of...

They entered the mine and gradually descended. Without a map of the old tunnel network, they just had to choose a direction at random and try not to get turned around in the sprawling network of passages.

"Night vision goggles!" Buffalo barked, slipping on his own. Though they'd all trained their eyes to see in relative darkness, the deeper they went into the mine, the fewer the light sources became, and in pitch darkness, you were never going to spot an enemy in time, no matter how great your vision was.

The three soldiers proceeded with caution, inspecting the underground vaults carefully as they went. They began to come across some unexpected things. The abandoned drills and various tools scattered around attested to the fact that ore mining had been in full swing here very recently.

Sometimes, they came across fires that were still burning, or a spot where helmets with built-in headlamps littered the ground.

"I think they gave us bad intel," Cobra said softly. "There are clearly more than ten people down here... or there *were*, at least," she nodded at the corpse of a miner lying nearby. She assumed he was a miner, at least; his uniform told her he definitely wasn't one of the Black Squad's new recruits.

"Definitely more," Buffalo agreed. "But where are they now? Could they really all have escaped? And more importantly, why haven't we found hide nor hair of that new recruit?"

"Strange, all of it," Cobra nodded, looking around at the cavernous space that felt like it had been bustling with life just a few minutes before.

Just at that second, a ball of energy whooshed past her face and exploded against the tunnel wall behind her. The sound of the blast made their eardrums hurt, but the three elite soldiers held their focus. Just in time, Cobra spotted a chunk of rock that had been shaken loose above their heads and was hurtling down on top of them.

"Scatter!" Buffalo yelled. "Ambush!" The other two, seasoned from countless tough battles, needed no more than a second to get their bearings and follow their commander's order. They dove for cover, and heard the rock come crashing to the ground behind them. Suddenly, hordes of grimy miners began streaming out of the endless network of tunnels and pouring into the cavern.

Cobra realised immediately who they were dealing with. You didn't just hire ordinary miners for an illegal operation like this one; anyone with half a brain knew that mining magical ore right on the Empire's borders was going to be exceptionally dangerous. That was why the pickaxe-wielding men advancing on them were not just miners, but experienced soldiers. And *that* was why they were also carrying weapons...

The shootout began. There were even a few gifted fighters amongst the enemy ranks who tried their abilities on the three Imperial soldiers. Soon, however, the element of surprise wore off, and the three Demons, though outnumbered and out-gunned, began to put up a serious fight.

"RAAAH!" a man jumped down from a tall ledge and slashed at Cobra with a long knife, almost slicing her in half with a single blow. At the last second, Cobra's impressive reflexes kicked in. Twisting and dodging, she knocked her attacker flat on his back with a swift kick. Then, she dropped her machine gun, pulled out her beloved daggers and buried them in the man's chest. A hail of bullets began to fly at her from every side. Activating her defensive artefact, she rolled behind the nearest rock.

"No sweat," she grinned. "These guys are small fry. We can do this!"

The fighting continued, and little by little, the three Imperial soldiers began to push the miners back. The miners might have had greater numbers, but the three brave Devils were superior fighters in every way. The Devils' gifts were stronger, their defences sturdier. Plus, they were staying cool as cucumbers, and aiming was a whole lot easier when you weren't flinching at every bullet that came your way.

But just when it looked like the battle was won, two of the mining horde's commanders appeared. The two big men emerged into the cavern and stepped coolly over to their soldiers, who were currently on the defensive. The first one extended a hand and engaged his gift for magnetism; he brought every metallic object within a ten-metre radius rushing towards him, and then, with one powerful burst, sent it all hurtling towards the three Demons. The second one didn't stay still for long; drawing two sharp knives, he began to dart around so fast that he actually seemed to blur. He swiftly closed in on the three soldiers, deftly dodging their bullets, and in the blink of an eye, he was locked in vicious close combat with Cobra.

"There's too many of them!" Buffalo roared, ducking out from behind his cover to fire off a long round at the magnetist. "We weren't prepared for this. They didn't tell us there'd be so many hostiles! We need to call for backup! We're fighting a whole damn mining company, here! We're taking those two down and then getting out of here. That's an order!"

As if to punctuate his words, Buffalo tossed a grenade, waited for the boom and then opened fire with his machine gun again. He was so focused on the enemy in front of him that he was almost blindsided by the new threat coming from their flank.

"Watch out! To your left!" Falcon yelled over the radio, and the other two scattered immediately. As she rolled, Cobra caught a glance of the New Imperial soldiers that had just come into view. They had emerged from the depths of the mine, and while they held their ground, the three War Demons watched the white-clad soldiers load up a shiny rocket launcher.

They heard a boom. A rocket went soaring straight into the roof of the cavern, where it exploded. Tens — no, *hundreds* of tonnes of rock began to rain down. All of this happened in the space of a few seconds, and Cobra had just enough time to register how cold-blooded these soldiers were... the way only New Imperials could be. They didn't give a damn that they were burying their own allies under the rubble. All that mattered was the mission, and limiting casualties wasn't in the job description.

An enormous boulder fell from above, almost crushing one of the gifted miners and tearing his hand clean off. His horrible shrieks of pain suddenly filled the cavern. Another rock flattened the man with the two knives, and the rest met even worse fates, buried under tonnes of earth where no one could reach them.

Illegal miners got paid handsomely, but it was a very risky gig, and you never knew what was waiting around that next bend in the tunnel...

The three Demons were also buried under the

rockfall. Falcon and Buffalo were unconscious, but Cobra had managed to hide beneath a ledge, her defensive artefacts and protective shields keeping her mostly safe. She'd still been hit in a couple of places, however, and blood was streaming freely down her face.

"Look!" one of the New Imperial soldiers cried joyfully. "This one's alive!" he kicked Buffalo's unconscious mass.

"Good," the commander replied. "Dig them out and tie them up. And you — sound the evacuation alarm and get the ingots out of here as fast as possible. The operation is over — we've been exposed!"

As he was barking orders, the commander spotted Cobra reaching for her pistol. She bared her teeth menacingly and tried to raise the weapon, but a white-suited soldier pinned her hand down with his foot.

"All the better," she spat. "We'll be coming back with ore *and* Newie scum. Today's a good day!"

And with that, she passed out.

When she came to, she was tied up tightly. Her hands were restrained with magical handcuffs that completely blocked her from using her gift. Her feet were bound securely with duct tape, and the rest of her body was firmly attached to one of the many columns supporting the cavern roof.

"Hey, assholes!" Cobra hissed at the others, trying to wake them up. No reaction. They stayed slumped against their restraints like limp ragdolls. She tried again, all the while trying not to attract any attention, but got no reaction from either of them.

On the plus side, the miners still hadn't noticed that *she* was awake. They were too busy packing up, and the cavern was a hive of frantic activity. Workers were hurriedly piling equipment and ingots into carts, trying to grab anything of value, and then hauling it out of the mine as fast as their legs could carry them.

All of this was knocking Cobra for six. Daring to mine such a rare and valuable resource right on the Imperial border... Those Newies really *were* getting brazen. Most mines like this one had lain empty since the war started, their proximity to the border considered too risky. At most, you might have a small crew working in secret, maybe transporting the ore out under the cover of darkness. *This*, though... they practically had a whole army down here!

Once upon a time, that wouldn't have been so unusual. The Empire also had mining operations, and in the past, these mines had been fought over endlessly. Both sides had sustained serious losses in these clashes, however, and over time, the mines had become a kind of no-man's land.

Cobra also happened to know that the Newies already *had* a bunch of mines like these on their territory. But the defectors had seized this one for a reason: this area contained exceptionally rich deposits of a variety of magical resources. There were only a handful of other magical mines across the whole vast territory of the Empire, which meant that they had to fight for every last one. That was probably why the Newies had decided to crawl across the border and steal it.

Cobra felt unprepared, and Cobra was usually prepared for anything. After all, she guarded a hundred-kilometre border zone, where she faced more shit in a day than most people faced in a month. You never knew what was waiting just around the bend…

"What happened?" Buffalo wheezed. He gave Falcon a stealthy kick, and the sniper also woke up.

"They blew us up," Cobra sighed.

"But we had defensive artefacts," Buffalo groaned through gritted teeth.

"Yeah, but then the roof of the cavern collapsed and we got buried. Plus, we were surrounded from the start," Cobra shrugged. "Looks like we're screwed."

The three soldiers fell silent, thinking hard. In fact, they were mildly in shock… they were supposed to be the best of the best, after all. Each of them had already served five years, and in that time, they'd seen every kind of mission imaginable. But they'd been woefully underprepared for the danger and complexity of this one, and right now, each one of them had questions for their high command. How could headquarters possibly have failed to detect such a huge concentration of enemy forces?

Soon enough, the Newies noticed that the trio was awake, and a white-armoured soldier approached them.

"Alright, I'll keep this brief," he said calmly. "You have a choice. Either you answer our questions voluntarily, or we torture them out of you."

"You won't get a word out of us!" Cobra spat blood at the soldier's feet. "You can torture us all you want!"

"Indeed," the man's nose wrinkled in distaste. "Well, either way, I'm going to get some answers. And as it happens, I only have a handful of questions. The first and most important is this: who is the soldier you sent down ahead of you? Who *is* he?"

"A dead man," Cobra scoffed. "I would have thought you knew that already."

The soldier produced a notepad and pen and began to write.

"Uhuh, Deadman, I see..."

"What, you're collecting the names of dead Imperials now?" Cobra sneered. "Don't you have anything better to do?"

"Very funny," he stashed the notebook away in a little bag. "Alright, let's move on. What is he in relation to you? What is his rank? Position? Gift ability level?"

"He's just some regular new recruit—" Cobra spluttered as the man kicked her in the stomach.

"Tell me the truth!" he roared.

"I don't *know* who he is! I told you — he's just a new recruit! This is his first mission!" Cobra hadn't planned on giving the bastards a shred of information, but right now, it hardly mattered, because *this* information wasn't worth anything to anyone. Plus, it let her stall for time; if their trio didn't report back within a certain time frame, reinforcements would be sent in automatically. Those were the rules.

"Don't play with me, worm!" the soldier thundered, delivering another painful kick. "Who is that man? Who did you send ahead of you?"

"Buddy, that's enough! Stop hitting her," Buffalo piped up. "She's told you everything she knows. The guy's a new recruit, and his group failed their mission. What don't you understand?"

"…Is this a *joke*?" a vein was bulging on the New Imperial's forehead. "A new recruit? The guy who's been running around down here evading us for two hours?"

"What do you mean, running around?" Cobra's eyes widened.

"I MEAN RUNNING AROUND!" the white-armoured soldier shrieked. Then, trying to compose himself, he continued: "Ok, fine… next question. Your comms hardware is encrypted. Which one of you can decrypt it and contact him? And do you think he'd give himself up if he knew we were holding you prisoner?"

Cobra could only stare at the man, blinking dumbly. The only thing she knew was that she had absolutely no idea what was happening. Not a clue. This was why they'd been miscommunicating from the start — they were talking about two totally different people!

The soldier kept on kicking her, but she decided to just ignore him. After all, she couldn't have told him anything else if she'd wanted to. Eventually, gunshots rang out in another cave and the soldier looked up.

"Looks like I need to go," he sighed as a voice squawked through his radio. "But I'll be back soon."

"Promise?" Cobra smirked.

"I promise, sunshine," he leered back. "I'm not done with you yet!" He turned to his assistant and pointed at the prisoners. "Knock them out for now. Let them get some sleep."

The assistant produced three syringes filled with a glowing liquid and injected each of the prisoners. Cobra didn't try to resist — she knew it would be pointless. She also recognised the liquid. They called it 'chamomile', and as far as she knew, one of the ingredients was the extract of a magical ore... Her consciousness faded rapidly into black.

In what felt like the blink of an eye, all three of them snapped awake at once, as if an alarm clock had just gone off.

"Those rats!" Buffalo cursed. "They pumped us full of chamomile!"

"Yeah, that shit hits hard," Falcon agreed. They all knew that a shot of chamomile could send you into a sleep deeper than anything any somnolist could conjure. They also had a rough idea of how much a single dose of chamomile could sell for. Maybe plain old magical ore wasn't what the New Empire was here for... The ore here was valuable, yes, but there were other materials worth far more. And yet, something here was clearly of great interest to the Newies... and headquarters would need to be informed about it.

"That asshole will be back soon," said Buffalo, trying to shake his head clear.

"What does he want us to say? We don't have any more information. But hey, more importantly — that new recruit is alive, and they're looking for him," Falcon remarked.

"Either that, or it's a different person," Cobra murmured, thinking. "Why did he have to kick me so many times, anyway?"

"Either way, we know the Newie will be back. We'll just have to improvise and try to stall him."

"He lied to you," the elite trio snapped their mouths shut and swivelled their heads in the direction of the unfamiliar voice. A dark figure slowly began to emerge from behind a rocky outcrop nearby.

"Uhh," Buffalo's brow knitted.

"Need me to repeat myself?" the stranger said, a little mockingly. "He *lied* to you. That guy's not coming back, trust me."

"Who are you?" Buffalo whispered.

"I'm the new recruit, the one they call — well, One," the stranger sighed heavily.

"One? The One who went down first and died?" Cobra couldn't believe her ears.

"Almost. The One who went down first and *didn't* die. Look," he stepped out fully from his dark hiding place and stood before the three fighters in all his glory. He was covered from head to toe in blood and gore, and his expression was very, very glum.

"How are you still alive?" Cobra whispered, astonished.

"How did you even *get* here?" Buffalo burst out. "Quick, you should hide!"

"Who from? I killed them all before I came here to you," One spread his arms wide.

"I think the chamomile did something to me," Falcon murmured, bewildered.

"You're not the only one," Buffalo grunted back. "Alright, hold up! You, One, killed them all, and now you're standing here, chatting to us? Have I understood correctly?"

"More or less, yeah," the miserable-looking soldier nodded.

"Commander, I have a question for him," Cobra said. Buffalo nodded wordlessly for her to go ahead. "One... If you completed your mission and you're standing here without a scratch, then... why are you so sad?"

"I bent my machine gun," One gave a sigh so pitiful that the others almost felt bad for him. He produced the gun and showed it to them. It was bent into the exact curve of some miner's particularly dense skull.

"Did you fight them hand-to-hand?" Buffalo asked incredulously.

"Uhuh!"

"You ran out of bullets, then?" Cobra guessed.

"Oh, no! I had enough bullets!" One shook his head fervently.

"I don't get it."

"Can't you see? The ensign is a good guy — I don't want to disappoint him!" One looked at them like they were three prize idiots.

"Hey, One, tell me something," Cobra sighed. "You're not crazy, are you?"

*  *  *

Crazy? What was she talking about? These guys were supposed to be seasoned vets, and yet here they were, asking me such ridiculous questions. Of *course* I was crazy! I was a demonologist! And why didn't they understand what I was telling them? What about the ensign? I'd told them the tragic tale! The man had looked after this gun, oiled it regularly, cleaned it and generally cared for it like a baby. Then, he gives it to me, and the first thing I do is *bend* it! How could I ever live this down?

There was no hope of explaining this to the three in front of me. These people clearly had no conception of how precious a person's property could be... I guessed they'd never been around students. You could have all your pollen samples sorted neatly into labelled jars, your vices and alchemical kits arranged carefully on the shelves and stored inside the special lock boxes, everything neat and orderly, and suddenly, you come back from a little week-long bender with Sanders to find — bam! Your laboratory has been transformed into a trash heap. Your students are sitting around, playing strip poker with a demon — all of them practically naked already, by the way — and all they say is: "Look, professor, look — we summoned him!"

In their defence, they did clean up nicely afterwards. Them, and the naked demon... And no, I didn't try anything weird!

"But how did you *do* it?" the big guy asked, sticking to his guns. I'd gathered that his call sign was Buffalo and that he was the unit's commander.

How *had* I done it? It was a good question, a clever one... and one I didn't know how to answer. Naturally, I'd run into some guards the moment I entered the mine. I'd said hello, they'd said hello back, I'd asked how they were doing, and so on, until we actually struck up a full-blown conversation. Then, some morons on the surface had started firing into the air, the guards had realised I wasn't one of theirs and everyone had started shooting everywhere. My demon had also informed me as to exactly who those morons were... Honestly, the backstabbing was a surprise.

I'd summoned a couple more demons and sent them into the fray while I slipped off to hide in the endlessly branching labyrinth of tunnels. I'd summoned yet more demons to scout the tunnel system for me, and they'd found me a secure hiding place sheltered away from prying eyes. I'd holed up there for a bit while they conducted sabotage and reconnaissance for me behind enemy lines. Who knew that setting a grenade on fire was just as effective as pulling out the pin?

While the miners hadn't been a problem, I'd known those New Empire soldiers might have some unwelcome tricks up their sleeves — especially that commander of theirs. He was a tough guy. I'd actually had to activate some magic marks and summon a couple of extra hefty demons to handle him.

"I got lucky — half of them left on the first batch of snowmobiles to transport the goods," I said. "These guys were the ones left behind."

"Of course," Cobra let out a sigh of relief. "Everyone was gone except a couple of miners. Well, that's that question answered. But can I ask one more?"

"Sure."

"If you've taken them all out, then why are we still tied up?"

"Ah... well, you could have attacked me, or who knows what. Better safe than sorry, right?" I said evenly. "But I can tell now that you're alright, so I'll untie you." I quickly slashed their ropes and — after a little fiddling — unlocked the handcuffs. Once the three soldiers had their bearings, Buffalo took off running for the surface, motioning for everyone else to follow him.

"We have to get back and report to command as fast we can!" he grunted.

What about me? Well, an order was an order, which meant *I* had to follow, too. I just fell in at the rear and did my best to keep up with the three brave elites. In my defence, the going was easier for them — they weren't even carrying weapons!

"On second thoughts, it seems like a *lot* of them stayed," Cobra said, her brow furrowed as she came across the tenth corpse in her path. And these were just the ones lying out in the open... she hadn't seen the half of it yet.

"*Holy shit!*" Buffalo cursed. "What the hell happened here?" He pointed to a razor-sharp stalagmite that was sticking out of the ground. It must have been at least four metres long and stretched almost to the ceiling. It also happened to have a dead Newie soldier impaled on the tip.

"You don't wanna know," I grimaced, making a mental note not to summon that particular demon again. And yet, it was strangely beautiful... Personally, I would have impaled the guy on one of the stalactites hanging from the roof — there were so many to choose from, after all.

"I count twenty bodies already!" the one called Falcon exclaimed.

"I, uh, just have really good eyesight!" I said, desperately trying to think up a plausible explanation for the carnage. But all three of them just turned to stare, first at me, and then at my bent machine gun. "Really, it's true! I jumped out at them from the darkness — they never even saw me coming."

We were drawing closer and closer to the surface when suddenly, we turned a bend to find a light like a street lamp shining in the cave. Falcon made a *listen* gesture, and the three fighters froze.

"Have you done a sweep of the area?" Cobra

asked. "Are you sure there's no one here?"

"Here? Yes," I answered honestly. The group relaxed and we continued on our way.

"Wait," Cobra froze. "Does that mean there *are* enemies somewhere else?"

"Yeah, at the exit," I shrugged.

"Why didn't you *say* that, you idiot?" she growled.

"A private shouldn't talk back to his superiors!" I said crisply, standing to attention. "The commander told me to walk, and I'm walking, ma'am!"

"Permission to punch him?" Falcon groaned, while Buffalo chuckled.

"Sure, go ahead, see what happens!" he nodded towards my mangled gun.

I didn't see what the big deal was. Sure, the bent machine gun had been a serious bummer, but everything else was going great! My life was suddenly filled with entertainment and excitement — how could I not be happy? And when my demon informed me telepathically that these three had obliterated my unit, well, that was the icing on the cake. That meant I could even skip being disciplined! Because I absolutely would have killed those traitors myself. They'd become dead men walking the moment they crossed me... I'd already drawn up a rough plan for when and how each one of them would die, which I thought was quite courteous of me. After all, I knew it wasn't very nice to get pissed on by an acid demon, or to be dragged kicking and screaming down to the lower demonic planes. From my side, those things were certainly a little tricky to execute, but I had time.

"We need a new plan," Buffalo said in a low voice. "First, we need to find some weapons—" he stopped short as I held out my bent machine gun.

"Here's a weapon for you, buddy. Take it at your own risk, though. And maybe you can tell the ensign it was you who bent it?" — my tone was hopeful.

"No, you can answer for that yourself," Buffalo shook his head.

"Fine," I huffed. "Let's come up with another plan, then."

"Way ahead of you. First, we need to go down and search the enemy corpses again. The Newies might have taken their weapons with them when they evacuated, but I bet they left something beh—" the big man's voice trailed off, and he fell silent. "One! Where did you get those gear bags? Don't tell me there's weapons in there!"

Had he seriously not noticed the three rucksacks all hanging from my shoulders at once? I dumped them on the ground, untied the drawstring of the closest one and pulled out a bundle of twenty-five assorted automatic weapons. I didn't touch the backpack I had stuffed into the bottom of the rucksack; I'd look through that one later and see if there was anything I could sell.

"What's this?" Buffalo asked, his voice tight.

"They're... trophies," I shrugged.

One thing I liked about the army was the many opportunities you had to collect trophies, and in that regard, the Imperial Army was head and shoulders above any other operation I'd ever served in. The trophy, you see, was a sacred object. Looting — that was, breaking into someone's home, robbing them and possibly even killing them — was strictly prohibited. But claiming the weapon of a defeated enemy? Now, *that* was a different story entirely. No one had the right to take a soldier's trophy away, and if it *was* taken, then the soldier was entitled to adequate compensation.

I was brand new to this town — to this entire world, actually — so I'd take everything I could get my hands on, including twenty-five machine guns.

"Just pick your weapon," I sighed.

"You got ammo?"

"Obviously!" I opened the second rucksack, which was stuffed to the brim with magazines and cartridges. There'd been no time to sort everything, so I'd just tossed it all in together.

"Let me guess," chuckled Buffalo, fishing a few magazines out of my stash, "You've got grenades in the third rucksack?"

"Why would I need grenades? It's full of ore," I replied casually.

"For real?" the commander whistled and then tried to lift the rucksack. Even for him, it was a serious struggle. "Why so much?"

"Why not?" I finished handing out the weapons, pulled the rucksacks closed and hoisted them back over my shoulders.

"Aren't they heavy for you?"

"Nah, they're a good weight," I said, giving one

of the bags a pat.

What these three didn't know was that my demons had already lugged dozens of bags like these up to the surface and stashed them in a nearby fox's den. That fox was certainly in for a surprise when it got home...

It was convenient that the New Imperials had been smelting their ore into three-hundred-gram ingots right here on-site. It was hard to even imagine how much one of those ingots must be worth. I, however, *could* imagine it, and I knew the exact price one would sell for. That was why fifteen bags crammed full of those ingots would be waiting for me in a secret location until the time came. I had a crystal-clear plan for how it was all going to unfurl...

Remember I said I liked how the Imperial Army did trophies? Well, they even had a special trophy storage facility back at base, and my current goal was to get all my new treasures back there.

I was also eager to start going out on proper solo missions. Most soldiers hated them, but I couldn't wait to wander through enemy territory all alone, free to display my true abilities without having to hide from anyone. And after that... well, it wasn't hard to guess who I'd run into out there...

"Change of plan. We have enough weapons, so we're going to meet the enemy here," Buffalo said as he looked around, noting that their current position was relatively secure. We swiftly set up some defences and settled in to wait for the enemy to fall into our trap.

It took about half an hour for the first miners to arrive. They were coming to collect the rest of the ore and ingots, which I'd long ago hidden elsewhere. Instead of their ore, the unlucky diggers got a round of hot lead.

All was still for a while, until a whole horde of enemies rushed us at once. Our defences almost broke, but in the end, the miners were no match for the three Imperial fighters. It helped that I lent them some of my artefacts, though only after they swore to return them in *exactly* the same condition they got them.

There was a reason I counted three Imperial fighters and not four. By the time the shooting started, I was already long gone! I could only hear a muffled yell in the distance as I ran…

"Where's that goddamn rookie? Where did he go?"

"To hell with him! Hold your ground — we have nowhere to run!"

*　*　*

Cobra fired off a few well-aimed rounds and then ducked back behind the rock, narrowly avoiding a spray of enemy bullets.

"Where did he go?" she yelled again.

"He bailed," Falcon sighed.

"He didn't seem like the type to run from a fight," Buffalo frowned. "Oh well, who cares? Just keep firing! Maybe he did run away…"

"We need to know!" Cobra shouted, leaning out

from behind the rock to fire off a few more shots. "He could attack us from behind!"

This operation was starting to stink worse with every second. They'd thought it couldn't *get* any worse — they'd thought they were saved! — but now here they were, back between a rock and a hard place again. The ammo the weird recruit had given them was running out, and while the enemy was weak, they had numbers on their side. And where was their goddamn backup, anyway? At this rate, they were going to be overpowered any second.

"We're going on the offensive!" Buffalo screamed, leaping out from behind his cover and clamping his hands around the nearest miner's throat. One clean twist, and the unlucky guy's neck snapped clean in two. Buffalo grabbed his machine gun and started firing into the mob, shielding himself with the limp body. "Behind me! We need to make a break for it!"

"Let's bury them!" came a distant cry, and it was only then that the three soldiers noticed the man with the grenade launcher. He was pointing it at the ceiling, and he had a nasty grin on his face. He was just waiting for the other miners to get out of range before –

A dagger plunged deep into his chest. A few nearby miners fell to the ground with him, missing their heads and limbs.

"Forward!" Buffalo roared, drawing a sword from his belt. "We're gonna tear them apart!"

* * *

"How did you do that? *How*?"

Oh, here we go again... I was just standing there, minding my own business, and then suddenly, that crazy woman was shaking me by the collar.

"I really don't understand the problem," I said, doing my best to deflect her pestering questions. "I already told you — I went behind them and then cut them down with this sword. That's all."

"But how? How did you get behind them?" Cobra insisted, still shaking the life out of me.

"What do you mean, how? That's what the second exit is for!"

Honestly, this was basic stuff.

"Guns aren't really my thing, see... for now, that is! I'll learn! Anyway, I got behind them, attacked from the back, and cut them all down on their way out the door. My energy is fully replenished, so it wasn't hard."

"But how? HOW? Buffalo, make it make sense, please!" Cobra howled.

"The bent machine gun was enough to make all my questions go away," the big commander shrugged. "Although, wait... Why didn't you tell us that this place had a second exit?"

"You think I'm stupid? You won't catch *me* out! I know how hierarchy works in the army!" I said, feeling pleased with myself.

All three of them opened their mouths to

speak... but there was nothing they could say! They knew perfectly well that I was right...

"Hey, kid, where did you serve before this?"

"Nowhere, really," I shrugged.

"Well, then how do you know so much about army procedures?" Buffalo narrowed his eyes.

"From jokes," I promptly replied. *Obviously*, I thought. But, to my confusion, Buffalo put his hand over his face. "I remember one, actually. It's the perfect illustration of why you shouldn't make your ensign mad. I can tell it if you—"

"No!" Buffalo roared. "Let's just get outside."

Shame — it was an enlightening joke. Still, getting some fresh air would be good, too; I'd had enough of these caves. And as a bonus, there were plenty of trophies along the way for me to collect.

"Ooh, a knife!" I squealed, running over to a body. "Ooh, another knife!" I gushed as I moved on to the next one. I didn't skip a single miner, and every one of them had a precious little something for me.

"Cut that out! We need to vacate this place as fast as possible!" Buffalo snapped.

"Yes, yes, of course. Whatever you say," I nodded. "Oh!"

"What? What is it?"

"A penny!" I cried, rushing over to grab the tiny coin. At that, Buffalo growled something under his breath and just increased his pace, trying his best to ignore my antics.

When we finally reached the surface, we ran for the snowmobiles. As soon as we reached them, however, the three soldiers all froze in unison, looks of amazement on their faces.

"But... when? When could you *possibly* have done that?" Cobra howled. "How the *hell*?"

"Huh?" I turned around. "Who, me?"

"Who else?"

"What's the problem?" I asked, totally mystified by her outrage.

"WHEN DID YOU DO THAT?" the poor woman seemed to have completely lost it.

"What do you mean?"

"When did you bring *those* up here?" she pointed a trembling finger at the snowmobiles, which now had a sledge piled high with big sacks tied onto the back of it.

"On the way..."

"You're telling me you were able to collect all that, unload the magazines, pack it all into bags, carry them on your back and fight at the same time?" her eyes were narrow slits.

"What can I say? I'm resourceful," I shrugged. I wasn't about to tell her that flying demons had done all the work for me. They could be very hard workers if you waved a little extra cash in front of their noses. All you had to do was give them instructions and they'd take care of the rest themselves. They'd even thank you into the bargain!

Buffalo only waved a dismissive hand, climbed onto the snowmobile and started fiddling with the tablet. Meanwhile, Cobra did some deep breathing exercises and managed to calm herself a little — or so it seemed from the outside, at least.

"That's it, you can't surprise me anymore," she said calmly. I raised an eyebrow.

"Uhuh, sure."

"Go ahead and try," she said, sticking her chin out. "It's not going to work."

"And if it does, what do I get in return?" I grinned. "Oh, I know! You have to eat lunch with me."

"Oh? Is the rookie asking me out on a date?" she suddenly smiled.

"Huh? Oh, no, you've got the wrong idea! It's just lunch..."

"Oh, sure! A lunch *date*," she chuckled.

"There's a caveat... lunch is on you!" I moved in close to her, touched a finger to her cheek and turned her head just a little to the side. I leaned in even closer, making her blush, and whispered three magic words into her ear. Her eyes grew wider and wider. She seemed more surprised than she'd ever been in her life. She drew a deep breath, looked at her two comrades and—"

"GET DOWN! SNIPER, EIGHT O'CLOCK!" she roared hoarsely, flinging herself onto the snow.

Lying on my side next to her, I propped my head up with my hand and smiled.

"Well? Were you surprised?"

"I'm going to strangle you with my own two hands when we get out of here!" she seethed.

"Not when — *if*," I corrected. "They've got reinforcements on the way."

"Well, then what should we do? Got any bright ideas?" Buffalo, hunkered behind his snowmobile, was suddenly glaring at me.

"Do you believe me?" I looked at the big man, who only started cursing under his breath. "Fine. In that case, no — I *don't* have any ideas."

"We believe you! We believe you!" Cobra shouted. "Now, do you have any ideas?"

"I do. We get on the snowmobiles and drive away right now."

"There's a goddamn *sniper*! He'll freaking shoot you!" she yelled back, but it was already too late. I stood up, strolled over to the snowmobile and hopped on. Surely, it couldn't be too hard to drive... I just had to find the gas pedal... Aha! Right there...

"Suit yourselves," I shrugged and reached for the ignition. "You don't have much time left, you know!"

The three fighters glanced at each other, jumped up as one and sprinted for the remaining snowmobiles.

"Well done!" I called. "Always listen to old Constantine, he'll never lead you astray. Just don't sell him your soul."

* * *

*The New Empire*
*Special Operations headquarters*

There were only two people in the office. The one in white armour standing in *front* of the lavish desk was currently explaining why the operation had failed. He'd been explaining for half an hour now... The one sitting in the tech-chair *behind* the desk was having trouble taking this explanation in. It made less and less sense with every word his subordinate spoke.

"How could that be? Let me say that again: *how could that be*? Our intel said there were only four of them, total! And you're telling me they took down the entire crew of thugs we hired to dig up sepheroth ore? Killing our operatives and destroying our equipment in the process? *How*?" asked the head officer yet again.

"They were an elite Imperial squad, sir," the armoured soldier replied, trying desperately to pull himself out of the hole he was, by now, at least neck-deep in. "Our experts are working as we speak to reconstruct the chain of events and get to the bottom of the incident. This will take some time, however... It's quite a puzzle, sir. But I can assure you that we have everything under control!"

"Fine, fine. Accidents happen, accidents happen," the man in the chair murmured, simmering down a little. "Forget the mine, there are hundreds like it. But I have one question... How did they manage to escape?"

"Sir... It was some goddamn voodoo!" the soldier burst out.

"...*Voodoo?* Soldier, my sniper was in position. I had everything in place! What HAPPENED?" he banged his fist against the table.

"I'm not sure, but the sniper took one shot and missed, sir."

"And may I ask *why* he only fired once? Dusk doesn't miss. And even if he *did* miss, he'd have another thirty bullets fired off in the space of a minute!" the man's patience was rapidly wearing thin again.

"Like I said, it was… well… *voodoo*," the soldier replied reluctantly.

"What the hell are you talking about? What do you *mean*?"

"Read for yourself, sir!" the soldier handed the head officer a copy of Dusk's first-hand report. The man skimmed the document, frowned and then read it more carefully.

"What does he mean 'I tried to fire, but two red men appeared and urinated on me'? And then they just up and vanished? What in the hell—?" the head officer scowled. "And what do you make of this report? Because I can't make heads nor tails of it!"

"Honestly, sir? The only part I'm clear about is Dusk getting pissed on."

# CHAPTER 9

"YOU... BENT it?"

"I bent it," I said miserably, staring at the ground.

"That's a shame," Birch sighed.

"Tell me about it!"

"What did you bend it around?" he asked, trying to disassemble the machine gun to no avail. Several of the parts were jammed tightly together.

"A head," I shrugged.

A smile spread across his face. "A New Imperial head?"

"Of course! What else would I bend a machine gun around?"

"Well, in that case, don't worry about it, son!" he said, setting the gun aside. "You were doing god's work... And I trust you're in one piece yourself?"

"All in one piece," I replied.

"Good."

Meanwhile, a whisper had started up in the line behind me. At first, the other soldiers had just been exchanging silent glances, but by now, they were openly staring, eyebrows raised in puzzlement.

"Is Birch feeling okay?" one soldier asked another. "I've never seen him give a crap about anyone before!"

"Hey, do you remember Squint?" the other replied. "He lost a magazine on a mission one time. That was also the mission where he lost his eye, spent a month in the infirmary. Anyway, he finally gets back on duty, and the ensign starts tearing him a new one! 'Where's my magazine, you asshole, go back out there and get it!'" the soldier chuckled.

"And? Did he go?"

"He *ran*! It was a miracle they even managed to catch him at the gates!"

All the while, I just kept handing Birch my gear. My uniform was soaked in blood, and the ensign only dealt with weapons, but that wasn't a problem; I'd just hand the uniform in elsewhere later.

"And the magazines? Are they all here?" he squinted at me.

"Of course, here they are," I held out the sack.

"Wait a minute... why are there fifteen too many?"

"Compensation for the gun," I shrugged. "I

have more, too," I handed him the rucksack full of weapons.

"Let's have a look-see," Birch yanked the rucksack open and started pulling out trophies. "Nice... Not bad... Huh! This is the model ER three-five-two!" he exclaimed, weighing a New Imperial pistol in his hands. "Amazing! You know, I'm supposed to file a damaged weapon report, but you know what? I can we can skip it this time. Sometimes things break — shit happens! My only question is why you have all your cartridges... Did you find extra somewhere?"

"No, I just didn't use them."

"Well, that was a mistake, Constantine," Birch frowned. "A big mistake."

"Am I actually hearing this?" someone in line burst out. "Birch just called him by his name! Not 'degenerate', not 'clumsy moron' — his *actual* name!"

"A big, *big* mistake." The ensign repeated, paying no attention to the commentary from the line. "Bullets are made to be fired, and every bullet must find its lamb."

"Its... lamb?" I asked blankly.

"You know, its Newie."

Aha, got it. They called the New Imperials 'lambs.' And 'Newies', too, it seemed. I guessed that the former must come from the colour of their armour.

"Anything else you need?" Birch asked.

"Yes, actually. I was hoping to get my own unit in the storage facility," I said.

"What? But this was your first mission! Are you telling me you brought home *trophies*?" I nodded. "Well, alright… come with me and I'll give you the tour."

"Hey! I've been standing in this line for forty minutes!" someone yelled, and the ensign's face darkened.

"Yell at me one more time, and you'll be standing there till tomorrow, you numb-skulled cretin!"

A sigh of relief went up from the line. "That's our ensign!"

Since I was still just a wet rookie, Birch gave me a personal tour of the storage facility. It was located deep underground. During the long lift ride down, Birch gave me a brief rundown of the system. I couldn't just stroll in and empty the contents of my backpack into my locker whenever I liked. Instead, each item would first need to be personally approved by the head of storage, which was to say, by the ensign himself. Since I had nothing to hide, I didn't mind opening my bags.

For the time being, I was given a little storage cell measuring one metre by one metre. While it could have been bigger, it *did* have a nice armoured door, and I wasn't planning on storing *all* my trophies away, in any case. Financially, it made a lot more sense to hand most of them directly over to the government and enjoy my fair compensation.

I pulled a string of grenades out of a bag and was about to toss them into the cell when Birch stopped me.

"No grenades down here," he snapped, narrowing his eyes. "Wait a minute... did you thread the cord through the *pins*?"

"It was easier," I shrugged. "Those rings are actually pretty hard to pull out, so it's totally safe!"

"If you say so," he muttered, carefully untying the cord and stashing the grenades well out of my reach. "Anyway," Birch emptied out the last rucksack and began to sort through the trophies. "Okay, this one is worthless... We can toss that one out... This one's interesting, I think it should go in the cell," he held up a powerful-looking white pistol, "and store the bullets somewhere nearby."

Some things went straight into my little storage unit, while others were put in a separate pile and carried off to be stored elsewhere.

An hour later, and the whole operation was finished.

"By the way, don't worry — your compensation for the items you handed in will be tacked on to your salary. And may I say, you'll get a nice price for them, too!"

"You know better than me," I shrugged. "By the way, do you mind if I ask you a slightly cheeky question?"

"Go ahead!"

"What other sizes of storage unit have you got down here? Are they all one-by-one?" I gestured to my little cell.

"Certainly not!" he exclaimed. "You insult me!"

He set off down the corridor, launching into a detailed explanation of the different types of units.

Apparently, you could actually store vehicles down here, as well as all manner of smaller items. There wasn't any strict protocol regarding who could receive which unit, either. This was the ensign's domain, and essentially, it was his to manage as he saw fit. He had the authority to grant access to different storage cells on the basis of rank, years served or honours received.

The biggest units were usually occupied by whole squads at a time, and were used to gather all of the squad's essential equipment in one place. High command didn't always give the green light for some of the riskier mission requests, and when that happened, your squad had to use its own gear. Other units held people's pension savings, personal items — more or less anything you could imagine.

"Now, *that's* what I'm talking about!" I whistled. "A three-room storage unit? For real?"

"It's one of the largest," Birch replied, his chest puffing with pride. "It's mostly used by the really big squads."

"This must be a hundred and fifty square metres!" I goggled.

"Yup!"

"You could park a tank in here!" I said, awestruck.

"Yes, you could," Birch grinned back.

"How many of these have you got?" I asked, already calculating that I'd probably need more space than this within a few months.

"Not many, but we tend not to need them as

much as some of the other bases do. Those Midnight Furies on the next base over are bona fide trophy fiends," he chuckled. "I talked to old Pistol over there not long ago, and he said a squad had just reserved *twelve* of these cells from him!"

All this was yet another reminder of why I liked the army so much. The whole trophy system was a bit convoluted, but it was fascinating! The thing was, you couldn't just go and waltz around town selling your trophies off willy-nilly. Or, to be precise, you *could* — depending on your rank and reputation. It was out of the question for me yet, which made me a little sad, but I knew it wouldn't take long. And once I made it, I'd be marching up the aristocrats' front drives with a display case full of weapons. The upper crust were willing to pay much more than government market value, not to mention the fact that doing business with them was a lot more convenient. For now, however, handing in the weapons was the simplest solution. The government handled the sale, and all I had to do was receive my share of the money. My ten Newie rifles would be put up for sale immediately, to be purchased locally, or perhaps, by buyers elsewhere...

"How much do I pay for the locker?" I inquired.

"Not much — two hundred a month," Birch said amiably.

"Alright. Can I give it to you later? Or do you need it right now?"

"Don't worry, we'll deduct it from your pay," he chuckled.

The fact that a new recruit was hauling so much treasure in didn't seem to be raising any eyebrows. Then again, these were the War Demons — they'd seen it all before. But the ensign did warn me that in the event of my death, all my property would go to the state unless I'd already signed a will bequeathing it to friends or relatives.

We finished up our adventure, all my weapons and cartridges stored away in my personal cell, and headed for the surface. Before we could step into the lift, however, Cobra came barrelling out of it. She was almost spitting with rage.

"Where the hell have you been?" she snapped at me, yanking me back into the lift with one swift grab. "I've been looking everywhere for you!"

"I was storing my trophies," I told her the truth.

"Trophies? What are you *talking* about? We were supposed to go straight to high command and deliver our report!" she fumed.

"But I told you my rucksacks were heavy," I shrugged. "So, I came to unload them... What's wrong?"

"I let you out of my sight for one second!" she clutched her head. "One *second!*"

"There, there," I patted her on the shoulder. "It's all okay, don't worry."

That seemed to calm the elite fighter a bit, but she still insisted on holding my arm with an iron grip until we reached Rester's office. It turned out that Buffalo and Falcon were both recovering in the infirmary, meaning we were the only two disposed to deliver the report.

Cobra and I stepped into the office and she summarised events for the general. She included the part about them eliminating my unit.

"I see," Rester nodded. "Interesting."

"Why is this debriefing happening without me?" the Bird came striding into the room. "I'm their captain, goddammit!"

"Simmer down, Joy," the general replied evenly. "Come and take a seat. And congratulations on losing six members of your squad today."

"Damn shame," the captain said, his tone surprisingly casual.

"They were traitors," Rester remarked pointedly.

"Oh, well in that case, good riddance!" Cardinal grinned and slapped me on the back. "Good job, kid! I know who's getting the *fun* missions from now on!"

"Don't execute him, you hear me!" Cobra burst out.

"Excuse me? Do I need to remind you that I outrank you, soldier?" Joy's face darkened.

"I apologise, captain." Cobra stood to attention. "Requesting that the boy be permitted to live, sir."

"Alright, I'll deal with you later," Cardinal shook his head. "But first, you." He pulled his chair up close and looked me in the eye.

"Are you going to beat me up?" I asked, my head bowed.

"Why would I beat you up?" the captain's brow

furrowed.

"Because I bent the machine gun," I sighed pitifully. "And I didn't take any prisoners, and I went into the mine alone."

"Did you have a choice?" the captain's eyebrows went up.

"Well, in theory, I could have trapped them down in the caves. I reckon it would have been difficult, but it was definitely doable."

The two senior officers sat in stunned silence for a few moments. Then, the general wordlessly opened his desk drawer, pulled out two cut crystal tumblers and filled them with whiskey. He handed one to the captain, and they drained the glasses dry in one gulp.

"I won't say we *never* see things like this," Rester eventually stammered, "but we certainly don't see them as often as I'd like! Therefore, I'd like to reward you — assuming Joy agrees."

"One hundred per cent!" Cardinal nodded.

"In that case," the general produced a notepad and scribbled something down on it. "Here, take this," he tore off the page and held it out to me. The message was brief but mystifying. 'Two months' was all it said.

"Two months? What does that mean?"

"It means that as of today, the length of your service has been shortened by exactly sixty-one days," Rester gave a stern nod. "Your achievement is impressive—"

"Two months, just like that?" I jumped up from my seat. "*Two whole months* just for a couple of caves?"

"I — think it's quite a — a small reduction, actually?" Rester stammered again, spluttering in surprise. "I would have given you six months, but you haven't been here long enough to qualify for that big a cut. That said, if you're planning on completing more missions as flawlessly as you did this one, I think we'll be giving you your six months soon enough."

"May I ask a question?" I waited for nods of permission from both the general and captain. "What's the maximum amount of time I can knock off in a year?"

"Well, that would be thirty years!" Rester chuckled. "But keep in mind that the risk level only increases with each new mission."

With that, I was dismissed. I headed off to get some rest. The only other point in my debriefing had been that the rest of our unit had also been sent out on a mission, and that out of eight people, only five had returned. No surprise there... Harsh as it sounded, natural selection was a pretty swift process around here.

I took a shower and grabbed something to eat. I liked the fact that food was always available here, and that it was decent in both quality and quantity. We had a huge canteen that was open around the clock, and you could pile your plate as high as you liked.

A strict routine was important for a soldier, but at the same time, we always had to be combat-ready. Many squads regularly went out on back-to-back missions, and everyone wanted a hot meal when they got back, day or night. We lived under pressure, knowing that we could be packed off on a dangerous operation at any time. This was the border zone, and skirmishes (albeit minor ones) broke out every day. Sometimes, they might even ship you off to some distant frontier, or even into central Circle City. There were rumours that an enemy sabotage group had been spotted inside the city, and that an elite squad of thirty War Demons had been sent in to neutralise them. As it happened, the entire squad had come back alive and unharmed, save for two with minor injuries.

There were also 'regular' (i.e., non-Demon) soldiers in our division, but their roles were very different to ours. They normally served as technicians and other support personnel. In theory, the Demons could be deployed anywhere, but were primarily utilised against the New Imperial troops. You *could* say we got the most punishing jobs, but somehow, we didn't seem to mind.

Once I'd eaten, I climbed into bed. Ah, this was the life... what else could a soldier need? Apart from needing to go to lineup, of course...

But when I woke up at five in the morning, the barracks was already empty except for the orderly. I asked him if everyone was already gone to lineup, but he wasn't sure. He did, however, reveal to me that the system here was much simpler than I'd first assumed. We no longer had to attend training sessions, and in the rare event of a lineup, we would be notified in advance. And if you were home from a mission and had been dismissed from duty, then no one was going to bother you at all — not about a lineup or anything else.

All this was according to the orderly, a soldier known as Nightstand, at any rate. He'd gotten his call sign for the fact that he liked to stand sentry on top of a sturdy little bedside table during his orderly duty. He'd stay up there for most of the shift, and it seemed to suit him just fine.

While lineups might not be scheduled, target practice was held at ten o'clock every morning. With my marksmanship leaving much to be desired, I decided I wanted to go along. So, at seven o'clock, I tracked down the Bird and requested to join the practice.

"No. You're on rest," said the captain bluntly.

"But I'm rested!" I protested. He only shook his head in reply. "Please? I really want to do it."

"If you're *doing*, you're not *resting*," he shook his head. "Oh, that reminds me — you don't have a squad anymore, do you?" He glanced around the barracks. "You can tag along with Veteran over there."

"Why's he called Veteran?" I'd learned by now that every call sign had a story.

"He served here for a year without anyone thinking up a call sign for him. So, they called him Veteran," the captain shrugged.

And just like that, I was led off to target practice. They handed us our weapons — mine was a shiny new machine gun — and we headed off to the training ground, ten kilometres west of base.

I understood now that target practice was essential. It wasn't wise to underestimate the power of these modern weapons… They were so *convenient*, for a start. Plus, Birch had told me to use my bullets, and I liked him too much to let him down.

I started by shooting at stationary targets, then moving ones, and then, I moved on to throwing grenades. That last part was easy, though; I'd tossed plenty of exploding artefacts at my enemies in my past life. Then, they showed us how to care for our weapon, demonstrating how to disassemble it, clean it and then reassemble it. That part was interesting, too.

Later, the Bird gave a short lecture about two different types of artefacts, complete with demonstrations. This rounded off a rich and interesting day of learning. Finally, we set off back to the trucks to make our way back to base.

There were four different companies in total at the shooting range. That made four hundred people under the captain's watch, excluding any in the infirmary.

"Hey, rookie!" someone called.

"Hi, I'm One," I held a hand out to the soldier.

"Whatever, that's irrelevant for now," he waved my hand away. "But hey, I heard you went in balls-deep on your very first day of service. Is it true?" his face was curious. I just shrugged. "Well? Tell us about it, at least!"

Well… what did I have to hide, right? I'd already told the story several times, so I told it again, more or less the same way, skipping the boring parts. If you really wanted to keep a secret, the best thing to do was act like you were just *dying* to talk about it. People might not even believe your story, but they'd stop asking questions, and that was the important part.

"Huh, you're in the right place — that's for sure!" the guy laughed. "You're just the kind of lunatic they need!"

"Who are you calling a lunatic?" I grumbled, offended. "I did everything by the book!"

"Then why did you go back to save the others when you knew the mine had a second exit? Huh?"

"Because they would have been captured or killed by the enemy."

"Yeah, and you would have been killed right along with them. You're not exactly the next great action hero, far as I can tell," he gave me an appraising look. "Or were you summoning *demons*?"

"What else would I be doing?" I frowned, and to my surprise, the young soldier burst out laughing.

"Oh, tell us another one! Hah! Summoning demons, he says!" he was clutching his stomach by now. "Keep this up, and we'll be calling you Funny Guy over the comms!"

"Quit running your mouth, Digger," croaked an old, battle-hardened fighter. "You ain't seen a demonologist fight."

"Yeah I have, but those were *powerful* demonologists," Digger replied, still chuckling. "And anyway, I doubt any of their kind could make it in the Black Squad — that's why they're all in the regular divisions."

"And what are we, the freak division?" I asked, confused.

"Oh, we're regular, too — our chances of survival are just a lot slimmer."

The trip back to base was swift, but just as we pulled up to the gates, the convoy stopped. Captain Cardinal jumped out of our truck and started speaking back and forth with someone over the radio.

"Something's wrong," he whispered as he waited for a reply, looking up at the helicopters circling over the base.

His suspicions were soon confirmed when headquarters transmitted details of an attack on the eastern outpost.

"Is there fighting currently underway?" the captain asked. "Understood... And the reinforcements are en route? You're sure we won't get in the way? Excellent! How many free choppers do we have? Hm? Sixty soldiers, got it!" he stuck his head back into the truck. "Veteran, Pacifist! Gather your troops and get over there. Are you fully equipped?"

"Yes, sir!" the two commanders replied in unison.

"Good! Get going!"

I didn't even have time to think. Another thing I liked about the army was that you didn't always have to. I just ran in the same direction as the rest, and soon enough, we were lifting off in a fleet of helicopters.

"Is this normal?" I asked Digger. I'd learned on

the drive back that his call sign came from his habit of endlessly asking questions. "Why isn't the Bird with us?"

"Don't panic, it's normal," he said dismissively. "Joy is gathering the rest of the troops as we speak. They'll be right behind us."

"Is this mission dangerous?" I went on. Digger wasn't the only one who could ask questions. Let *him* do the answering for once...

"Relax! We won't all make it back, though, that's for sure," he slapped me on the shoulder. He thought I was scared. In reality, I was crossing my fingers for the deadliest mission possible. I needed to knock two months off my contract every single day...

"And it's alright that I'm still wet behind the ears?" I asked, just to be sure.

"Yup. I had the same thing — three of these missions in my first week!" he chuckled. "And look at me, still breathing! I *have* had thirty concussions, though."

Out of the corner of my eye, I noticed a second helicopter. It was Pacifist's group. Just then, an energy pulse exploded next to them, soaring up from somewhere in the forest. Smoke suddenly started streaming from the helicopter's engine. The chopper began to plummet towards the ground, leaving a black trail in its wake, and then crashed down hard between the trees.

"Pilot!" Veteran yelled. "Listen carefully! We're going to go down and land next to them. We need to cover them!" He turned to the rest of us. "Alright, boys! Strap in, because this is about to get bloody! But we must help our comrades. We disembark in two minutes, so prepare. All clear?"

"Yes, sir!" the entire unit shouted in unison.

I swivelled my head to stare at the two imps perched on my shoulders. No one else could see them, of course. But I was a little concerned that they might be able to *hear* them, especially given the cheerful "YES, SIR!" they'd just squeaked along with everyone else.

"What was that?" Veteran's eyes narrowed.

"Must have been the wind, sir!" I said. "There's a terrible draught in here."

# CHAPTER 1∅

WE CIRCLED OVER THE CRASH SITE, the pilot searching intently for a place to land until he spotted one a few hundred metres from the other helicopter. No sooner had we turned for it, however, than his control panel started beeping shrilly, and he had to use all his skill to dodge as a missile hurtled past us. We were all thrown sideways, and then, there was a deafening blast. But even over the roar of the explosion, the pilot's furious cursing carried clearly, and you could tell he meant every word...

"What the hell are they shooting us with?" Veteran spat. "Our shields can't handle it! Descend, now!"

In fact, the flank shields had weathered the first attack quite well, and that had even been a direct hit... but I wasn't going to say that out loud.

This was the army — no one was looking for my rank-and-file opinion.

I looked behind us and saw that we were being followed by five more helicopters. They were also under attack, and were being forced to dodge, duck and manoeuvre, activating heat traps and throwing up smoke screens as they flew. But only *we* were descending; the rest were continuing their westerly course, heading for the outpost, where the fighting was still in full swing.

After a few circles of the uneven clearing, our helicopter was finally able to land and everyone jumped out. Veteran roared some rapid-fire commands, and we got to work doing our job. One group formed a defensive ring around the site, four others left to scout the area — one in each direction — and the rest of us ran straight for the downed chopper. And ran. And ran, and ran. We brought with us some stretchers, medical supplies and a full complement of weapons. I had no idea what was happening — but hey, I was having fun! I just couldn't understand why everyone else looked so glum and serious... Did they have a problem with the commander's orders? Well, I agreed with them there. If *I* were commanding the unit, I'd have done things very differently. For starters, I would have directed the helicopter straight to that spot where the enemy had shot at us and taken them by surprise. By now, the enemy would have moved, so trying to track them in the forest would be pointless. We were being forced to play by their rules, and in war, you couldn't let that happen. It was essential to retain the upper hand and force the enemy to play *your* game. On top of that, I reckoned the wounded could wait. Doing things my way would have protected any surviving soldiers in the helicopter, anyway.

Nonetheless, I knew this line of thought was getting me nowhere. I knew that saying it out loud wouldn't get me anywhere, either, because no one was going to listen to me. And even if they did, it was too late — the enemy forces had long since melted away into the forest and were already elsewhere, gearing up to finish us off.

We covered the two hundred metres in a flash, and the crashed chopper soon appeared between the trees. The defensive artefacts had obviously held the machine together until the last second, but its body had buckled and crumpled on impact with the ground. The metal had been shredded in some parts and torn away completely in others, but overall, it was in better shape than I'd expected.

Some of the surviving soldiers had already formed a defensive circle around the crash site, while others were busy pulling the gravely wounded out of the smoking wreckage. There were also plenty of concussions, and a few soldiers were lying unconscious on the bloodstained snow.

"Damn," Veteran muttered. "That was a serious strike — they killed this bird stone dead." He stepped up to the chopper and stuck his head inside. "Glad to see you're all alive, at least."

Once he was done surveying the crash site,

Veteran got straight down to dishing out more orders. He sent the four scouts out again and tasked some others with setting up the stretchers, while the medic rushed off to deliver first aid.

"You go and do some reconnaissance, for now," I ordered my two imps quietly. They gave me two snappy salutes, opened their buzzing wings and flew off in opposite directions. They flew with such precision... admittedly, one of them *did* hit a branch and go tumbling into a snowdrift, but it picked itself up and flew off again.

We loaded the wounded onto stretchers and set off back to our own helicopter, praying we'd get there before the Newies showed up. The scouts had reported that our white-armoured enemies were gathering a large force nearby, and that they could attack at any second.

When we reached the helicopter, we started loading everything up, while Veteran paced up and down and cursed at us to go faster. He also cursed at how heavy the loaded helicopter was, nervous that the machine wouldn't make it into the air.

"That's it! We're airborne!" he shouted the second we lifted off, slamming a hand against the back of the cockpit. "Get us out of here!"

The pilot revved up the engines and radioed through to headquarters, reporting our approximate trajectory and our aircraft number. We hovered briefly, and then... he began shutting the engines down again.

"Permission to fly was refused," he said gravely, taking off his huge headset and resting it around his neck. "Take-off is prohibited until further notice."

"How could we be refused?" Veteran burst out.

"I spoke with high command. We're not permitted to become airborne under any circumstances," the pilot shrugged helplessly. "According to intelligence, enemy forces have two Fighter Bird choppers in the area, so it's too dangerous to try and fly — they'll just shoot us down."

I'd read about this type of helicopter. The Fighter Bird was a serious machine, equipped with techno-magical surface-to-air missiles. Missiles like that could penetrate even the strongest artefact-based defence system. In fact, there wasn't much it *couldn't* blast apart, and our helicopters evidently weren't on the list.

"That's a death sentence!" Veteran yelled. "I've got sixty soldiers, here! I've got twenty wounded!"

A vein was pulsing in the commander's temple, but he knew that getting angry wouldn't help. He took a deep breath and tried to pull himself together. "Alright, everyone but the wounded — out! We're going to establish and fortify our position, set up patrols, and then split up into twos and threes. You four," he tipped his chin at a group of soldiers, "help the medic, and then get to work on camouflaging our bird."

"My artefact is drained!" the medic cursed. "And my bandages are running out! I have no supplies!"

"Anyone with a first aid kid, hand it over," Veteran ordered. "Do it!" he yelled, and the whole unit sprang into action, all detaching the little sacks marked with the red cross from their uniforms. All except me.

"Why aren't you doing it, numb-nuts?" Veteran scowled. "Don't want to say goodbye to it, or something?"

"I, uh," I gulped. "I dropped it somewhere on the way…"

"I'd shoot you in the knee, but we're short on bandages," Veteran hissed at me through gritted teeth. "Yes, come on, go and take up your position, moron! Go with him!" he shouted at another soldier. "And you three, you hold down the southwest. But it's gonna get busy down there, so be ready!" He looked back to me and sighed. "Rookie… you take the west. That'll be the safest direction, so you should be able to handle it. I'm not expecting any action on that side, but still, keep your eyes peeled. If anything happens, just start shooting, and we'll come help you."

"West?" I repeated

"Yeah. Off you go," Veteran nodded.

"Alone?" I asked, just to be sure I hadn't misheard.

"Yes, alone — now go!" he said impatiently, already waving me away.

"Don't you think I could take the east instead? Or the north, maybe?"

"No, that's where we expect the brunt of the attack to come from," Veteran replied, speaking fast. "And why are you arguing with me? Get out of here and go carry out your orders, jackass!" he yelled.

"Fine, fine!" I put my hands up, already turning to go to my post.

*Why west?* I wondered... Base was to our west, of course. The only catch was that it was over forty miles away. Also, the New Imperials had figured out our commander's plan, which meant that the main thrust of the attack was going to be directed right here — where a single, solitary new recruit was waiting.

Alright, admittedly, I wasn't complaining. This new recruit would have his demons with him, and Veteran, unbeknownst to himself, had actually made the only viable choice available to him. Still, the Newies were going to attack from three sides at once — or at least, three was how many units my imps had spotted so far. It was possible that reinforcements might arrive, but that was a problem for later. The problem right now was that most of our soldiers had been posted exactly where no enemies were (or would be) planning to attack.

"Listen, there's something we should consider," I said over the radio, trying to make my comrades see sense. "What if they attack from the south-east and the north simultaneously? And then, they'd obviously attack from the west, too."

"Great contribution, private!" Veteran exclaimed. "Now shut your goddamn mouth, or I will shove my foot in it and shut it for you!" This was followed by a string of the foulest obscenities I'd ever heard.

The way Veteran spoke was so deeply expressive that even the word 'foot' sounded like an expletive coming out of his mouth. It was a very impolite way to speak to a demonologist, but in another sense, it was entirely appropriate. Veteran did outrank me, after all, so he was fully entitled to curse me out if he wanted to. In a sense, his words weren't even disrespectful; in a situation like this one, hurling curses and obscenities at someone could actually be seen as a sincere expression of concern. If the commander had known the full extent of my combat experience, however, he would have been expressing that concern in considerably different terms. I was pretty sure the entire unit would have been standing to attention at the mere sight of me, in fact. Oh well, whatever — I'd have more fun on my own, anyway.

I got into position, assessed my situation, sat back and waited for the imps to report back with more details. They soon came to tell me that a group of New Imperials were heading my way and would be here in roughly forty minutes. Good, then I still had some time to prepare.

Presently, four track-tread armoured tanks rolled up. These were some seriously impressive machines. Each one had a rapid-fire multi-barrel machine gun mounted on the roof, and each had space for around six to eight soldiers inside...

They were going to tear me to shreds! Unless I went in all guns blazing, that was... but revealing my full power in front of these New Imperials would be a huge mistake. I didn't want anyone to know that our army suddenly had a mighty demonologist in its ranks, if for no other reason than that I still needed time to develop. My body was still extremely weak, far too frail to let me access my skills to their full extent. If I fought hard now, I would also be unfit for my next fight — and there *would* be more fights, that was for certain. Joining the army to escape imprisonment for killing a petty aristocrat, well, that was one thing. But attracting the attention of every aristocrat and upper-echelon individual in the Empire, or possibly even this entire world? Now, *that* was a different game.

Anyway, down to business. I'd been given my orders, but no one had specified how I was to carry them out. So, I was going to do things my way.

While I still had time, I sprinted back to the helicopter and gathered up all the weapons that had been abandoned in the rush. I was starting to understand why the ensign just yelled obscenities at most of the recruits instead of saying hello when he saw them. Honestly, how could seven different people have dropped their damn machine guns? Not to mention the sea of magazines and cartridges littering the floor of the chopper. I quickly loaded up a rucksack full of guns, ammo and all the grenades I could find!

"Some of your troops are already in combat," one of the pot-bellied imps stuck its head inside the chopper.

"Really? I haven't heard any gunfire, and the radio's quiet, too," I said, puzzled.

"Well, then they must already be dead," the imp shrugged.

"Got it. Where were they?"

The imp gave an approximate description of the two unfortunate soldiers' location on the far side of the helicopter, and I nodded and grabbed my radio.

"Bluey and Petro! Do you copy!" I said into the common channel. "Bluey! Petro! Come in!" Silence. "Anyone know where they are?" Radio static. And then:

"No, but we're nearby! We can go and check! Over!"

A minute or two later, the channel exploded with noise, and I heard gunfire somewhere in the distance.

"Enemy presence! Bluey is dead! Requesting backup!" someone yelled. I turned the volume down on my radio. I didn't want to get distracted, now, did I?

As I exited the chopper, my rucksack bursting with all manner of weaponry, I looked back at the wounded machine. I couldn't leave her like this... We'd camouflaged the other one, so there was a chance that the enemy wouldn't find it, but something had to be done with this one. If nothing else, the column of smoke rising from it was surely going to act like a smoke signal and attract unwanted attention. Towing it away wasn't an option, either...

I quickly drew a small summoning circle on the ground, poured a few drops of energy into it and summoned one of the cheapest demons I could think of. It was about three feet tall, hunchbacked and very, *very* stupid. You could see in its eyes that there was hardly a single brain cell bouncing around in there.

"At your service!" it squeaked.

"Good," I nodded. "Here — take this rock," I pulled the pin from a grenade and handed it over to the demon. "But hold it tightly!"

"At your service to hold the rock!" the demon squealed with delight.

"Good job!" I slapped it on the shoulder. "Count to two thousand, and then let go. Got it?" The demon nodded, still grinning from ear to ear. I narrowed my eyes. For a creature this stupid, it seemed to have understood my instructions awfully fast... .

"Do you know how to count?"

"At your service to count!" it nodded rapidly. Fine — I knew it wouldn't lie to me. I hoisted my rucksack onto my back, stepped out of the helicopter and immediately heard a grenade go off behind me. Well, it hadn't lied... it just hadn't told me how *high* it could count. Not up to two thousand, apparently.

I didn't have a problem sending demons to their deaths, but that wasn't because they were bad. On the contrary, the stupid demon behind me wouldn't have harmed a fly! I'd even go so far as to say that the creature was good by nature. But the thing was, it hadn't actually *died* just now. The grenade had only destroyed its physical form in *this* world, while the demon itself had respawned, safe and sound, on its own infernal plane. Sure, dying was unpleasant for them, and respawning cost quite a bit of energy, but I compensated for those expenses. It got more complicated with higher-order demons, admittedly; they required a lot more energy to respawn, and the process also took some time. Anyway, it was certainly *possible* to kill a demon, but it was no easy feat.

In any case, dealing with demons was complicated, but the main thing to keep in mind right now was that I could afford not to skimp on the bargain-basement options. I could easily cover their costs, the terms of which were inscribed within the demon's pentagram itself. That was why my demons were so keen to work for me and carried out my orders so willingly — even orders I hadn't inscribed in their summoning circle.

The other soldiers had no idea how badly outnumbered we were. Ours wasn't the only chopper that had been forced to land, and by now, it was blatantly obvious that the Newies had set up a flawlessly-calculated ambush. They'd sent a chunk of their soldiers to attack the outpost, knowing that our guys would immediately send in reinforcements. Then, they'd hidden themselves in the forest, armed with cutting-edge anti-aircraft missile launchers. As far as I could tell, our commander was the only one who'd realised what we were up against, and he was keeping that information to himself so as not to sow panic amongst the troops.

With all these thoughts still swirling in my head, I climbed to the top of a small hillock and

looked out over the trees. About two hundred metres away, I could see a narrow track. It looked to
me like the perfect place to stage an ambush. If *I*
were the enemy commander, I'd certainly have ordered my troops to stop and attack from there...
Since there was no space for vehicles to manoeuvre through the surrounding forest, it would force
our soldiers to approach on foot.

I cleared some snow from the base of a few
trees and then quickly summoned four new demons. Admittedly, they were pretty unimpressive
beasts, and I wasn't expecting any of them to start
slaying hordes of enemies single-handedly. They
were just puny, skinny little things with horns,
barely five feet tall. They wouldn't even be much
use for carrying things, but hey — work with what
you got, right? I couldn't afford to take any risks
right now, so I'd decided to just go for the old
reliables.

That said, the demonic plane attached to this
world boasted a pleasing diversity of creatures,
and I sometimes summoned some interesting
specimens... Unfortunately, most of them were
hopelessly stupid and totally useless, but even so,
I felt a little thrill of the unknown with every
summoning.

I'd originally summoned five of these demons,
but one of them had turned out to be a three-
armed demonic tree climber. Two arms to hold
onto the branch, and the third arm to pelt the
enemy with stones... Under other circumstances,
I would have been delighted, but for this particular

job, I had to send it back.

"Alright, boys, listen up!" I said, lining them up in a row... Why was I talking like that? Had I suddenly been possessed by the soldier's spirit? Was this some kind of karmic payback for choosing to join the army? "Your task is simple! On my command, you will pull this thing and start shooting," I showed them the trigger. "Are we clear?"

"Don't we have to aim? Those are fire sticks — you can kill with them!" the demon's eyes were shining.

"You can aim if you like, but don't expect to hit your targets," I said. "And remember — if you find yourselves in danger of being detected, fall back." I'd already left plenty of traces behind me back in the mine, but still, I preferred not to give the Newies any more reasons to hunt me down.

The demons took up their positions, while I readied my gun and took aim, pointing it roughly in the direction I expected the enemy to attack from. Not five minutes later, I heard the revving of engines, and four armoured all-terrain tanks appeared in the distance. They were hurtling towards us at top speed, spraying an impenetrable cloud of swirling snow up behind them. It was mesmerising to behold... What could I say? This world had some cool technology.

The demons, however, were not so charmed by the spectacle.

"Uh, Master, do we really have to fight *them*?" one of them wrinkled its nose.

"Just fire into the air, that's all you need to do," I sighed. "Time for me to get outta here!"

"But when should we start firing?" another demon asked.

"I'll give the order telepathically. For now, just sit tight and wait." With that, I left the defensive post. Even with four demons, there was no hope of defending it — but I'd been ordered to hold out to the bitter end and repel any attack coming from this direction. That meant there was only one thing I could do: follow my orders.

As I walked, I summoned the two imps, and they landed on my shoulders. They were shivering.

"Want to go home?" I smiled at them. They nodded their heads emphatically.

"Of course we do! It's warm at home!"

"Well, then, grab this rock and fly on over to that big tank."

"No way!" they protested. "You can't fool us! We saw what those rocks of yours do!"

"Oh, fine," I sighed. "I guess I'll have to do it myself."

* * *

The four powerful all-terrain tanks sped along the snow-swept track. Their bluff had worked, and they were rapidly approaching their target. Inside each tank sat eight fully equipped and armoured soldiers, the main strike force for this prong of the attack. And every single one of those soldiers was out for blood... in their minds, the Imperials deserved only one thing, and that thing was death.

"I hope we make it in time," — one of the soldiers was bouncing his leg impatiently.

"We'll make it," his commander answered, his voice steely. He knew he'd brought his column on a detour, but it would be worth it. The Imperials would never expect an attack from the direction of their own base... Plus, he wanted to avoid crossing paths with the Imperial reinforcements that would arrive in a couple of hours.

It was a risky manoeuvre, but the rewards fully outweighed the risks. It would let them strike the enemy from behind and wipe out the Imperial troops without sustaining a single loss of their own. All they had to do was act fast and go in hard.

"Alright, load out!" the commander ordered. The trucks came to a sudden stop. White-clad soldiers immediately began to pour out of them and file into battle formation, ready to move out. "We'll go on foot from here. We need to stay undetected." He glanced at the small screen mounted on his helmet. "Seven hundred metres to the target. And it looks like they have no idea we're coming."

They forged carefully ahead, constantly monitoring their surroundings. And yet, we *still* caught them off guard...

"Contact!" was all the commander could cry before the hail of bullets hit. Most of them flew harmlessly past the troops, but a few pierced some unlucky soldiers' defences. "I can see four firing points! Advance! Suppress them!"

The troops launched their assault. In their haste, not one of them noticed a human-shaped figure emerge from the snow at the very edge of the track.

*   *   *

I knew this was the perfect place! The New Imperial commander obviously thought so, too, I mused, as I watched the tanks stop just a few metres closer than I'd predicted.

I had to admit that the imps had overdone it slightly; I'd given them one shovel to share, and they'd buried me in the snow so enthusiastically that I'd barely made it out again. But no harm done...

While the Newies were all busy attacking the four reluctant demons, I moved swiftly for the tanks. Three soldiers had been left on guard, and all three of them were currently climbing out of the tanks to meet me. I was glad they hadn't gone straight for the mounted machine guns and started firing; those things looked incredibly threatening, and I hadn't even seen one in action yet.

As soon as the three soldiers' feet hit the ground, my first magic mark went off. Beneath the snow, a complex pentagram flared into life, immediately spawning a raging fireball of hellish flames that began spewing out a thick red mist. This formed an impenetrable cloud which rushed towards the guards, carrying with it a shower of scorching sparks. I stepped smartly aside and waited... and it worked! The guards started firing into the cloud, thinking I was hiding in there somewhere.

The cloud closed in rapidly, and just before it reached the guards, angry little imps brandishing knives began leaping out of it. They hacked at the soldiers' armour and tried to gouge out their eyes, an endless stream of them crawling out of the red depths to hurt the enemy any way they could. I loved open contracts — they let me do things like declare a monetary reward for the demon who caused the most chaos. This had really boosted the imps' motivation, to the point that they were now hurling themselves straight at the machine guns like halfwits, not giving a damn whether they got hit or not.

One of the soldiers suddenly screamed and toppled over into the snow. Meanwhile, another one was busy trying to pull a bunch of the irritating little demons off him, while the last one was just firing in all directions — until he ran out of bullets, that was. He tried to make a run for the nearest tank, but the door slammed shut right in front of his face. A pudgy little imp appeared on the other side of the porthole and waggled his tongue at the soldier. Looked like I had a winner!

Then, the *real* fun started. The gunfire here had attracted the attention of the main group, and the three soldiers had begun to retreat, which meant that the whole squad would be here soon. I got the demons to trail the three and give me a running commentary on what they saw. I found out, amongst other things, that the squad had already neutralised my demonic machine-gun crew and had retreated deeper into the forest. But I'd left a nice little surprise waiting for them there...

By the time the white-armoured bodies appeared between the trees, I'd already climbed inside one of the tanks and was pointing the gun turret in their direction. The squad may have been shielded head-to-toe with defensive artefacts, but that wasn't going to help them.

It took no more than thirty seconds for the four heavy machine guns to finish the job quickly and effectively, me controlling mine and the imps controlling the others.

The funny thing was, I'd just barely had time to figure out the controls myself; as for the *imps*, all I could do was tell them to hop in and figure it out on the fly. I'd never expected them to actually *manage* it...

I ended up christening one of them 'Rambo', and boy, was the name well-earned!

Now, a name bestowed by a demonologist was not the same as a military call sign. Along with its name, the demon would receive a wide range of perks, not to mention some handsome bonuses. For example, one minute earlier, Rambo had been your average, chubby little demon spawn running around with a pocket knife. Now, his horns had elongated and twisted, his body was significantly stronger and his once-puny arms were bulging with muscle.

And why did I choose 'Rambo'? Well, this imp had hopped straight into the gun turret control seat and started pulling levers with perfect confidence, sending a stream of hot lead straight at the enemy with an aim any tank-combat vet would be proud of. Also, he was wearing a little red bandana. And *that* was just for starters…

Anyway, in thirty seconds, we'd obliterated the entire squad without a trace — quite literally. Most of the bodies were no more than scraps. Those guns really *could* pump out two thousand rounds, after all…

And what had I learned from all this? Just one thing: I needed to make some cash and buy myself some decent artefacts *fast*. I realised now that my chances against this kind of kind of firepower were slim. I may have had powers of my own, but they just couldn't save me from that many bullets… yet.

"We're out of ammo!" Rambo squeaked, clambering out of the tank next to mine. "Permission to reload and ready the machine gun for combat?"

"You know how to do that?" I asked, raising an eyebrow.

"No, but I'll figure it out," the three-foot-tall creature said nonchalantly.

"Rambo, stand down!" I ordered. Despite the fact that I also had no idea how to reload a tank gun and was itching to watch and learn, I said: "We don't have time for that right now."

"What, then? Collect more vehicles?" he asked.

"Vehicles," I mused. "No, there are no more vehicles for us to take around here," Rambo's face fell. "But our *enemies* have vehicles!" the imp's frown disappeared and his eyes lit up.

"We'll kill them and take their vehicles as trophies!" I liked the way this little guy thought. The name *really* fit... "Just give me a knife and I'm ready to go!"

"We don't have any knives," I frowned, looking around at what was left of the New Imperials. "Oh, but there's a machete lying over there! Will that work?"

"I mean, it's not a *knife*," Rambo said, sucking his teeth, "but it'll do."

While the attack from this direction may have been quelled, the sound of gunfire was still thundering all around us, which meant that the battle was far from over. We were under attack from plenty of other sides, and after that, there would still be the final push: the push to get everyone out of here.

I, however, *was* finished; all I had left to deliver was one final flourish. I traced a long line with my foot, filled it with energy and watched a sophisticated hexagram blaze into life in front of me. The earth cracked open and tongues of infernal flame burst forth. A cloud of scorching steam rose from the depths, spewing out hundreds of tiny demons.

"Don't worry," I grinned. "We're going to make it work."

* * *

Veteran had lost all hope, but he wasn't letting it show. His soldiers didn't need to know that backup wouldn't be here for over an hour, or that their chances of holding out till then against the superior New Imperial forces were slim to none. As for breaking out of the circle, well, there wasn't a chance in hell. The Newies had them surrounded on all sides, and beyond that, the forest was infested with small, concealed groups of Newie soldiers in every direction. They would attack out of nowhere and then melt back into the trees without a trace, making it impossible for the Imperial troops to relax for even a second.

Veteran also knew that sooner or later, the enemy was going to bring out the big guns. He could have gathered all his able-bodied soldiers and retreated, but that would have meant leaving the wounded behind, and Veteran wasn't that kind of leader. If only they'd had some ground vehicles, they could have tried to break through the circle and at least evacuate the wounded. Then, they could have split up into small groups and snuck to the evacuation point on foot...

Veteran glanced at the tablet on his wrist and suddenly grinned.

"Way to go!" he cheered, looking at the picture of a Newie truck that had been shot to bits. The image of the battered vehicle had been sent straight to the group chat, which they used to keep track of enemy kills — and of their own losses, too. "Well, that's heartwarming," Veteran sighed, "but we're still up shit creek without a paddle."

He radioed yet again to request any kind of backup at all, hoping that someone would respond. However, high command clearly couldn't help him right now. Any chopper capable of facing down the New Imperial's Fighter Bird was probably already in use. Or maybe they didn't want to put their aircraft at risk... Whatever, there was no point guessing.

Veteran understood now that they were going to have to stick this out to the end. He cursed under his breath; out of sixty soldiers, he reckoned no more than ten might make it out alive. But no matter what, they had to stand firm — and never fall into enemy hands! Victory, or death!

He heard a notification. A new message popped up in the chat. He stared at it in astonishment.

"Commander! I have a proposal for how to get out of here!" the face of that new recruit appeared on his screen.

"If you can magically conjure up some tanks for us, I'll name my first-born child after you!" Veteran laughed. "Can you do that?"

"I'm not sure about that," Constantine paused. "But take a look at these — maybe you'll find something you like in there."

The call dropped and Constantine's face disappeared. A number of images popped up in its place. They showed six New Imperial all-terrain tanks, standing empty, the bodies of enemy soldiers strewn all around them. The message below said simply: "Need these?"

"Stay where you are! Do you copy?" Veteran roared into his radio. "We're coming to you! Cartridge! Busher! The rookie's found us some transportation."

* * *

Ah, the wintry forest... it was beautiful, no doubt about that.

I was walking along with two other soldiers, one of whom had been shooting me furtive glances for a while now. Eventually, his curiosity got the better of him.

"Hey, Constantine," he said, tugging at my sleeve. "Don't you think it's kind of unfair?"

"I don't mind," I shrugged.

"No, but... it really *is* unfair!" he declared.

"Relax!" I tried to wave him off. "Honestly, it's fine."

"But you were the one who got us the tanks... and now, you're *walking* back to base!" he exclaimed. I just smiled.

"A nice walk out in the fresh air is good for the constitution," I declared.

If I was honest, though, I'd actually been a bit surprised myself. With all the injured loaded into the tanks, they didn't have space for the rest of us, so me and twenty other soldiers were heading back on foot. We were heading to the evacuation point, which Veteran had shown us on the map. According to the latest intel, it was free from enemy forces. That much happened to be true; the area really *was* empty. The only forces in action were two demons, who'd been sent to load rucksacks up with Newie gear and find a place to stash them. *Good work, Rambo!* I said telepathically. He was a very promising little imp, that one. I liked his hands-on approach.

"Glad to be of service!" he squeaked back next to me, pulling his bandana a little tighter and stroking his pistol.

"Huh? What was that noise?" one of the soldiers grabbed his gun.

"Just the wind, I'm sure," I smiled. Being able to hide the little imps and demons from view was convenient. It was important that they didn't come into physical contact with anyone else, and ideally, I liked to have them stay as close to me as possible. That made it easier to keep up the invisibility part. "You know what, *I* have a question," I turned to the soldier. "They told us to travel to the evacuation point in small groups of two or three, right?"

"Yup!" he nodded.

"Right. Well, then why the hell are you all following *me*?" I turned around. All twenty of them were filing along behind me.

"Well, damn, who knows?" another soldier shrugged. "You're a good luck charm!"

"I see. Off we go, then," I grinned. "Uncle Constantine will get you home safe!"

"Hey, one more question!" someone else piped up. "Are we *supposed* to be walking in the opposite direction to the evacuation point?"

"Of course. I'd rather not have to trek all thirty kilometres on foot, you see," a smile spread across my face. "A little bird told me that if we just take this four-kilometre walk south, we'll be cruising all the way home..."

# CHAPTER II

YET AGAIN, WE FOUND OURSELVES a few seats short... Couldn't the Newies just have left a few extra trucks lying around? That would have made our lives a whole lot easier...

Admittedly, this time around, we hadn't robbed our all-terrain vehicles from the Newies at all. We'd had to grab whatever was closest, and we'd come across some... well, they were either bandits or vagrants, living in the forest. They were in pretty bad shape themselves, and the vehicles were even worse, but they could still manoeuvre through the snowy forest, and that was all we needed.

Having to drive these hunks of junk stung when we had a next-to-new helicopter nearby with barely a scratch on it. My little collaborators, however, had reported that our side had, in fact, been forced to booby-trap and abandon the chopper. Get within ten metres of it, and the thing would explode, destroying itself irreparably in the process. And I had a feeling that sooner or later, someone *would*; that bear, perhaps, or those curious squirrels, who were sure to pop their heads in looking for a snack. Plus, there were still plenty of Newie soldiers around, and one was bound to get curious.

It was odd, when I thought about it. Lose your knife, and your superiors would be hurling abuse at you for days. You'd be a butter-fingers, a moron, a knucklehead, an idiot — and the names would only get less affectionate from there. An endless torrent of new and innovative insults would rain down on your head. In fact, I sometimes got my demons to record the ensign's inventive turns of phrase so I could save them for later use on the demons themselves. In the interests of furthering our professional rapport, of course...

But lose a *helicopter*... well, to put it simply, I was pretty sure no one was going to say a word to Veteran over this. They'd just nod silently, write off the whole machine (which cost a fortune) and then ask the Imperial government for a new one.

The difference was that losing your knife was your own *personal* failing, caused by your own carelessness, and this was true no matter how high up you were. The helicopter, on the other hand, would be considered lost in battle. This was something a soldier had no control over, so there was no sense in reprimanding them for it. It was just another piece of equipment destroyed in combat, something that inevitably happened.

"How did you know we'd find trucks here?" the soldier riding next to me in the back seat nudged me with his shoulder. "They were hidden."

What was I supposed to say? Tell him I summoned some demons and sent them out scouting? That would be the honest truth, but he'd never believe me, and I had no intention of revealing my powers to him.

There had originally been four trucks, but the vagrant-thieves had destroyed two of them — not because they'd wanted to, but to sabotage us. Not wanting to use my gift in front of the other soldiers, I'd had to storm the camp the old-fashioned way, without any demonic assistance. As a result, it had also taken longer to secure the vehicles than I'd hoped.

I could have *talked* about my demon-summoning powers till the cows came home, and people might have listened, but no one would have actually believed me. But were I to *demonstrate* those powers — well, that would be a different story. The questions would dry up pretty fast, and that could spell trouble for me.

For starters, I knew there was an unspoken hunt for powerful people underway in this world. Everyone was looking to procure the most impressive entourage, and the competition was fierce. In this world, you never saw a powerful healer operating independently, for example. They'd all been snatched up by the influential bloodlines and the secret government agencies. Not to say that they were mistreated; they were paid handsomely, at least. But they weren't exactly free, either.

I'd also read stories about some demonologists of reasonable ability. It was a rare gift, and freely available information on the art of demonology was impossible to find, even online. Still, I'd gleaned that a few natural talents still popped up from time to time, bright sparks who could not only summon demons, but also command them. They got up to such entertaining activities as driving demons out of the possessed, of whom this world had plenty.

But where *were* those natural talents? Nowhere! As far as I could tell, all of them were either dead, or had disappeared without a trace. It wasn't hard to deduce, then, that my unique powers would be in high demand here, but still, it would be better not to broadcast them to all and sundry. Since my body was still relatively weak, that was what most people were seeing. But my knowledge... my knowledge was far beyond superior.

We soon reached the New Imperial lookout point I'd had my sights on. There was enemy gear just sitting there waiting for us, and all we had to do was grab it. I knew there'd be no one to bother us, because we'd already received the location of every enemy soldier in the vicinity. The hardest part, in fact, was trying to explain to my comrades exactly *how* I knew about all these secret enemy locations...

Once we'd swarmed the lookout, we inspected

all the gear we'd managed to grab, loaded it into the trucks and set off back to base. We carried only the very weakest soldiers in the vehicles, meaning some of the others had to go on foot. We gave them our defensive artefacts to help them on their way, but I knew they were big boys and girls who could take care of themselves. Plus, my demons had already cleared the way for them...

As we went, the trucks would occasionally break down. Luckily, we had a decent mechanic with us. His expertise was evident from the stream of obscenities he used to describe any conceivable component of a vehicle. I was astonished at how he could use the same expletive to refer to multiple parts, and yet, we all knew exactly what he was talking about. I guessed it was something to do with his intonation, or maybe his facial expression... hmm. I still had a lot to learn about this world... it was so much more complex than I'd originally thought.

Finally, we made it back to base. We'd warned high command of our arrival in advance, even describing our commandeered vehicles in detail so they wouldn't shoot us down on sight. Once the sentries had let us through the gates, the rest of the group was dismissed and sent off to rest. I, meanwhile, was dragged off to headquarters. Apparently, they were very eager to speak to me...

"Much as it pains me to say it," Rester sighed, hitting me with an appraising stare as soon as I stepped through the door, "you did well. This is the second time I've had to praise you, and I promise you, it makes me sick to my stomach. If it were up to me, I'd be making you clean the toilets! But, according to the rules, I have to tell you what a good little soldier you are instead."

He wanted to praise me, really — I could see it in his eyes. In order to maintain his authority before the new recruit, however, the general was obliged to express his displeasure. And so he should; war was a serious game, after all, and one needed to stay on one's toes. But how could you keep your balance if your head was all swollen up like a pumpkin with praise? Why would you bother trying if you were already the best?

"I don't know what kind of miracle you performed out there, but you managed to stop quite a sizeable enemy unit," Rester rumbled.

Just then, Captain Cardinal entered the room.

"Carry on, don't mind me. I just wanted to listen in," he said quickly, taking the nearest available chair. "Well? Tell us! How did you do it?"

"I got lucky, I guess," I shrugged. To my surprise, both men simply nodded, and the conversation moved on. Just like that, they lost interest... *how convenient*, I thought. Apparently, they didn't actually *care* how I'd done it — all that mattered was that the mission was complete. The enemy had been defeated, the casualties were minimal, and everything else was irrelevant. Plus, the army may have been all about obeying orders, but in the Black Squad, you didn't pry into another soldier's secrets or interrogate a person about their past. You let the past lie, and you respected everyone's right to a new life with a clean slate. We'd dedicated our lives to military service, and for that, the Empire rewarded us handsomely, not only with money, but also with those particular privileges. Most of these suicide soldiers would die with those privileges, after all. Such was the price of freedom.

I could, of course, have taken a different path and avoided the army altogether. It would have been easy; my past was clean as a whistle, my body had no relatives, and restoring its old owner's title and estate would have been a piece of cake. But I'd wanted something new, and I didn't regret my decision for a second. This life was simpler, more *honest*, somehow...

"Here's your reward," the general held out two scraps of paper to me. Another month reduced from my contract... I paused for a second. An anxious feeling was creeping up on me. At this rate, I'd have my whole contract struck off within a year. I didn't want that! What would I do then? Where would I go? I liked it here. I wanted to stay put for the foreseeable future!

Obviously, no one was actually going to kick me out once my contract ended. I could stay with this division if I wanted, or even move to another. I could go and serve in the emperor's personal guard, or I could form my own company of soldiers. Once that contract ran out, I'd be my own boss, free to do whatever I pleased — so long as it wasn't illegal, of course.

Still, I wouldn't get so much enjoyment out of it anymore. And that was what I was here for, after all! More specifically, I was here to escape the endless boredom of the dead world my own body was currently stuck in. But when my contract died, a lot of the attention I was currently receiving would die along with it, and *that* would be no fun...

I turned to leave, feeling disappointed, but just at that moment, the door of the general's office swung open and Birch rushed in. I was well aware that despite his comparatively low rank, the ensign had a certain status around here — one that excused him from such formalities as, say, knocking on doors. He was free to go where he pleased, dishing out orders to all around him. Given that strict hierarchy was the backbone of military life, it was an unusual case, but the man had earned it, through his actions rather than through his words.

"Constantine!" the ensign burst out. "I've been looking for you everywhere! Why didn't you come to me first?"

"Birch!" Rester roared. "How many times do I have to tell you? I summoned him to the office, which means that his first duty was to come to *me*!"

The ensign looked at me. I just shrugged. What could I do? My hand had been forced. I'd never have come straight to the office otherwise — my trophies were far more important!

"It's just that the kid's brought home several brand-new New Imperial all-terrain tanks," Birch appealed to the general. "Aren't all-terrain tanks more important than office meetings?"

The poor ensign — no one else in the room got it. The upper ranks operated on a completely different plane, and they tended not to concern themselves with such logistical trifles as having enough tanks. Those *trifles* fell squarely on Birch's shoulders...

"I also brought home a couple of trucks, actually. And I still have a few more things to hand in," I added.

"Well, then what are you standing *here* for?" the ensign huffed. "To the storage facility, now! On the double! And no more busting my ball—" Rester frowned, "...my balloons."

Birch's special status aside, rank really *did* confer privilege in the army. For example, only the higher-ups had the right to use the more... *expressive* parts of their vocabulary, and even then, only in the presence of those of a lower rank. I, for now, could only speak that way in exceptional cases where doing so was unavoidable.

"Wait a minute, where do you think you're going?" Captain Cardinal shouted after me. "At least read the second piece of paper first!"

Of course — the general had handed me *two* scraps of paper. I'd been so upset about losing a month off my contract that I'd clean forgotten to read the second one. It surprised me even more than the first! The little handwritten note authorised me to leave the division's territory for exactly twenty-four hours. As in... a *day off*?

"Uhh," I hesitated. "Do you think I could swap this for, I don't know, another mission?"

"...You *can*, but you don't have to," said Cardinal, quickly masking the astonishment on his face. "Take a day to relax — after a mission like that, you need to let off some steam."

Well, if you must, you must. There was no point arguing with my commanding officers. And anyway, I wouldn't mind taking a little trip into town. I had some unfinished business there, and once I took care of it, I'd be coming back a better soldier than ever...

"Well, then let's go!" Birch huffed impatiently. "You can admire your bits of paper later. It's time for you to show me all the good shi—" Rester frowned again — "uh — trophies!"

* * *

With the new recruit gone, Cardinal got up to leave, too.

"Not so fast," Rester beckoned him back. "We need to discuss the details of the last mission."

"What is there to discuss?" the captain sighed, sitting back down all the same. "Those Newies are getting bolder and bolder! It's high time we step up the pressure and show them their place, or they'll start thinking they're invincible!"

"I understand, but right now, increasing the pressure isn't an option. I haven't received the order to do so," it was Rester's turn to sigh. Not at liberty to divulge details, he said no more.

In fact, all was not going as well as it seemed for the Empire. Meanwhile, the New Imperials were in excellent shape. Not only had they recently stepped up their efforts internally, but they were bolstering their own troops with expert assistance from outside.

The general and the captain discussed the mistakes that had been made during the operation. Rester expressed his displeasure at how quickly Cardinal had given in to the New Imperials' provocations.

"Listen, they're gearing up for something. For whatever reason, they obviously want the frontier bad." 'The frontier' was how everyone here referred to the ill-defined border zone we were stationed in. There was no clear demarcation line between where the old empire ended and the new, breakaway republic began. Instead, there was the zone, which was about a thousand kilometres long and roughly a hundred kilometres wide. It had, until recently, been considered neutral ground. The details of the very recent (I gathered) coup d'etat seemed to already have faded from people's minds, but this expansive border zone had nonetheless been established to prevent the outbreak of war.

But there was a big difference between a real front with thousands upon thousands of soldiers doing battle, and a no-man's-land like this one, where at most, you might have small raiding parties occasionally clashing. So, in a way, the war was both happening and not happening at once in this place…

General Rester was aware that they were walking a razor's edge, and that their petty skirmishes could blow up into a genuine conflict at any time. But orders were orders, and he'd been explicitly forbidden from advancing beyond the fringes of the frontier. Even in the fringes, he could only carry out minor operations.

"According to intelligence reports, incidences of neutral mines being seized are occurring more and more frequently," Cardinal reminded the general. "But the takeovers are being carried out by bands of illegal miners, with minimal direct involvement from the New Imperials...

"Yes, those bastards are a sly bunch," Rester nodded. "You leave the dirty work to someone else, and you save yourself the casualties in the process," he sighed heavily. There was nothing he could do. He was haemorrhaging men, while the enemy wasn't even showing up to the fight. And there were still as many people looking to make a bit of quick cash as ever, so the number of mines being seized was only going up. "We'll deal with it somehow," he said firmly. "How about you tell me what you think of that new recruit? What's his name again... There have been so many Ones through here lately, we need to start adding on decimals!"

"We'll he's definitely going to be useful," Cardinal shrugged. "He's strong, for sure, but there's something *else* about him... something I can't put my finger on yet."

"He'll tell us if he wants to," Rester leaned back in his chair. "You know we don't pry around here."

"Of course not," the captain replied. "But, as

he's been declaring to anyone who'll listen, he has the gift of demonology. As in, he summons a demon, and then the demon does all the work for him. All *he* has to do is stand there and watch, basically."

"Hah!" Rester guffawed. "Is he kidding? Pull the other one! You know as well as I do that if he had even the slightest gift for demonology, then he wouldn't be here. He'd be welcomed into the fold by any *one* of the bloodlines," Rester trailed off, deep in thought. "If he's *running* from something, though... No, that seems unlikely. I don't take him for a fool — if he were on the run, he wouldn't be openly advertising his gift like that. Everyone knows there are no free demonologists — not skilled ones, anyway."

"Maybe he *is* lying," Cardinal shrugged. "But one thing I can say for sure is that mentally, he's strong as an ox. If you yell at him, he smiles. Make him do four hundred push-ups, and he thanks you," Rester chuckled, recalling the recent incident on the parade ground. "Birch is right — he's the perfect soldier. *He* found those tanks for Veteran, and when Veteran told him he had to *walk* back to base, he smiled and thanked his captain! He said he was glad to get some fresh air, and that he could do a bit of mushroom-picking along the way! Madness! And Veteran only meant it as a *joke*!"

"Indeed," the general's brow furrowed. "And did he pick the mushrooms?"

"Yes, he did! Plucked them right out from under the snow!" Cardinal exclaimed. "He dropped a basket of them into the kitchen!"

"Where did he get a goddamn *basket* from?"

"How should *I* know where he got the damn basket? It's like he just wove it himself, right there on the spot!"

"He's an odd fish, that's for sure," somehow, Rester's brow furrowed even deeper. "*Very* odd. But promising... once he's back from his leave, let's send him on a solo excursion."

"I'm with you. I think the team is holding him back, too," Cardinal nodded.

*   *   *

"Why did you bother lugging all this back?" the ensign sounded puzzled. "It's just junk..."

"You can sell junk, you know," I replied with a frown. "And anyway, it's not like I had to carry it all on my shoulders, so why not?"

"Fair enough!"

Now *here* was someone who spoke my language. The long line of people waiting to hand in their weapons and trophies behind me was once again starting to grumble, but any complaints voiced were quickly quashed with a few choice words from Birch. Meanwhile, he was singing my praises for bringing back fewer bullets than I'd gone out with. The truth was, I'd stuffed them into one of the rucksacks and handed them in along with my trophies. In my defence, I'd taken my enemies down using my demons *and* a machine gun, so my conscience was clean. Hell, I'd fired off two thousand rounds today, hadn't I?

Once I'd handed in all my trophies, with a promise from Birch that my cut would be transferred soon, I headed back to the barracks. I needed a shower, a change of uniform and a good meal.

Once all my needs had been attended to, I set off for the main gates. In my three months of service thus far, I'd racked up quite a decent amount of pay. I'd made even more again from selling my trophies, and overall, my plan seemed to be working. Every tank I brought back was worth at least a cool fifteen thousand. Weapons were worth less — around a hundred dollars each — and the cartridges weren't even worth counting. In comparison, however, the monthly pay for a private of my current rank was only around a thousand dollars a month. It was decent money, but for such a dangerous job, it definitely could have been more.

Ultimately, though, all my cash combined was still just small change. Plus, I already had plans to spend every penny... In my defence, I hadn't expected to make it to the city so soon, since rookies like me weren't normally given leave. You usually needed five years of service under your belt first, but in my case, concessions had been made. Presumably, the general had been loathe to slash yet another two months off my contract, and had decided to compensate me this way instead.

"Hey, One!" Cobra called out as we crossed

paths by the gate. She was still on leave after our last mission, and with nothing better to do, seemed to be roving around the base harassing new recruits. "Where are you off to? You're gunning for those gates so fast, I'd almost think you were going to the city!" she said, smirking at her own joke.

"Oh, uh," I hesitated. "Is it that obvious?"

"Is what obvious?" Cobra looked at him quizzically.

"That I'm going to the city."

"Hah! Are you kidding? You're not getting out of here for a *long* time yet — not until you're good and worn down first!" she laughed, but her grin was fading by the second. "Wait... you didn't hit your head and forget where you are, did you?" her face grew serious.

"No, no, nothing like that." I pulled the slip of paper from my pocket. "I have official leave — look."

Cobra re-read the scribbled note several times, even examining the stamp, and still couldn't believe her eyes.

"But... you haven't even served two *months* yet!" she exclaimed.

"Uh, three, actually," I showed her more slips of paper. I wasn't sure why I'd brought them with me. Somehow, it felt reassuring.

I continued on my way, leaving Cobra to pick her jaw up off the snow-scattered ground. My beeline for the gates was obviously too conspicuous, however, since I soon got waylaid again. It was a couple of the guys I'd gone through training with, though I didn't recognise them straight away. We'd ended up under different commanders and thus, had parted ways. Right now, they appeared to be working on some kind of advanced tactical technique. I watched. Something about... how to move in formation through marshy terrain while under gas attack? Hmm, that was *sure* to come in handy...

The reason I hadn't recognised them right away was, in fact, because they were all wearing gas masks. They were also wading back and forth in formation across a shallow pit filled knee-deep with water. As far as I could see, they'd dug the pit themselves; snow and dirt had been shovelled into two separate piles on either side, meaning they could simply fill the hole back in once they were finished. Hmm. Their commander was a clever one, that was for sure.

"One!" it was Hot Cross. "Where are you headed?"

"Into town," I said, rerouting over to them.

"Well, screw me sideways!" another rookie whose call sign I couldn't remember chuckled. "Know where you're going, already? It's a big city... To a brothel, am I right?"

"Nah, there are a few places I need to swing by." Since the addresses escaped me, I showed them the two locations on a map. The spots I pointed to were approximate, but there was a jewellery store and a pawn shop in that general area. "I'm just doing some shopping."

"Huh. Well, have fun!" the kid grinned. "But if you come back late, don't tell them your car fell through the ice and got stuck in a bog," he sighed, "or you might end up like us," he made a sweeping gesture at the watery hole. "And we weren't even coming home from leave — we were just transporting shells to the outpost!"

I left them with a nod and carried on my way. As if I needed jewellery and other people's pawned trash! Why would I *buy* weapons when I could get them from my employer for free? As for jewellery, well, the army also gave me everything I needed or wanted to wear.

With the money I'd saved up from my trophies, I could even have bought property, but why would I? Now *gold...* gold was a different story. I needed *lots* of gold, and unfortunately for me, gold was expensive. But there was no way around it... my demon army didn't come cheap, and it ran on one of two things: energy, or gold. The horned ones would not accept any other currency — I'd tried and failed to change their minds on that front more than once.

Since my energy was extremely low (I was barely scraping enough together for each summoning) and I also needed it to strengthen my body, paying in gold was my only real option. It was more convenient, anyway.

* * *

As a reward for wading across the knee-high bog hole faster than the rest, Number Five was excused from the very important gas-mask training exercise early. He practically sprinted to the barracks, got changed, shut himself up in a toilet cubicle and then whipped out his phone.

"Serge!" he said in a whisper. "Hey, Serge! It's Cyril! Yeah, that's right... Oh, you're still working there, huh? Wow! Amazing! But listen, that's not why I'm calling... Go back? Why would I want to? I'm a War Demon now, and I'm gonna work my way up through the ranks!"

He listened for a while as Serge went on about how great their old workplace was and how well they paid, but the whole speech fell on deaf ears; after all, there was no way out of the Black Squad.

"Listen, Serge, I'm calling because I just stumbled across an opportunity for both of us to earn some serious cash. You remember that incident in the laboratory? Remember they were looking for some kind of weird guy? The one who ticked off the Count, somehow? Well, I found him!"

Suddenly, Five's ears pricked up and he fell silent. He listened hard for a few seconds... but the noise from the corridor had already died down, and when he peeked out of the stall, he saw no one in the bathroom.

"Anyway, it's really him!" he continued. "He's always going on about being a demonologist, and

I've even heard him describe the estate — he burnt it down himself! Look, I can't talk for long — it's against the rules here. You know whose estate I'm talking about, and you know the incident I mean. And this guy, he's going to be in the city today... I'll send you all the details."

With that, Five hung up. With a smile on his face, he messaged Serge the fee he was offering and the locations Constantine would be at. Then, he fished a small cigarette case from his boot, opened it and pulled out a cigarette. Smoking in the toilets was forbidden, but come on, it was cold outside! Leaving the barracks every time he wanted a cigarette was a pain in the ass. Plus, the commander loved to catch people on their smoke break and send them off on pointless menial tasks. So, Five preferred to smoke in here, sitting on the toilet, nice and cosy.

And as for reprimands — who cared? Five certainly didn't, even though the punishment for smoking in the bathroom was crazy harsh. Come to think of it, the punishment for getting caught on your phone in a non-designated area was just as rough... The bathroom was for bathroom business only, according to high command.

The entire barracks was also fitted with sensors, since there was always some idiot who considered themselves above the rules. Five, however, was no idiot — not in his own mind, at least. Before he lit up, he pulled out a miniature artefact shaped like a cigarette holder. This would eliminate any smoke or odour, leaving nothing for the sensors to detect. Well, they hadn't been triggered *last* time, at any rate, so he was sure there was nothing to worry about this time.

That said, one rookie *had* been caught recently, and he'd been sent to a disciplinary camp for ten days. A disciplinary camp was a terrible place where you were forced to carry out a brutal training regime day and night. They said it took a lot of guys a few days to remember how to speak once they got out.

And while the ban on smoking in the toilets might have seemed stupid, or even patronising, the higher-ups didn't see it that way. Rules were rules, they were there for a reason, and they had to be strictly adhered to. How were you supposed to have your comrade's back on the battlefield if you couldn't even stick to smoking inside the designated areas, moron?

But Five didn't give a damn about the rules. He lit up, took a deep drag and closed his eyes in satisfaction.

Suddenly, sirens blared into life throughout the whole building! The ceiling lights began to flash, bells began to ring, and all of a sudden, a bunch of soldiers burst through the bathroom door. After them rushed in the commander of the entire squad. He kicked down the stall door to reveal poor old Five, frozen in horror, the cigarette still smouldering in his hand.

"NEW RECRUIT!" the commander roared. "Private! You dipshit!" he was a man of few words, but then again, he didn't need many; the situation was crystal clear to everyone present. "Tell me, you pea-brained imbecile — you haven't even been here a month, so why are you acting like you've been acing deadly missions for two years? Huh?"

Five, overcome with shock, said nothing. Was the commander implying that you had to survive two *years* here just to smoke on the toilet?

But Five didn't get much time to reflect on this revelation. He was swiftly grabbed by the armpits and hauled off to the disciplinary camp. The commander, meanwhile, stood in the bathroom a while longer, trying to understand what went on in some people's heads.

As Five was being led away, the only question in his head was why his artefact hadn't worked this time. The answer was simple: Five had failed to notice the little imp perched above him in the bathroom stall, a red bandana around its head and a huge cigar dangling from its lips.

# CHAPTER 12

I HAD EVERYTHING LAID OUT and my plan of action ready, but a setback had just hit me in the form of some bad news: I didn't have as much money as I'd thought. And I'd only found this out on my way through the front gate...

Apparently, the vehicles I'd brought back would need to be officially sold to a new owner (or owners) before I could get my share of the money, minus the costs of refitting them up to Imperial standards. The process for the weapons and other equipment was a little easier, since the government would simply buy them up directly. The problem, however, was that the New Imperials weren't always packing the latest, shiniest gear, and on top of that, I hadn't had enough hands to get everything back to base without a scratch. As for the magical ore and ingots I'd picked up in the mine, I knew it was wiser not to sell those in a hurry. I was saving them as a future asset.

Oh well, I still had *some* money, even if it was nowhere near enough for everything I'd had planned. Plus, I still had the entire day free, and I intended to spend it wisely.

Right outside the gates, I faced my next challenge: how was I supposed to get to the city? It wasn't that far away, but getting there on foot might take me half a day. It was currently snowing, and trekking the snowy roads on foot was going to be a lot less fun than speeding along inside a warm, cosy car.

I stood by the security hut and considered my options. There was a guard standing nearby, taking pensive pulls from his cigarette.

"Hey, how do people normally get to the city?" I asked.

"By car," he shrugged.

"Oh? So, not on foot, then?" I said, deciding to play his game.

"Not on foot," he shook his head. "By car."

"By car?"

"By car."

It was quite a meaningful exchange in its own way, conducted in true army spirit.

"And where can I find a car?" I asked, not really expecting a useful answer.

"Over there, in the parking lot," he pointed to a spot behind me. It was true; a dozen identical black cars were parked just opposite the front gates. "A couple of bucks, and one is yours for the day."

This army really did think of *everything*, down to the very last detail. Anyone going on leave could grab a car for practically nothing and use it however they pleased. Convenient, indeed... but only if you knew how to drive. My sorry experience on the moped had been more than enough driving excitement for me, and I had no desire to get behind the wheel of any vehicle for the foreseeable future. I made a mental note to get some driving lessons soon, though — if for nothing else, then to be able to show my demons how to control these mechanical steeds.

The army cars were very popular and much appreciated by the base's population. They were also a favourite of high command, who couldn't have thought of a better way to keep tabs on their soldiers. Every car was fitted with multiple sensors that constantly relayed information back to headquarters, so it was advisable to stick to the rules of the road. Otherwise, you could expect an awkward conversation with your commanding officer when you got back...

This setup also had its advantages, however. Every person in Circle City knew that these were army cars, which meant you didn't have to worry about run-ins with locals or trouble with the police. The army was well respected in the city, and for good reason.

Sadly, a car wasn't going to suit my purposes today, which was a shame — it would have been convenient. I thought about getting the bus, but the nearest stop was several kilometres from here. The soldiers at the base didn't visit the city often enough to merit a regular bus route. And anyway, most of them knew how to drive!

Twenty minutes later, I was still debating over whether to walk or just abandon my plans for the day altogether. But just then, a guy came through security and made a confident beeline for one of the cars.

"Hey, Scruff's heading into town now," one of the guards called out to me. "Go ask him if he'll give you a ride."

"Hm?" hearing his call sign, the guy turned around. "What's up?"

"This recruit here doesn't know how to drive," the guard smirked, "but he wants to go into town. Can you take him?"

"No problem," Scruff nodded amiably. "Come on, kid, let's get going."

And that was that. I hadn't even had to open my mouth — the problem had practically solved itself! Glad to accept the offer, I hopped into the front passenger seat. I'd worry about the trip home later. Getting there was the most important part, and the rest would follow. Worst case, I assumed they had taxis in the city, and I could get back using one of those — *if* I had any money left, of course.

"First time on leave?" Scruff asked after a minute of silence.

"Yup!" I replied. "Rester insisted. Said I needed to unwind".

"Sure, like you put up a fight!" Scruff chuckled. "For my first two years, I *dreamed* about the moment I'd get that permission slip. How long have you served?"

"Three months, give or take," I said, bending the truth a little. In fact, I'd barely served a week, but they'd already cut three months off my contract, which meant that officially, I *had* served three months.

"Yeah?" Scruff whistled. "What did you do to earn a day's leave, then? Steal a tank off the Newies, or something?" he chuckled.

"With *my* driving skills?" I smiled.

"Huh. Well, in *my* day, they didn't dole out those permission slips so easily," he sighed. "Look at you, just three months under your belt — you barely even have your bearings! Yeah, it's all a piece of cake now... when I was a rookie like you, we were *real* War Demons. And we lived in hell, too! The time they stormed the southern outpost — you should have seen it! Endless waves of enemy soldiers coming at us from every side! Tanks, shell fire, aerial assaults! I took multiple gunshots to the arm. I even got hit in the *head*, but I kept on fighting! Earned myself a well-deserved day's leave. Took it just as soon as I got out of the infirmary," he gazed misty-eyed into the distance, recalling old times.

"Lucky you," I sighed. "Sounds like fun."

"I'm starting to understand why they let you out," Scruff said, one eyebrow raised. "But don't worry, your thirst for action will soon pass. If only you'd seen the horrors I've had to witness..."

He carried on telling tales of all the different conflicts and clashes he'd lived through. There were brief skirmishes against New Imperial soldiers, as well as raids on illegal mining outfits and other criminal enterprises. There were countless combat missions, both solo and in groups, even over his relatively short period of service. And every one of his experiences was carved deeply into this veteran fighter's memory... He'd certainly have some stories to tell the grandkids.

Not for the first time, I thought about how I'd well and truly fallen on my feet. It was undeniable. It wasn't that *I* was made for the army — more like the *army* was made for *me*. It was the perfect place for a demonologist, and I was very glad I'd chosen it over the aristocracy. The aristocrat's life was one of constant inter-family intrigue and affairs, balls and etiquette and being bored to death! But war... war was a different beast. War was a simple game, no place for lies or deceit — or not in large doses, at least.

On top of that, the best way to develop one's gift was through battle, and a war zone was the very best place to do that. In the space of a few short days, I'd fought in two heavy clashes and completely replenished my energy; in fact, I'd taken in so much power that I'd actually *increased* my energy capacity. And yet, the adventure had only just begun...

In the blink of an eye, we'd reached the city. Scruff dropped me off at the right spot and then headed off about his business. Meeting him had been a piece of good luck; a good-natured soul like that would always be ready to lend a helping hand.

I oriented myself and set off for the first address. I'd been there before, and the old man behind the counter smiled when he recognised me.

"Well, well! I reckoned you were a soldier, alright!" he called out as I approached. "So, come to buy some more artefacts, have we?"

"I'm here about something else this time," I shook my head and placed a small bag down on the table. "I'd like to sell something, in fact."

I'd brought some of my weakest artefacts to sell. The stronger ones might come in handy, plus, once I sold them, I could expect an upsettingly high price tag if I wanted to buy them back. The old man had to put food on the table just like everyone else, after all, which meant there was quite a price difference between the goods you sold and the goods you bought.

And yes, I was aware that I wasn't supposed to be selling my own trophies yet. I knew it wasn't permitted until I'd done two years of service, but hey — if you don't get caught, it didn't happen, right?

Getting the artefacts off the base had been simple. A certain imp, making himself invisible to the eye, had spirited them effortlessly away. Rambo knew his stuff; he was a master of covert operations and a specialist in sabotage. As for where he'd picked up all those skills... well, I had a feeling I didn't want to know.

I'd ordered him to fetch the artefacts right after I'd learned how much money I had in my account. I was a little insulted by my meagre balance, but, still wanting to make the most of my day, I'd decided to adjust my itinerary.

"Hmm... I'll examine them immediately," the old man said, gazing at my offerings. He pulled out a special instrument designed to measure their energy levels. "But I can tell you right now that I can't give you much. These aren't exactly the best quality... you understand."

"Yes, of course. I specifically brought the least valuable ones — the stuff I know I'm never going to use."

"I can give you three thousand for the defensive ones," the old man replied after a silence, setting the artefacts aside. "And the cigarette holder... twenty, maximum."

"Excellent," I said. I had no intention of haggling. You get what you pay for, as the saying went... "Say, would I get a better price for selling in bulk?"

"Potentially. We can discuss that when you've got the artefacts," the old man gave a thin-lipped smile. "Anything else I can help you with?" he finished counting out the bills and handed them to me. "Some more powerful defensive artefacts, perhaps? Or something attack-based? A soldier like yourself might also appreciate a household artefact to help with chores — makes life much easier out on those long campaigns, you know."

"I'll pass, thanks," I shook my head. "I have

enough artefacts for now. I found a place where you can get them for free."

"Now, would that be the kind of place you might also get yourself mauled by a bear or freeze to death?" the old man chuckled. "Lucky for you, I also have just the artefact for that!"

"You could freeze to death right outside," I said, tipping my chin at the door.

In fact, this was becoming a real problem for me. My demons were always so cold that they were almost useless. It wasn't that I was concerned about how they *felt* — more that the cold made their productivity tank, and I couldn't afford to summon them for long. Snow demons, meanwhile, were still way out of my budget for now. Plus, they were tough to control, and I was still so weak.

"By the way, do you sell gold?" I asked the old man on my way out.

"Not me," he waved a hand, "artefacts only. But I can recommend a few places that won't rip you off."

*  *  *

The city streets were bustling with people. Everyone was hurrying about their day, all trying to get out of the cold as soon as possible. The weather was certainly nothing to write home about; a howling blizzard was pounding the streets, and the whipping wind kept driving tiny snowflakes into my eyes, nose and mouth.

The people here were used to these conditions, however. Ignoring the foul weather, they wrapped themselves up in warm coats and simply got on with their business. And no one, as it happened, had business with the lonely black minivan parked alone on the side of the road... and why would they? It was just standing there, after all, minding its own business The windows were all tinted black, and whatever might be going on inside was of no great interest to anyone.

What *was* going on inside was twenty men in serious-looking suits surveilling the street outside through a big bank of screens. They'd been there for the last half-hour, and all cameras were currently pointed to the front entrance of the artefactor's store their target had just entered. They had clear instructions: trail the victim, and if possible, capture him. However, since the mark was a soldier — and a War Demon, no less — they'd also been advised to exercise extreme caution.

The target emerged from the store and disappeared around the corner of the building. After a pause, the minivan began to crawl slowly after him, keeping its distance so as to remain undetected. The mark walked for some time, making several turns, and then disappeared into an inconspicuous store.

"What's that?" one of the men raised an eyebrow. "One of those places where they sell coins?"

"A coin collector's store, yeah," the group leader replied. "Huh, what would a War Demon want with old coins!" a small chuckle rippled through the minivan.

"To pay Charon! The ferryman! Because he'll be down in the underworld pretty soon!" one of the men joked, and this time, a burst of real laughter erupted. The only one not smiling was a young man at the back. He'd only joined the group recently, and he was trying hard to hide his gift. The kid could see spirits, and right now, he was staring wide-eyed at the shadowy figure behind his colleagues.

"Hey, guys? Um... maybe it's a bad idea to joke like that?" he said, his voice wavering, but this only made the others laugh louder.

They spent a while cracking jokes at their victim's expense, each one more hilarious than the last, while they waited for him to come out of the coin store. Suddenly, the leader wrinkled his nose and looked around.

"Hey, who let one rip in here?" he yelled. "Georgie, turn on the air con unit, or we'll all suffocate!" he ordered the driver. A few seconds later, the fan whirred to life and began sucking the stink out of the van. As soon as Georgie switched it off, however, the smell returned.

"Which one of you knuckleheads is *doing* that?" the leader roared.

"Maybe we should just... ignore it?" the kid suggested. Instantly, the others all decided they'd found their culprit. They didn't kick him out, though, settling for some vicious mocking and a nasty new nickname instead.

The thing was, the kid really *had* caused the smell. He hadn't meant to, it was just that the spirit standing silently behind his snickering colleagues... happened to look an awful lot like Charon.

At that moment, the target emerged from the coin store. All joking instantly ceased. All eyes flicked to the screens, and the driver shifted into gear, ready to take off. But the target just stopped dead outside the store and started looking vaguely around. Eventually, he spotted a nearby taxi rank and set off briskly in its direction.

At the same time, inside the van, the leader was suddenly struck by the perfect plan. Their van was exceptionally inconspicuous — there were hundreds of them on the roads of Circle City, and most of those were *taxis*. If there was a better way to nab their mark, he couldn't think of it.

*　*　*

The old man had been right — the store hadn't ripped me off. That said, the prices were still pretty high, since the coins were all masterfully crafted collector's items. But demons didn't give a damn about craftsmanship — they just wanted the gold. What shape it came in was irrelevant. As a result, I picked out only those coins made of solid gold and, ideally, with as little collector's value as possible.

I was almost out of cash, but at least I'd be able to pay my demons now. Plus, I'd be racking up more funds in my bank account soon enough; I was quickly coming to realise that the army was an easy place to make a buck. And all I had to do was do my thing! I had one job: kill the enemy and bring back trophies, and let the government worry about the rest.

Now that my bag was jingle-jangling with solid gold coins, I reckoned it was time for lunch. I wasn't sure where to go, so I turned to the internet for help. The closest decent-looking place on the map was all the way over in the next neighbourhood. There were a couple of greasy diners closer by, but judging from the reviews, eating there was a guaranteed ticket to indigestion city.

I didn't want to waste time walking there. I spotted a taxi rank just down the street. Hmm... I decided to take a whirl on it. Maybe it would be fun! Never too late to try something new, right?

No sooner had I reached the rank than a black minivan appeared, as if out of thin air. It seemed to already have some passengers inside. But something was off... When it pulled up to the curb, a guy tried to hop in — or, to be more precise, he *did* hop in, but he stumbled back out again a few seconds later, white as a sheet and drenched in sweat. Hmm. Maybe it was hot in there... Whatever the reason, the guy took off in the direction of the bus stop, his cap clutched in his hands.

"Where ya headed, buddy?" the driver said, stepping out of the van. He was wearing a serious-looking, though clearly cheap, suit. I noted that it was the same style of suit the bodyguards of aristocrats tended to favour. Hmm, funny coincidence.

"Barrow Street," I said, which was true.

"Well, what do you know! That's where *we're* going!" he pulled open the back door and waved a hand for me to get in.

"Oh, wait, not Barrow Street — I meant Bowler Street! I always get those two mixed up," I gave him a sheepish smile. "Shame we're not going the same way."

"We'll take you to Bowler Street *and* Barrow Street, if that's what you need!" he came closer and put a hand on my shoulder. "Come on, hop in. We'll figure it out on the way!"

Well, alright then, since he was so insistent — why not? Business must be bleak if he was fighting this hard for fares. Deciding not to argue, I climbed inside the van and looked around.

I'd never been inside one of these vans before, only read about them. These minivan taxis were all over the cities in this world. They followed a set route, picking up and dropping off passengers for a reasonable fare. They were a bit like buses, only faster and better at dodging through traffic.

I'd been reading a lot lately — maybe even too much, in fact, since I could have been using that time to meditate and hone my skills. Then again, I knew hardly any competent demonologists who'd been killed in battle. Meanwhile, I knew *plenty* of demonologists who'd been killed by their own ignorance, so it was probably prudent to learn as much as I could about the world around me.

There were ten people already inside the van. All of them were sitting and staring blankly out the window. These must be passengers, then. One of them had a machine gun barrel poking out slightly from under his seat, while another's hand was buried in his pocket and clearly gripping a pistol.

I knew Circle City was a dangerous place, but *this* dangerous? Was everyone really so scared they had to carry a weapon at all times?

"Quit standing there and take a seat, buddy!" the driver barked. I quickly sat down in the nearest empty seat, next to a burly guy in a suit. Now that I thought about it, they were *all* wearing exactly the same suit... The suit store must have been having a sale, and a serious sale, at that.

And since *they* were all acting so serious, I decided to activate *my* defences, too, just in case. Surely, they were packing all that heat for a reason.

"So, where are you headed, again?" the driver turned to look at me once more. "Bowler Street, right? Which address?"

"I'll just jump out when we reach the street — I can make it the rest of the way by myself," I said casually. "I'm just hungry, is all, and I heard the place I'm going makes excellent curry!"

Some of the comments *had* also mentioned that the curry was better going in than coming out, but since I didn't know what that meant, I'd decided to just ignore those ones.

"You got it, pal!" the driver declared. "We'll be there in a jiffy!"

The minivan pulled away from the curb and sped off down the road. I looked out the window for a bit, admiring the local architecture. After a while, however, it struck me that we were taking an unusual route. I took out my phone and pulled up the map. Hmm... that was strange. If the map was to be believed, we weren't headed anywhere *near* my curry house. Either I was confused, or someone here was lying to me...

I decided it was probably fine. After all, I wasn't a local, while the driver clearly was... maybe he was just avoiding traffic! I was sure he knew better than I did. Still, I decided to ask if he might be lost, just in case.

"We're definitely going to the restaurant, right?"

"Of course!" the driver grinned. "Where did you think we were going?"

"Oh, nowhere!" I raised my hands apologetically. "It's just that we're almost in the slums, and — well, it's just wasteland after that."

The driver only chuckled in response.

Soon after, the van rolled to a stop. As expected, we were surrounded by wasteland. Behind us lay the city's poorer neighbourhood, a maze of ramshackle wooden lean-tos. Funny... I couldn't see a single person anywhere, no matter how hard I looked.

"Here we are!" the other passengers began to climb out and walk away until only three men were left inside. They pulled three machine guns out from under their seats and pointed them at me. "This is your stop, buddy! Out you get!"

"Um, no, I think it's *your* stop — *you* can get out, if you like," I said, turning back to the window.

"I don't think you understand. *This is your stop*," one of them snarled through gritted teeth.

"No, it's not," I protested. "I told you, I'm going for curry, and I'm pretty sure there's no curry house out here. And you know what?" I shot the driver a reproachful look. "I don't think much of your driving. You don't know your way around this city at all!"

The guys looked at each other, dumbfounded.

"Are you stupid, or something?" the biggest one said after a pause. "I told you — this is your stop, and you're getting *off!* Or don't you realise what's happening here?"

"No, what's happening?" I frowned.

"Wow, *definitely* stupid," the big guy grimaced. "Either that, or he's messing with me," he leaned in and pressed the barrel of the gun to my forehead. "You've got ten seconds to stand up and get out of this vehicle. Trust me, I'm serious."

"Alright, alright!" I put my hands up. "No need for violence. Couldn't you just have told me to get off?"

I was not, in fact, stupid. Well, I *could* be a little slow to take in new information, but that was different. Anyway, I'd realised they were trying to kidnap me pretty fast. At first, I'd thought the passengers were just a bunch of hot-heads, until it started to dawn on me that they weren't passengers at all. I'd figured they weren't the driver's bodyguard, either, not with the kind of small change the minivan was carrying.

I stepped out of the van and immediately sank

up to my knees in snow. I was suddenly surrounded by a ring of armed thugs. One of them
pulled out a radio and relayed our coordinates. He
reported that the 'target' had been successfully
captured and requested a convoy.

And me? I just stood there, drawing patterns
in the snow with the tip of my shoe. God, I hated
waiting.

"Who are you guys, anyway?" I asked their
leader. "I understand that this is a kidnapping and
all that, but... who *are* you?"

"You don't need to know that," the leader
growled. "You'll find out soon enough, anyway," he
tore a black patch off his shirt and held it out to
me. It looked like some kind of chevron. "Recognise
this coat of arms? Hmm?"

"No... ohhh, right!" I stepped closer and took a
better look at the patch. "Yeah, when me and my
demons were on that killing spree down in the
basement, the soldiers had that same insignia on
their uniforms! But I don't know whose crest it is,
if I'm honest."

"It belongs to Count Serpentine," the man
scowled. "So, that really *was* you? I lost a lot of
friends that day, you son of a bitch!" he yelled, and
then punched me swiftly in the stomach. I doubled
over and... straightened back up. It hadn't hurt
much — five out of ten at most. They hit us harder
than that during training.

"These things happen," I shrugged. "But I'll let
you in on a little secret," I crooked my finger to
beckon him closer. "Just between you and me,

those guys weren't anything special," the leader punched me in the stomach again.

"Shut your trap, you pig!" he screamed in my face. But I wasn't in the mood to be quiet. *I* was the one being kidnapped — the least they could do was entertain me!

"Aren't you all nervous about kidnapping me?" I smiled. "You know I'm a soldier. And not just any soldier — I'm a War Demon. You know what's going to happen to you for kidnapping a War Demon?"

They looked at each other. I could tell they knew *exactly* what would happen to them and were fully aware of how risky this was. If this got back to even a single soldier, every one of these guys would be getting executed where they stood. Their employer could expect trouble, too — and we weren't talking about a stern scolding.

If their employer was very lucky, then the Imperial chancellery would be the first to hear the news. If their employer was *unlucky*, our high command would find out first. In that case, the general would have sole discretion on how to resolve the matter. And I reckoned Rester might just happen to have some squads between missions who'd be happy to raid an aristocrat's mansion and obliterate anyone who dared stand in their way... *unavoidable collateral damage*, they called it.

"Who's going to find out?" the leader scoffed, but he sounded nervous. "You thought you were getting into a regular taxi, but this one just so happens to be completely untraceable. It's not registered anywhere. It wasn't even made in a factory — it's a custom job, built specially for this operation. It's armoured, reinforced and has a jumbo-sized, turbo-charged engine."

"Why are you telling him all that?" one of the thugs said sharply.

"So that he knows he's being kidnapped in style!" the commander guffawed. "We can just shoot you, you know, and walk away scot-free."

"Sure about that?" I cocked my head toward the slums. "What if someone looks out a window and sees us?"

"Look up," the man smirked. "There's a blizzard on the way, see? Once it hits, no one will be seeing anything."

"Fine, then we'll wait for the blizzard," I shrugged, then went back to drawing my designs in the snow.

"Tough guy, huh? Check his pockets," the commander ordered.

"I don't have any weapons," I said to the two guys who immediately came over to frisk me. "I don't even have a knife on me. I have my mobile, but I'm not getting any reception out here... Oh, yeah, my coins!" I declared as one of them fished a handful of gold coins out of my pocket.

"What's this?" the commander's eyes narrowed as he came closer. He picked out a single coin and began examining it carefully. "What's wrong with this one? Why's it all covered in blood and little patterns?"

"It's enchanted," I said, which was true.

"You really are a total halfwit, aren't you?" the commander made a face.

"I'm not a halfwit! I'm a demonologist!" I burst out. "I'm the one who enchanted it!"

"Oh, yeah? And what does it do?" he scoffed. "Summon demons? Hah!"

"Toss it on the ground and find out," I shrugged. "Unless you're too much of a coward."

"A coward? A COWARD?" he grabbed me by the collar and started shaking me.

"Listen here, you little whelp! If this coin hits the ground and nothing happens, your teeth are gonna hit the ground after it! Got it?"

"Go ahead!" I waved a and. "I bet my teeth you'll be amazed!"

The commander smirked again and flipped the coin into the air. A moment later, it landed squarely in the snow. His eyes slowly travelled up to meet mine.

"Well?" a smile spread across his face. "Looks like you're about to lose some teeth."

"How heartless you are…"

"Oh, I have a heart," he grinned darkly. "It's just black."

"No, it's definitely red," I nodded at his chest. "See for yourself."

He looked down, and I watched the shock spread across his face. There was a clawed paw sticking straight out of his chest, his heart clutched in its grip.

"What the fu—" was all the commander managed before slumping unconscious, hanging limp from the mighty paw of the demon I'd summoned.

"Ah, and here comes the blizzard!" I smiled. I looked around the circle. "Alright, boys, time to have some fun!"

It took the thugs a beat to process what had just happened, buying me some extra time. I used it to bring a bright ball of demonic fire to life in my hands. Meanwhile, an infernal blood-red mist began to rise up all around us, thick enough that only me and my demons could see through it — thick enough that not one of the many bullets suddenly flying at me from all directions could hit me.

One of the thugs ran to the van and grabbed the radio, desperately trying to contact the count's people. Rambo snatched the receiver out of his hand. The demon tutted softly, shaking his little horned head, and then plunged his army knife into the guy's throat. When he was done, he trotted over to me with the radio.

"They won't be needing that," I said, giving the demon a satisfied nod. "Otherwise, they might tell their buddies it's too dangerous to join the party. And what do we say about parties, Rambo?"

"The more the merrier!" the demon squealed.

# CHAPTER 13

WITH EVERY PASSING SECOND, the red cloud spread out further, swallowing my enemies one by one. Meanwhile, I sprayed them with hellish flames, shifting constantly around the battlefield to dodge the random barrages of bullets. Even so, a stray bullet would still bounce off my defensive shield every now and then.

The cloud itself was also toxic... unless you were a demon or a demonologist, that was. *We* were in our element in this mist, able to sense our enemies more sharply and see more clearly than on even the brightest day. Meanwhile, our opponents were gasping for breath, unable to see even an arm's length in front of them. I liked to call it a demonic veil, but for some reason, my enemies tended to use different words for it — or, at least, the words they were screaming right *now* were different.

As I was releasing more bursts of fire, I suddenly sensed danger approaching. I swiftly ducked to my left and heard something whistle past my ear. Hmm, that meant this person could see me... I shot a few bursts of flame back in reply as I tried to put some distance between us. Surely, two metres would be enough to lose this attacker... but it seemed that one of these guys was more powerful than the others. He easily deflected my flames and continued darting around in the mist, brandishing his sword.

"Ahh!" I heard a scream and saw Rambo slicing through the tendons in someone's leg. He then disappeared into the mist, popped back up in front of the guy and stabbed him in the chest.

The imp looked up at me and understood without words what I wanted him to do. He quickly tossed me the fallen fighter's sword. It was a pretty shoddy blade, but it would do. Things were about to get a lot more entertaining...

*Swing,* and one enemy collapsed into the snow. *Swing,* and the blade struck another enemy's defences, failing to pierce them — but I was stubborn, and five more *swing*s later, cold steel bit into soft flesh and a trickle of blood hit the snow.

I could have imbued the sword with energy, yes, but that would have been an unnecessary expenditure. It was better to save my energy for summoning than squander it foolishly in battle. For as long as the mist held, I could engage in as much close combat as I liked with no bigger threat than the occasional stray bullet chipping at my defences. Even *with* the bullets, my defences would be solid for a long time yet.

Demonology could be a lot of fun — the carnival unfolding all around me was proof enough of that — but only if you had two specific things: a body full of energy and a head full of knowledge. Right now, I only had one of those things, namely, the knowledge. I was sorely lacking on the energy front, but that was a problem for later.

Again, I sensed danger, and I dodged the whistling blade just in time. This guy, again?

"Back off!" I yelled, aiming a blast of fire into his face. I slashed my sword across his chest and saw sparks fly from the blade, the steel almost snapping. I backed away swiftly and dashed off to find some other targets. This guy was one tough cookie — better let him wear himself out for a while.

While I darted about delivering the occasional backstab, I watched Rambo out of the corner of my eye. He wasn't flying; in fact, he'd tucked his wings away and was sprinting around the battlefield in short bursts. He was doling out swift but minor attacks aimed to slash tendons and inflict nasty leg wounds. Then, as soon as his target fell, he would deliver the finishing blow. I saw one guy bend over and clutch his leg, and then watched Rambo instantly ram his horns right into the guy's backside at full speed. After that, someone grabbed him, and I had to come to his aid, yanking him by the hooves to free him from captivity.

I couldn't resist thinking about how I might upgrade my faithful demon. Imagine poisonous horns! Those would really suit this kind of fight... but I shuddered to think how much they'd cost.

Demons worked a little like cars. You poured energy and gold into them, and they got fitted out with all kinds of enhancements back in their own plane. It could be anything from poison horns to a more advanced muscular system. You could give them skin designed for invisibility, increase their wing span for long-distance flights — anything you wanted! You could spend months just *researching* all the possible modifications!

My problem — still — was that my energy was practically drained dry. And my gold reserves were starting to dwindle, too... Using that coin up earlier had broken my heart, but there'd been no way around it. I'd traced a summoning circle on it as we were driving, crafting it exclusively for the demon I'd had in mind. The handy thing about this particular summoning circle was that you could use it in different ways. For example, if *I* was the one to activate the coin, the demon would appear and carry out my command. If someone *else* activated it, the demon would automatically deliver that person a swift and sudden death instead. This was what had happened earlier, more or less. I hadn't ordered it to rip out the guy's heart, though — that part was improvised.

This battle wasn't going to last long. Our blinded enemies were helpless against our relentless attacks, and I was pretty sure they were doing more damage to each other than we were to them. At least four guys had gone down with bullet wounds, and I knew I'd only shot two of them.

All the same, my artefact eventually ran dry and crumbled into dust. That meant I'd have to face my last few opponents with only my inner shield for cover. I was slightly annoyed — I'd paid a pretty penny for that artefact, after all. I could have used that coin to buy gold and strengthen my demons, or even to summon something special. But hey, no use whining about it now... and anyway, the thing had probably saved my life today, since I was pretty sure my inner shield couldn't withstand more than a few rounds of bullets.

I didn't have time to summon any more demons, so I'd just have to work with what I had. On the plus side, I could feel my energy replenishing with every enemy I killed, even if the flow was more like a trickle. Soon, that energy would be absorbed, metabolised and begin to surge through my energetic channels. My internal energy reservoirs would start to expand and stretch, becoming elastic and flexible, and I knew exactly what to do to maximise results.

There was just one opponent left, but it was my tough cookie, and he was a force to be reckoned with. I hadn't been able to pierce his protective shield even once, and it looked fully intact.

The mist was starting to disperse, and finally, the man locked eyes with me.

"What are you waiting for? Come at me!" he roared. His gaze shifted over to Rambo. "So, you

weren't lying, after all... You really are a demonologist. Come on then, you freaks!"

I looked at him, and then at Rambo.

"Well, go on, get over there!" I told the horned
imp.

"Me?" he said, eyes wide.

"He said *freaks*, didn't he? That counts me
out," I shrugged.

"It counts *me* out, too!" Rambo squeaked, looking insulted.

"Ok, let's be objective here. Look at me, and
now look at yourself."

Rambo sighed loudly, pulled out his army
knife and trudged off towards the man while I
chuckled behind him.

"Alright, you don't want to have to respawn, I
get it. He definitely meant *you*, but I'll go, too," I
sighed just as loudly and set off after the imp. "Uncle Constantine will take care of it, don't you
worry!"

I got into fighting stance and pulled out my
sword. My opponent bared his teeth and charged
at me, then made a deft lunge and tried to stab me
in the stomach. I somersaulted backwards, landed
and then swung my blade. The steel connected
with his shield. Though it didn't leave a scratch,
this riled the fighter up, and he howled and un-
leashed a rain of rapid sword strokes. But his efforts were futile... My movements were light and
fast, and every stroke missed me by just a few centimetres. Meanwhile, I was striking his impenetrable shield again and again, riling him up even

more.

"Enough with the fancy footwork!" he growled. "Stop dancing and fight me!"

"Dancing? *This*?" I said in a wounded voice. You've just insulted a world champion martial arts master of the swallow-tail style!"

"The *what*?" the man frowned. I did a couple more somersaults and landed back in fighting stance. "Stop prancing around and just fight normally, already!"

"Fine," I switched my stance again. "Let's do it your way!"

I went right back to dodging every one of his blows. Given the poor and weakened condition of my body and my pathetic energy levels, I was surprising myself. But the skills I'd honed over centuries of gruelling training were still sharp. And, of course, like any self-respecting demonologist, I devoured any information about the art of battle I could get my hands on, no matter what kind of weapon was involved. Well, except for firearms, maybe... I'd have to rectify that in the future.

"What the hell are you doing?" he cursed. "Cut it out!"

"You don't like this style? Well, then let me show you the berserker style!" I grinned. "Although, hmm, I'm not *quite* immortal yet... so, maybe I should wait with the freestyling."

To make the guy happy, I started fighting 'normally', but he still couldn't land a single swipe with his sword. After a while, he got angry again — so angry that he actually hurled his sword at me in frustration. I skilfully knocked it aside, but failed to notice the fighter closing in on me until he had one hand tightened around my throat and the other clamped down across my sword arm.

"I've got you now!" he shrieked and lifted me off the ground, squeezing my throat with an iron grip. Rambo rushed to my aid, but the man pulled me close, using me as a human shield to fend the imp off.

"You know what?" he leered. "I'm not going to kill you. That would be too easy. I think I'll hand you over to the *count's* people. Believe me, they'll lock you up so far from civilisation that no blood-hound will ever sniff out even the slightest trace of you. And they'll keep you for a long time, too. They're going to torture you, experiment on you. The count is obsessed with demonology, and I promise you, he won't show mercy until he's dragged every last one of your secrets out of you. And once you've told him everything you know, *I'll* tell him you know even *more*! And he'll torture you again! He'll tear you into pieces, heal you, and then tear off *new* pieces! He'll study your flesh and do horrific things to it! That's the fate that awaits you, asshole!" I was barely listening to this long-winded ramble. I almost dozed off twice, but just about managed to keep myself conscious, assisted by the icy wind that was blasting me steadily in the face. "Why so quiet, hmm?"

"What is there to say?" I shrugged. "Except goodbye, I guess."

There was a sudden *cling*, and the man looked

down in time to see a handful of golden coins scrawled with a strange script land in the bloody, trampled snow.

I'd just thrown away a hundred grams of gold. It was worth it, though.

There was a flash, a mighty bang, and two enormous, hulking figures reared up behind my opponent. For a few seconds, my face turned pale and my body went limp. I didn't have enough gold for these two, so I'd had to cover the extra with energy, but in this moment, I had absolutely no regrets.

"What the—" the man managed to splutter before something grabbed him by the shoulder. The hand around my throat loosened, freeing me from his murderous grip. Then, they grabbed him by the other shoulder.

My opponent was a big guy, well over six feet tall. He clearly worked out, and his shoulders were easily twice as broad as mine. But right now, standing between the two pumped-up, grinning demons I'd just summoned, he looked like a skinny little dwarf — but a very *brave* dwarf, I had to admit, as I watched him boot one of the demons in the leg as hard as he could, putting every drop of power into his kick.

"Let's pretend that hurt," the horned beast said cooly. Then, they turned and began dragging the courageous dwarf by his arms into the portal that had just sprung up behind them. The guy kept on struggling, but the demons didn't seem to notice.

Suddenly, they stopped and looked back at me.

"Hmm," one demon looked at me appraisingly. "You think we should take that one, too?"

"Well... he's the one who summoned us. It would be kind of rude," the other demon said in a gravelly voice.

"He's a weakling, though, and his summoning is sloppy. We *could*," the first said with a slight shrug. My eyebrows shot up.

"Excuse me?" I stood up and stared at them. I dropped the concealments around my soul and revealed it to them, letting it radiate in all its glory. "Aren't you both getting a little above your station?"

"No," the first one shook its head at its companion. "I think he wants to do the same thing to us as we're about to do to this one," it said, shaking my hapless opponent like a ragdoll. "Let's not take the risk."

They turned and resumed their exit.

During all this, Rambo had been perched nearby on a warm corpse, cackling with glee as the scene unfolded.

"Yeah, and don't come back, you jerks!" he cried after the two enormous demons. The huge creatures paused again, this time, turning to look at imp. Meanwhile, their captive was still trying to break free, jerking his body, screaming and hitting them, none of which was having any effect at all.

"Want to come with us, little one?" the second demon rumbled.

"Nah, I'm with him," Rambo shrugged. "So go on, hit the road!"

"Lucky for you, you little runt," the huge creature scowled, shooting me a glance, and then the two continued on their way.

"Freaks! Why isn't my magic working? You bastards! Why can't I *hurt* them?" the man screeched. The demons just kept dragging him closer and closer to the portal.

"Wait!" my little imp cried out when the trio was almost through the portal. "You haven't apologised! Turn around right this second and beg your master for forgiveness!"

"Maybe we *should* take him," the first demon mused, regarding the tiny imp.

"Rambo, that's too far, even for me," I shook my head. "Let them go, it's fine."

With that, the two muscle-bound demons and their prisoner disappeared through the portal, leaving me and my imp alone. I sat down next to him and smiled. For whatever reason, the demon smiled back. I let out a long breath, and Rambo did, too.

"Tired?" I asked.

"Nah," he shook his head.

"You haven't had enough, have you?" I sighed.

"Nope!"

I'd really hit the jackpot with this one — he was the most bloodthirsty little lunatic I'd ever met! He was truly crazy, even by demon standards! But war was clearly his calling. I'd seen him in action. Hell, I'd seen him pull the magazine out of a man's gun, run up behind him and stab him multiple times in the back, all while moving at speed! He moved coolly, quickly and efficiently. He'd slash one opponent's tendons, scrape a second one's face off with his claws and drag a third one to the ground to finish him off. And most importantly, I could see how much he enjoyed it.

"Don't worry, Rambo," I slapped him on the shoulder. "There's plenty more coming. And soon, too—" I broke off as the radio in the minivan crackled to life. A voice came across the airwaves.

"Messenger, come in! Do you copy? Messenger!"

I picked up the radio, considering my options. I had to do something... I pushed the talk button and rubbed the microphone against the car seat for a bit.

"Messenger, I can't hear you! There's interference! Stay where you are — we'll be there in five minutes. Wait for us, and do not move! Over and out!" the voice on the other end finished hurriedly, and then the connection cut out.

Phew, pulled it off! But if I was going to pull the *rest* of this thing off and make the second round go my way, then we'd need to be prepared. I didn't know who was coming for me or how it would all go down, and unlucky for me, I was fresh out of coins...

While his reckoning may have been epic, I knew my recent opponent's fate was going to be utterly wretched. I didn't even want to think about it...

What he'd passed through wasn't a portal to 'hell', as they liked to call it around here. The people here told all kinds of tales about the infernal plane, each one more farfetched than the next, but in reality, the infernal plane was simply a place inhabited by beings totally unlike them. Inhabitants of the infernal plane ran on a different form of energy, their bodies were constructed in a different way, their magic took a different form, and so on. It was just a different dimension, plain and simple!

Incidentally, the inhabitants of the infernal plane also seemed to be surprisingly imaginative. Some of them had even come up with the idea of keeping little beasts as pets! As for what might await my burly enemy... well, I could only guess.

"Alright, Rambo! Enough lounging around — let's get ready to fight," I gave the little imp a shove, and he eagerly scampered off to scavenge weapons.

"But isn't Master tired?" the imp asked, circling back. "Maybe we should retreat?"

"Of course I'm tired," I shrugged. "But if we retreat now, we'll miss the best part! No, retreat is not an option," I murmured. This thought was exactly what had landed me in that dead, isolated world in the first place. Sometimes, retreat really *was* the smarter choice... But that just wasn't how I rolled.

* * *

The two huge demons were draped across a pair of deck chairs and admiring the view. This uninhabited island was far, far away from civilisation. Here, you could listen to the ocean and watch the waves break across the sand without a soul to disturb you.

The demons were having a great time, tanning themselves in the baking heat wearing nothing but loincloths. The loincloths didn't actually hide much, but the two muscle-bound monsters couldn't have cared less.

"How much time is left on the contract?" the first demon asked, cracking one eye open.

"Twelve more hours," the second demon sighed.

"You know what? I like this place," replied the first. "Sun, sea... We don't have that back home," he turned his head to look at the camping tent that was pitched in the shade of a nearby palm tree. "Hey, human, good news! We've got twelve more hours!" There came the sound of a tent flap opening, followed by a sob. The demons burst into laughter. "Relax! I've only just finished my cigarette!"

# CHAPTER 14

"AND THAT WAS ALL THE LATEST NEWS from here in the Philippine Republic!" the television presenter announced, waving his hands enthusiastically. "And now, dear viewers, everyone's favourite segment — Weird and Wonderful! A fishing boat has rescued a half-naked man from one of our beloved homeland's many islands! Here is a photograph."

An image of a clearly spooked and very pale-faced man appeared on the screen.

"And what's *weird* about this, I hear you ask? Everything! And we're here to tell you all," the presenter's round, cheery face reappeared on-screen. "The man — whose name is Valentine — has said he is a citizen of the Rusan Empire. However, no one knows how he ended up here, on an uninhabited island, thousands of miles from home! This report was made possible with the help of a translator. The man in question also received a sachet of our own signature tea blend, made by Fili-Mili Teas. Find them in stores throughout our great nation!"

The feed cut to a clip of some smiling people who seemed overjoyed to be brewing tea, smelling tea, sipping tea and generally engaging in any conceivable tea-based activity. The message was clear that this tea was the source of all their joy, the key to every success and happiness in their lives.

"Choose Fili-Mili Teas to help you rewind and relax... But wait, there's *more* to this story! Initially, the translator was reluctant to repeat to us what the man had said. In fact, he demanded we call a psychiatrist first. Apparently, our guest declared himself to be a faithful servant of one Count Serpentine, and claimed he had been forcibly brought to the island by two enormous demons. Being kidnapped by demons, can you imagine? And then brought all the way here to have some fun in the sun!" the presenter gave a genuine peal of laughter. After all, who *wouldn't* laugh at a story like that? "And can you *imagine*? He even said it with a straight face! He said that once they got there, the demons pitched a tent and set up deck chairs for themselves! And it doesn't end there!" the presenter cried. "The man claimed that the demons had kidnapped him for a reason," the presenter's face contorted into an expression of theatrical intrigue, though he couldn't stifle his laughter. "He claims — *can you imagine this?* —

Mister Valentine *claims* that the demons had him cracking coconuts, mixing cocktails and acting as their personal masseur! All of which has left him deeply traumatised!"

The man's picture appeared on-screen once again, though smaller this time.

"If anyone recognises this man, we suggest you contact emergency services and get him the psychiatric care he clearly needs, since only an unwell mind could concoct such a tale as this, I'm sure we all agree. And *that* is all the news we have for you tonight," the presenter beamed, spreading his arms wide. Suddenly, his face grew serious. "But! If we discover this story to actually be true, and we find out that this man really *was* abducted by demons," he grimaced goonishly, pausing to increase the suspense, "then this will cease to be a laughing matter. However! Our good friend Valentine shouldn't be worried! If he really *has* been massaging demons day and night, then he must be a great masseur by now! He'll be able to get a business going over here — and Focus law firm can help him! Focus — get fast, reliable legal support for the business of your dreams!"

The screen went black, and a thick, tense silence filled the room.

"What did I just see?" the captain of Count Serpentine's guard said finally, managing to keep his voice calm. "Why is he in the Philippine Republic?"

"He... appears to be the only survivor of the group, sir," one of the captain's subordinates said warily.

"And if he hadn't managed to bribe the nurses in that Philippine hospital, we'd never even have found him!" the captain scowled, stroking his thick beard. "Hmm... are you thinking what I'm thinking?"

"You mean, about how he earned the money to bribe the nurses? Yes, I'm also thinking about that, sir!"

"No, you idiot!" the captain huffed. "I'm thinking that the guy we were supposed to kidnap must dabble in demonology! Or that maybe he does a whole lot more than dabble, and he's connected to the disaster at the laboratory!" he began pacing rapidly around the room. "And the death of two squads, to boot... There's something fishy here, I can smell it! We need to capture him at all costs, but next time, we'll be better prepared."

"Well, we'll have time for that," the guard said wryly. "He's back at the military base already, and who knows when they'll let him out again. New recruits almost never get leave."

"You don't understand," the captain of the guard shook his head. "Our count has more resources at his disposal than you can imagine. And if *we* can't nab that little upstart, then our partners on the other side can. If you know who I mean..."

* * *

"Are you *sure* that's going to help us?" I pointed at the small demon. It was skinny, battered and struggling to stay on its feet. Its horns also appeared to be cracked. I looked at Rambo, who only shrugged as if to say *we'll see.*

I was pretty sure I'd seen enough already. Before me stood twenty imps, each one in worse shape than the last — and the first one wasn't exactly fighting fit. Every one of them looked dirty, beaten down and miserable. In a word, they were pathetic.

"Rock bottom," I muttered to myself. I put a hand over my eyes and let out a heavy sigh. "Alright, folks! Let's whip you into shape." After all, it wasn't like I had a choice. I'd just have to work with what I had. "Rambo! Assemble your soldiers here and get to work. You know what needs to be done."

"Yes, sir!" the little imp shouted, standing to attention, and then began barking orders at his subordinates. Meanwhile, I got to work on the payment. I worked up a small ball of energy and flicked it at the first imp with the tip of my finger, then another at the second, and at the third, until I'd gone all the way down the line.

Yes, I'd spent some huge sums of energy today, but that was during battle. The sad little creatures lined up before me were still getting paid crumbs regardless. In my position, every penny counted, and since I had some time to prepare for the next clash, I planned to take every energy-saving precaution possible.

I'd spent a lot more energy than I'd gained over the past few days, so by now, summoning anything resembling a normal demon was totally out of the question. My only option now was to make do with barrel-scrapers like these, and they could be difficult to work with. Their physical frailty seemed to go inextricably hand-in-hand with an incredibly low intelligence. In a way, this was actually a good thing, since stupidity also went hand-in-hand with courage. They were also incapable of bargaining. There were always perks to summoning an idiot.

Soon, I'd be back out on the battlefield, and out there, there was no room to cut corners. You always needed some aces up your sleeve, and the more you had, the better your chances of making it back alive (and with some trophies to show the ensign). That was why, this time, I'd turned to Rambo for help. He'd assembled some of his buddies, and I'd been able to save on searching, summoning and transportation costs right out of the gate. The only thing I'd had to pay was the hiring fee, and that was usually well within my budget. Apparently, it paid to get friendly with a demon or two.

And who knew Rambo had so many connections? I wondered if I should start making more demon contacts myself, maybe some gun demons or demonic snipers. I could really set up some nasty traps with those...

Anyway, there was no use complaining now, especially given the peanuts I was paying. This was what I could comfortably afford right now, so I was going to make it work.

One of the imps slipped and dropped his

machine gun, which went off and hit another imp in the horns. They started hurling abuse at each other, which escalated into fisticuffs, but Rambo quickly broke them up. He'd probably been no stronger than them until recently, but getting his name had made him grow, and he was now a head taller than the rest.

A real dream team... All the same, they piled the scattered bodies up quickly behind a nearby hill, checking their pockets well to collect a pile of valuables for me. They also laid out all the weapons they found on a patch of flat ground so we could easily grab them later.

I sat behind the wheel of the minivan, trying to remember what I'd learned in our vehicle training session at base. It hadn't been a *driving* lesson as such, but I knew the basic mechanics of how to control this thing, at least in theory. There was the steering wheel... you turned that to make the car change direction. Then, there were the two pedals... but shouldn't there be three? Oh well, it was probably fine.

Now to start the engine. What was it the sergeant major had said? Let me see... you insert the... something... into the... something... and then... hmm... Ah! I noticed the key sticking out of the ignition. All I had to do was turn it! That certainly made things easier.

A second later, a deep, rhythmic rumble started up under the hood of the van. There — half the work done already! All I had to do now was press the clutch, shift into first gear and... after that, I wasn't so sure. The training hadn't prepared me for this. I'd learned to operate *three* pedals — no one had said anything about two! But not to worry, I'd just use what I remembered. I knew that the right-hand pedal was to make the car go, so by that logic, the left-hand pedal must be the brake.

I decided to leave my door unlocked, just in case I screwed up; better to end up face-down in a pile of snow than go speeding to my demise.

I tried to pull up some instructional videos online, but it took me a while to get around the signal jammer. This was installed in the van to prevent victims from ringing for help. As it happened, I knew my way around signal jammers fairly well, since our training in such systems had been a lot more thorough than the vehicle training — probably because everyone else already *knew* how to drive...

I pressed play on the first video I found, hoping for instructions on how to get the car moving. A cheerful young chap appeared on the screen. He spent the next two minutes failing to tell me anything useful. He *did* talk about the importance of wearing your seatbelt, using your turn signals and correctly adjusting your seat. Oh, and he also mentioned the mirrors, but not until after the advertisement for brake pads, by which time, I'd already adjusted them.

Cursing to myself, I typed 'how to drive a car' into my search engine. Links to dozens of sites instantly popped up, each one promising to explain the whole process to me in detail. The first site forced me to read all about the history of the automobile, as well as telling me who invented the car wheel. I also learned about lots of different makes of cars, and absolutely nothing about how to drive any of them. It might have been further down in the text somewhere, but I was too pressed for time to find out.

In the end, I decided I'd just have to figure it out by myself. Fortunately, it didn't seem too hard. The most important thing was not to make any sudden movements...

BANG — the van jerked backwards, and I swiftly slammed the brakes. I'd only hit one imp. It was currently sitting on its backside in the snow and shaking its head, looking dazed and confused.

Learning from my mistake, I did everything right the second time. I soon had the vehicle rolling, and cruising smoothly, I steered it behind a dilapidated building nearby and parked it away from prying eyes. I locked it, checked all the doors and then walked back to the battleground.

When I got there, instead of the crowd of imps I was expecting, I saw *people*. They were all dressed in white camouflage uniforms, holding weapons in their hands and sweeping the area. There were no more than fifteen of them, but they were all armed. On the other hand, I didn't think they were much of a threat. Only one among them was gifted, and weakly at that. I didn't think much of their readiness for battle, either; they were all bunched up together and clearly didn't know what they were doing.

I guessed these soldiers had been sent as nothing more than a delivery crew, and that the *real* work would be done by professionals later. The brand-new car standing nearby with the coat of arms emblazoned on the hood and doors indicated as much. From what I could sense, the vehicle had a special artefact-based device installed that blocked magic. In my current state, even a trivial little gadget like that might stop me in my tracks... I made a mental note not to end up inside the car.

Meanwhile, what did *we* have at our disposal? Nothing! And what did *that* mean? We'd have to experiment on the fly!

I decided my first experiment would be to set the imps on our new arrivals. My expected imp survival rate was zero, but they knew what they'd signed up for. I'd given them so much energy that even if they 'died' they'd still be in the black, so none of them were about to kick up a fuss. And anyway, now that they were armed with guns and a crash course in marksmanship from Rambo, they might even stand a chance.

I gave Rambo the order telepathically, and he led his troops into battle. They popped straight up out of the snow, aimed their weapons and started firing erratically. This took the guards by surprise, and they, too began firing wildly in all directions. Panic, chaos, gunshots and screams all blended into one, and the battlefield grew thick with smoke from the guns.

I decided to hang back and watch from the

sidelines. I wasn't going to be much use, and there was a decent chance of ending up riddled with stray bullets. Even at a hundred metres away, bullets were *still* whistling regularly over my head and burrowing into the snow behind me.

The imps had seized the element of surprise, and that wasn't only thanks to the ones who'd buried themselves in the snow before the fight. They were also cloaked in a kind of invisibility spell. The spell dispersed as soon as they launched their attack, but in fact, this was ideal, since invisibility spells cost a crippling amount of energy to maintain.

As soon as the shooting started, a thin stream of energy began to trickle into me. I closed my eyes in pleasure. I *hated* spending energy... but accumulating it was one of the sweetest feelings I knew.

When the imps ran out of bullets, they just hurled themselves at the enemy soldiers, who were frantically trying to reload their weapons. Even from here, I could see their hands trembling, fumbling hopelessly with their magazines. *These* were the guys they'd sent after me? Seriously?

My kidnappers must have reported back to their boss that the target was weak and unarmed, which was why the count's guards had come so poorly prepared. Bad call — *very* bad call! And I knew they were a bunch of weaklings, too, because my imps had actually taken them down! My imps should never have stood a chance! To my astonishment, two of the little creatures had even survived — along with Rambo, of course.

My favourite part had been when the commander of the guard unit started shrieking and trying to crawl away when one of the demons came running at him with an axe. Then it was all *no* and *please* and *don't harvest my soul, I beg you...* ridiculous. A demonic entity doesn't harvest your soul when it kills you — that's just not how it works! But apparently, this guy didn't know that, because he died of a heart attack right before the axe split his stupid head in two.

Once the fighting was finished, we set to work on cleaning up the evidence. I had to spend some of the new energy I'd accumulated on speeding up the process, because sooner or later, the count would send more people, and the next batch would be much better prepared.

I sat in the van for half an hour and meditated. This was essential if I wanted to replenish my energy. Then, I got out, pricked my finger and began to paint a rare and complex summoning circle in the trampled snow. It was composed of a series of looped, interlocking magical chains. It was as complex visually as it was in design; summoning such a specific type of demonic entity required great specificity and an awful lot of symbols.

As I drew, I listened carefully to the conversations taking place over the radio. We'd had two days of training on radio equipment, and we'd gone into quite a lot of detail. We'd learned how to retune a New Imperial transmitter to the Empire's frequency, how to intercept enemy communications, how to encrypt our own transmissions and more. Thanks to that, I'd figured out the van radio in no time, and now, I was using it as an advance warning system for approaching enemies.

As soon as I finished the many-looped circle, three higher imps appeared within it. Higher imps were a little taller and broader than their lower counterparts, though they still weren't as big as your average demon. Their distinguishing feature, however, was something else. Not only were they stronger than lower imps, but they were also much smarter. They weren't much use in a fight, since they lacked the idiotic courage that was the main appeal of using regular imps in battle, but on the other hand, you could actually talk to them.

"I have a job for you," I said in greeting. "Here's your payment — get started."

"That's not much!" one of them protested.

"Just take what you're given and do your job!" I snapped.

"That's not much!" all three of them repeated in unison.

"Excuse me? Is that insolence I hear?" for just a moment, I gave them a glimpse of my soul. I wanted them to know exactly who they were talking to. "You signed the contract! So, take your payment and *get to work.*" They just stood there staring at me in silence, not moving a muscle. "Fine. I'll throw in a bonus," I grabbed three machine guns and held them up. "Will that do?"

"That's not gold," the scrawniest one shook its

head.

"They're *better* than gold!" I cried, but the imps didn't seem to agree. "Want me to prove it?"

"No, don't," I pulled back the bolt on one of the guns and cut the imp off with a well-aimed shot straight to the knee. "Ahh!" the felled imp screamed, while the other two tried to break out of the circle and attack me. Despite their best efforts, the circle's protective dome held them back.

"You really think I'd forget the dome?" I shook my head. "Listen, you can either take the guns or get out of here. I'll cover your energy costs for the round trip. What do you say?"

"Oh, we're going to get you—" the hissing imp stopped short as I pointed the barrel of my gun right between its eyes. "Yes, we're going to, uh, get you *all sorted out*! Yes, sir, we're going to clean this whole mess up so spick and span, you'll be fit to faint!"

"That's more like it," I waved a hand and the summoning circle dissolved. "You may begin."

They immediately sprinted off to start collecting corpses, not forgetting to search through the guards' pockets and make small piles of the various valuables as they went. It was a pleasure to watch them work; unlike the lower imps, these three thought of everything, down to the smallest detail.

An ordinary soul could never have conceived of the true profundity of a demonologist's power, nor of the things that power enabled a demonologist to do. Currently, for example, that power was enabling *me* to sit back in a camping chair and watch a bunch of imps do all my hard work for me. Summoning demons didn't always have to be about war and fighting; the horned beasts could make excellent cleaners, too.

Valuables in one spot, weapons and magazines in another, corpses into the portal — and in the blink of an eye, we were standing in the middle of a perfectly empty clearing. Even the blood-stained snow had been carefully sprinkled with clean snow from the next pile over, and then trampled on so as not to stand out from the rest.

My total haul of valuables was three gold bracelets (which the imps eyed enviously) and four thousand dollars in cash. The special forces guys from the van hadn't been carrying any money, but their weapons were more valuable than the others. Aside from that, the imps had collected a random assortment of radios, intercom devices, telephones — basically, any other junk that I could sell.

I dumped the trash into the portal after the bodies, then carefully packed the firearms into four gym bags and threw them into the van. All that was left was the coat of arms-adorned car. Since I didn't know how to drive two cars at once yet, I just set fire to it instead.

I'd settled my accounts with the higher imps and was just about to get behind the wheel of the van when...

"You owe us compensation," I heard one of the three grumble. "You shot one of us in the knee."

"Compensation, huh? Where did you learn

such a big word?" I laughed.

"Let *me* settle this one, Master," Rambo grinned, pulling out his knife as he moved for the demons.

"Wait," I stopped him. "They're a decent little crew — I think we'll have use for them in the future." I produced a little ball of energy and tossed it at the wounded imp.

"My gratitude," the imp nodded, and a moment later, all three disappeared into thin air.

The energy I'd given the imp wasn't much, but I thought it was fair. They really *had* done excellent work, taking care of every last detail. You could have searched the place with a fine-tooth comb and not have turned up even a single shell casing, never mind any traces of blood or other evidence.

With that done, it was about time to head back to base. But just then, I realised... I hadn't eaten yet! Oh well, the canteen food back at base would do just fine. I got into the van, turned the key in the ignition and watched Rambo hop up into the passenger seat.

"Listen, are you sure you want to come with me?" I asked. "You know I can't drive, right? I figured I could practice on the trip back. Maybe you should go back to your own world and rest for a while."

"I like it here," the little creature shrugged his shoulders.

"Hey, is that a new knife?" I asked, the blade stuffed into his belt catching my eye.

"Uhuh!" Rambo grinned. Suddenly, I slapped a hand to my forehead — I'd completely forgotten!

I got out of the front seat and opened the side door of the van. I rummaged around briefly until I found what I was looking for. I had no idea what it was doing here, and I didn't really want to think about it.

"Here, try this!" I grinned.

"What? Why? What is it?" said the imp, looking puzzled.

"Have you seen yourself lately? Come on, you'll be safe and comfy in this child seat!" I said, attaching the device to the front passenger seat and stepping back for Rambo to get in. This was a game-changer!

And the gifts didn't stop there. On the trim of the dashboard, I inscribed a small pentagram in blood and then tapped Rambo on the shoulder.

"Touch it," I nodded at the pentagram.

"Touch it?" he frowned. "Why?"

"Not scared, are you?" a smile spread across my face, but the demon really *was* regarding the portal with a hint of fear.

"No!" he tightened his bandana, stretched out a clawed paw and... nothing happened. Nothing except for a faint spark as the spell was activated... "What *is* this?"

"It's your own personal portal," I said. Rambo's eyes widened. For a moment, he stood speechless.

"That's possible?"

"Yup, imagine that," I chuckled. "Only *you* can use this portal. And I think you have a reason to try it out," I held a bundle of rags out to him.

He unravelled the rags to find fifteen shiny new army knives. I noticed he was trying not to cry.

"Are these all for me?" his lip began to tremble. When I nodded, he jumped up and dived straight into the portal.

A few minutes later, the portal flared into life again and Rambo came tumbling out, this time, without the bundle. I guessed he'd taken it home and hidden it well.

"Thank you, Master!" he squeaked, fastening his little seatbelt. In some ways, demons were a lot like people. They, too had homes where they liked to keep all their personal things. Of course they did — where else were you supposed to keep your weapons?

You could easily lose a weapon in battle, and you mightn't always have the energy or gold to buy a new one. For that reason, smart demons always kept a knife or two stashed away somewhere. If you ever summoned a demon and it showed up empty-handed, that meant it had lost all its weapons and didn't have the resources to obtain new ones, and *that* meant it was either weak or stupid. To buy weapons, you needed at least some amount of energy — either that, or gold, which demons also used as currency.

That was one odd thing about demons. I was familiar with many schools of summoning, not just within the realm of demonology, and creatures of other kinds could often be summoned using silver or platinum. Demons, however, cared only for gold. They *might* be persuaded to accept a few other extremely rare metals; while creatures of the light tended to favour mithril, for example, the only thing demons liked more than gold was adamantium. Unfortunately, both those metals were highly prized in every world I knew of and were almost impossible to get one's hands on.

There was a time when I could have thrown four hundred kilos of gold down on a single high-level summoning, and I could have repeated that summoning six times in a single day. But that was in my youth... For the last few hundred years, I'd been paying my demons exclusively in energy. The good thing about energy was that you could use it to summon any type of demon, even those of the highest order.

With that, Rambo and I set off back to the base. We *could* have driven back through town, but considering it was my first time behind the wheel, I decided not to risk the welfare of the citizens of Circle City.

As predicted, I broke multiple red lights, drifted into oncoming traffic more than once and even managed to break the speed limit. I only discovered this last part when the cops pulled me over.

"Oh, you're a soldier," the officer waved me off immediately at the sight of my uniform. "On your way!"

My eyebrows went up.

"Aren't you even going to fine me?" I asked.

"You're a War Demon, your life is already

tough enough," he replied. "On your way — but easy on the accelerator, demon!"

I didn't know whether to be pleased or disappointed. I'd seen the pity in the guy's eyes. On the other hand, that pity had saved me from a fine.

Grateful for the officer's kindness, I stayed below the speed limit all the way home. The speedometer hovered at fifteen kilometres as I diligently maintained a safe and steady speed. Meanwhile, my fellow motorists showed their support, driving behind me at the same speed and honking to express their admiration for my driving skills!

I didn't notice the time passing on the drive home. I just kept looking straight ahead, occasionally glancing at my map, and all of a sudden, I was pulling up in front of the security hut, where the very same soldier as before was standing and pulling leisurely puffs from a cigarette.

"You're back early," he raised an eyebrow.

"I got hungry," I shrugged.

"Why didn't you eat in town?" he laughed.

"I'm used to the canteen food, I guess."

"Huh? That's the craziest shit I've ever heard! Hey, Carp, get a load of this!" he turned and yelled to another soldier. "This guy prefers our canteen slop to city food!"

"*You're* the crazy one," I pointed at him. "The canteen's got mashed potatoes, pork chops, juice boxes — mmm. And all for free!"

"Aren't you sick of that stuff?" he stared at me, scratching the back of his neck.

"You're all so spoiled," I sighed. They'd clearly

never been to the Middle Ages — now *there* was some real slop. Here, you ate better than a medieval lord.

Giving the car back was simple — I didn't even have to show vehicle registration papers or anything. I supposed the number of soldiers stealing cars to get back to base was pretty low. The guards just directed me to the parking area for soldiers, and, out of concern for the other vehicles, even helped me park the thing.

My first order of business was to see Birch. Despite the late hour, I found him down in the storage facility. I knocked politely on his office door, triggering a string of expletives that only stopped when he saw that it was me standing in the doorway.

"Apologies, sir, but I need to ask a... delicate question."

"Soldiers can't normally just stroll into my office like this after work hours, you know," he sighed. "Well, I suppose they *can*, but I'll tear them a new one for it — verbally, of course. Otherwise, you get pestered to death, distracted from your business," Birch smiled. "But I like you, so come in," he waved me into the room and then fixed his gaze on me. "Well? What is it?"

"I'd like to know if I can store some weapons here—"

"Did you hit your head in the city, or something? Did you lose all your brain cells in a bar fight?" the ensign frowned. "You've stored plenty of weapons here already — of course you can!"

"No, you don't understand," I shook my head. "I know I can store weapons I bring back from military operations... but what about weapons I bring back from town?"

"Huh?" After a few moments of reflection, Birch clarified: "What the hell are you on about?"

By way of explanation, I pulled four machine guns out of my bag and laid them on the table.

"So, you're saying you went to the city, found these guns and now you want to store them here?" he asked. I nodded. "Tell me, how exactly did you get through the medical exam? How on *earth* did you get through the psych evaluation? You bribed them, didn't you? I thought I'd seen it all... Soldiers usually bring things *into* the city to sell on the black market. This is the first time I've seen someone bring something *from* the city back to base!"

"I value you as a business partner. I only want to trade with you," I shrugged.

"I bet you also value the fact that I won't ask questions about where all this came from," Birch arched an eyebrow.

"Well, that too."

"Mm-hmm... Well, then. Four machine guns. Must have been some fight!" he exclaimed.

"Four?" I said indignantly. I picked up the other bags and emptied them onto his desk. One bag of grenades, one of pistols, one of knives and one with the rest of the machine guns.

"Holy hell... now I *definitely* don't want to know," the ensign shook his head. "Let's just register this, lock it up and speak no more of it."

And with that, my very eventful day came to an end.

Back in the barracks, I lay in bed, smiling and content. And why wouldn't I smile, when I'd had raspberry jelly for dinner? I was living the dream! And there was even more excitement to come...

Captain Cardinal had summoned me to share the good news that I was being sent on a solo reconnaissance raid the very next morning. I let my mind wander, thinking pleasant thoughts about the day ahead. I had a feeling it was going to be an eventful one...

No sooner had I closed my eyes than I heard a strange sound coming from above me.

"Psst! Psst!"

I opened one eye and found Rambo standing over me.

"Master!" he whispered. "I brought you a gun! Here, you can sell it!"

I blinked in the darkness and saw that the imp was, in fact, holding a machine gun in his hands.

"Where the hell did you get that?" I hissed in surprise.

He shrugged. "Over there, in the corner."

"Holy shit!" I burst out, shooing him off my bed. "That's not how we do it! Put that back, right now!"

# CHAPTER 15

BREAKFAST WAS LONG SINCE OVER. In fact, even lunch was nearly finished by now. And yet, here I was, still lying in my bed with no desire to get up. Outside the window, I could hear the sound of boots marching, soldiers assembling in formation and the day's orders from high command being read out. Now and then, a battered-looking new recruit would come into the barracks after some training session or other and glance enviously in my direction.

About fifteen other beds were also full, but all of *those* guys had been serving a long time, so the new recruits were mostly jealous of me. If you asked me, though, that jealousy was a waste of time. If they just opened their eyes and cottoned on to what the army was all about, then *they* could be sleeping late, too! It was that simple!

Instead, they sat on their bunks, furtively whispering that I was crooked, that I'd pulled strings to get here, that my life here was too easy. Unlike me, they had to train every day, had to go on patrol and night duty, and all that was a damn sight harder than lying in bed until midday staring at the ceiling.

The fact was, they just didn't know what streamlined military procedure looked like. If you had a mission coming up, the best thing you could do was put all the less important stuff on hold and conserve your energy. Rest, sleep, relax, eat... the time before your mission was entirely yours, and you were entitled to spend it however you saw fit. You might head down to the storage facility early and inspect all your weapons and equipment, for example. Or, you might like to talk with some of the more experienced recruits, discuss the potential challenges ahead and get some advice on how to tackle them.

A soldier had to embark on a mission full of strength and determination, not stumbling in exhausted from the parade ground, the firing range or a gruelling training session. The system here reminded me of how the Order operated... In fact, the Order and the army ran on very similar principles, which might have been a hint as to why I felt so at home here.

Being accepted into the order I belonged to was considered an incredible achievement, like winning a golden ticket in the game of life — but only by those who got rejected.

There were plenty of other orders, clans and enclaves in my world dedicated to demonology, but ours was considered the best. And yet, those happy few who drew the golden tickets quickly discovered the harsh reality behind the glittering facade. I'd seen that look of pure disillusionment in the haunted eyes of my students and followers many times... though it always morphed into despair soon enough.

The Order's philosophy could be described in two words: 'iron' and 'discipline'. Iron discipline was the key. Woe betide you if you tried to do so much as take a piss outside of the Order's appointed schedule. But this was for good reason. Demonology was a very exact science, and its disciples needed to have discipline instilled in them from day one. Discipline had to become a demonologist's second nature, because one wrong word, a single clumsy movement, and you'd find yourself a corpse.

The Order's teachings brought this to life. One wrong word in front of a teacher, and your life would be a whole lot harder for a few months. But instead of lecturing our students, we liked to have them learn through experience. This didn't just come in the form of physical trials, however. In some cases, outright punishment was necessary.

I remembered one follower, a guy called Wales who'd barely even been with us twenty years. Wanting to celebrate something or other, he'd smuggled alcohol onto the grounds. He'd spent the next six months in a specially commissioned cell custom-made by the Order of Architects. Its clever structure meant that the three higher-order demons who'd been summoned within it couldn't physically harm the boy... but they knew how to hurt him in other ways. After all, they were called *higher* demons for a reason.

Without spilling any order secrets, it would be fair to say that those six months were... *difficult* for the unfortunate young follower. The demons had all the fun they could with him, trying to lure him over, getting their friends to join in, even bringing in a couple of demonic banshees. By the time Wales got out of there, he was a completely different person. Every trace of his old, slovenly attitude was gone, and his long, thick hair, previously black, had turned white.

Anyway, it was time to get out of bed. I was well rested and recovered by now! I'd spent the whole morning laying back and enjoying the other new recruits' furious glares. I kind of enjoyed how much they hated me.

I got up and set off straight for the Bird's office to receive my mission.

"Huh, ready already?" he said with surprise. "Well, then — come with me!"

The captain led me out of his office, through the long, winding corridors and into a stuffy room that was buzzing with life. It was crammed with people sitting at desks, on calls with other military branches. Some of them were being briefed for missions, while others were waiting their turn for the phones or even arguing with the person next to them about the finer details of some tactical manoeuvre or other.

"Seriously?" a guy standing in line exclaimed. "They're sending new recruits on solo missions, now? Wow, are we really that short on personnel? He doesn't even know how to march in a straight line yet, and you're sending him out into the *forest*? Gimme a break!"

"Allot that one enough ammo for three missions," Cardinal ordered a clerk sitting at a desk nearby. "If he has the energy to run his mouth like that, he's better off using it on the battlefield."

"I apologise, Captain Cardinal, sir," the guy said, dropping his gaze. "That was out of line."

"*Way* out of line, soldier," Cardinal replied, thin-lipped.

"He *is* a new recruit, though," the soldier said again. "I mean, look — his chevrons are empty. He doesn't even have the little bald demon!"

I looked down at my chevron patch and realised the guy was right. My chevrons *were* totally empty... I started to feel a little mad. The joker in front of me had a demon on *his* chevrons, and it had horns and everything!

"I'll get my demon," I called out, "and it'll be bigger and meaner than yours!"

"First of all, this recruit already has two missions under his belt, and heavy ones, too," Cardinal cut in. "And second of all, this isn't your call, Cornflower." Then, he led me away and sat me down at a table. "Listen, kid, I've sent all the information you need to your wrist tablet. But keep in mind that as soon as you leave the territory of the base, everything will be wiped. First, though, I'll brief you in my own words... Do you have a question?" he asked, noticing me fidgeting in my chair.

"Yes, sir! When will I be able to leave the base with the tablet? To go to the city, I mean," I said rapidly.

"Are you getting impertinent, private?" the Bird frowned. "Why would you need it in the city, anyway?"

"It's more convenient than a phone," I shrugged.

"More convenient? Seriously? That's military technology!" he exclaimed. "Theoretically, it's after two years of service," he chuckled softly. "But you're a special case. For you, let's say a year."

"Hmm... I think I can do that in a month," I nodded to myself, and the captain burst out laughing.

"That's a little over-confident," he shook his head. "Anyway, let me tell you about the mission ahead."

The captain gave me a brief rundown of my mission. I could tell he was just waiting for me to shake my head and ask him to send someone else. Not a chance... I couldn't wait! I was also enjoying watching the other soldiers' faces. I could sense their shock as they eavesdropped. The captain was really sending a new recruit on a full-blown reconnaissance mission!

Once I was finished with the Bird, I went to see Birch. I found all my stuff already checked out, laid out and ready to go.

"Is this all for me?" I asked, just to make sure. It seemed like a lot.

"Well, it's no easy task you've got. You never know what might come in handy," the ensign shrugged.

"I get it, but... what about that guy?" I pointed to a soldier standing by a meagre pile of equipment nearby. He was gazing longingly over at us. "Don't you think he needs it more? And why is it all brand new? I'm only going to break it!"

"Forget about the others!" Birch huffed. "That soldier is heading four kilometres out, and he's taking a tank!"

"Why's he going out that far?" I frowned.

"There was an explosion out in the minefield. We need someone to go and check it out," the ensign explained impatiently.

"Why not send a drone?"

"You don't think there are system jammers out there?" he arched an eyebrow.

"Well, now I know," I smiled back. "Okay, well, thank you very much. I'll try to return everything safe and sound."

"You bet your ass you will!" Birch waved a threatening finger at me. "This isn't the cheap stuff. Look at this one, for example."

"Oh, wow... a knuckle duster! That'll come in handy. And it fits like a glove!" I cried, grabbing it from the table. "Thank *you*, ensign! I promise to smash the skulls of all my enemies with it."

"*That* is the latest remote gesture-control system for your personal drone!" Birch snapped, snatching my new toy away from me. "You won't be needing it, though — the drone's not even operational yet," he said, picking a few other unnecessary items out of the pile.

"Want to give me a grenade launcher instead?" I asked, deciding to try my luck.

"Why would you need one of those? You're going on reconnaissance," Birch frowned.

"What if something happens? The grenade launcher would be peace of mind," I shrugged.

"You know what? Why not," the ensign chuckled and ran to fetch one. "Here you go. If you can lift it, you can have it!" he smiled, holding the enormous tube out to me with effort. It really *was* a serious piece of equipment. It weighed more than a hundred kilos! Nevertheless, I hoisted it onto my shoulders and took it for a walk. "Amazing. It's yours!"

"Thank you, sir!" I grinned, brimming with joy.

For transportation, I ended up with a snowmobile and a sledge, both piled high with all my equipment. They also gave me a top-of-the-range rifle (which I quickly stowed away so as not to lose it), a few boxes of assorted electronics, a camera and various other useful items, such as a tent, a sleeping bag and a tinderbox. I was then escorted to the front gate, where I confirmed one last time that I understood my assignment, and off I went. The adventure had begun...

Basically, I had to take as many pictures as possible of the enemy base that had been under construction nearby for the past six months. Our attempt to storm it had ended badly, so we were only conducting reconnaissance missions for now.

You didn't want to send a crowd on a mission like this. The enemy would soon spot even a small group and would only send a bigger unit out to destroy you. Alone, however, it was easy to sneak in close — *if* you were a top-class, well-prepared scout, of course. Not if you were a new recruit...

According to Cardinal, I was unlikely to meet any trouble en route. The path had been cleared by an earlier group, and I could travel along the road for most of the way. This meant I wouldn't have to worry about unexpected landmines or other such surprises. All I had to do was get in, take some photos from a distance and then high-tail it back to base. High command desperately needed intel about the progress of the construction, and they needed it fast.

All this had been told to me in confidence, and when I asked what the photos were for, I was met with silence. It didn't take a genius, however, to guess that command was planning to storm the base, and that my images would be used to craft the plan of attack.

The assignment was tough, yes — maybe even impossible — but surely, others had been on similar missions before me. And while *they* might have had years of service under their belts, but none of *them* were three thousand years old! I certainly was curious to see how things would unfold...

Another thing I liked about this mission was

that it had no expiration date. When I'd asked Cardinal how much time I had, he'd said I could wander around in the woods for a week if I wanted to. As long as I came back alive, preferably with some photographs, no one cared. As for how to actually *get* back — well, that was my problem.

How many photos I took was also at my discretion. Coming back with one would be less than ideal, but still acceptable. Beyond that, the more the better. And if I could cover the perimeter of the base and take snaps from different angles, that would be the bee's knees. The only minor inconvenience was that I'd probably die five hundred times in the process, since the base was not only guarded by troops, but also surrounded by landmines. On top of that, it was constantly monitored by cameras, drones and all kinds of other tech.

It was also important for me to get pictures of people. Their faces could be used to deduce which units were currently stationed at the new base.

Cardinal had smirked a little when he'd told me to just do as much as I was comfortable with. He was probably thinking I'd take one picture and then scurry home with my tail between my legs. Meanwhile, I was just dreaming about the grenade launcher...

It took me about a day to reach my target location. In that time, I encountered seven hundred and forty-seven squirrels, thirty-one bears, twenty-seven snow wolves, twenty-one brown wolves and three gigantic magic wolves. I lost twenty-one imps and discovered six frozen corpses, two of which were Imperials and the rest Newies. I noted the coordinates of the two Imperials for future retrieval, while from the Newies, I recovered three machine guns, four knives and a handful of grenades. I didn't take any trophies from *our* two guys — that was against the rules. It wasn't forbidden by the Empire per se, but it went against my personal moral code.

I reached the location quicker than expected. Estimated travel time to the base had been two days, but that was travelling by road. I'd taken a different route, one that went straight through the forest. Travelling by road was boring, plain and simple, while the forest held all kinds of adventures.

I parked the snowmobile, grabbed what I needed and stashed everything else securely nearby. Then, I set off for the base on foot at an easy pace. I still had a half day's walk ahead, since there were ten kilometres of dense, snowy magical forest between me and the base. To protect myself against traps, I traced a couple of pentagrams in the snow and summoned twelve flying imps. I sent them off to reconnoitre the area while I walked. Only Rambo stayed alongside me, but he was a more interesting travel partner than most of his kin.

The little imp was clever, quick and reliable, but he couldn't work miracles. So, I'd come ready with some other tricks up my sleeve, just in case. I'd prepared well for this operation.

The last leg of the journey was the toughest. We were forced to make wide detours around dozens of detection devices, which led us into mine territory more than once. But this mission was important, and I couldn't let myself get caught.

It was late by the time we reached the base. I'd hoped to get there sooner, but the reconnaissance drones flying overhead in the forest had forced me to bury myself in the snow and hide multiple times. Just in case the drones had aura scanners, I'd also cloaked myself in demonic energy. That way, even if they'd detected me, they would have taken me for a demonic beast or something of the like.

Presently, I reached the first line of defence around the base. The land here was riddled with mines and there were tripwires concealed everywhere. I decided to use the reconnoitred route I'd been shown back at headquarters. But the reconnaissance hadn't caught everything... Suddenly, I found myself in a densely packed minefield. I couldn't take a single step!

In the end, I had to send Rambo to tunnel down and dig the mines out of the ground. Yes, I knew they might explode, and so did he, but what could I do? Hand him a shovel and tell him to dig — that was my only option. And anyway, Rambo turned out to be handy with more than just a knife. The engineer's shovel became like an extension of the little imp's arm, and the earth, hard and frozen as it was, was soon flying in all directions.

"Where should I put this?" Rambo asked, holding up a mine.

"Just take it away somewhere," I waved a hand. "About two hundred metres from here. And you can put the rest with it."

As I set off through the minefield, I realised I had another problem. The base was only three kilometres from here — close enough, you would think, to photograph. The thing was, it was completely hidden amongst the trees. I'd have to climb a hill...

By now, I was close enough to run into an enemy patrol, but I'd already been warned about them, so they wouldn't take me by surprise. The commanders had informed me of them back at base, and I had my imps to alert me out here. As a result, it was no great effort to avoid them. When you knew the location of every patrol, and even every detection device within a hundred-metre radius, a reconnaissance mission becomes a walk in the park.

A half-hour later, I was cresting the ridge of a small hill. From the top, I had a perfect view of the base — or as good a view as I was going to get, at least, since the complex was surrounded on all sides by high walls plated with thick metal shields and dotted with watchtowers.

I pulled out my camera, screwed off the lens and began to snap picture after picture, a victorious grin on my face. I took close-ups of one building after another. I captured some soldiers' faces, and then turned my attention to a building at the edge of the base that was still under construction. Ten photos, then twenty, a hundred, a hundred and thirty...

... and that was it! The mission was complete!

I sank down into the snow to rest for a moment. I opened my thermos of hot water and took a sip. Rambo sat alongside me, rocking slightly to fend off the cold.

"They sent me all this way just for this?" I sighed. "Pathetic."

"Is Master disappointed?" Rambo gave me a sideways glance.

"Not *disappointed*, exactly," I said, frowning. "But I *would* like to know when they're actually going to give me a challenge. They promised me this mission would be a hard one, but look at us now."

"Is a walk through the forest *supposed* to be challenging?" the imp shot me another glance.

"Don't forget, this is a high-risk, covert operation!" I stuck a finger dramatically in the air as I repeated the captain's words. "And they told me it was going to be tough."

"Do humans think a walk in the forest is a covert operation?" my horned companion tittered.

"Seems so," I sighed heavily. What else could I say? Ashamed as I was to admit it, it was true.

"BORING!" Rambo hollered, just as disappointed as me.

I had a thought and started rummaging through my backpack.

"Want a candy bar?" I said, producing a couple from my top pocket. Rambo nodded hesitantly. I handed him one-half of our feast, and as we sat there chewing, I started thinking. We sat in silence for several minutes.

"You know this is an enemy base, right?" I tipped my head towards the complex. "If they find us here, they'll obliterate us!"

"They'll obliterate *you*," Rambo corrected me. "They'll send *me* home. I wouldn't like that, though."

"If I got obliterated?" I laughed.

"No, I wouldn't like to go home," he admitted. "It's boring there. At least here, I get to have new experiences. Even if it *is* freezing..."

This wouldn't do, not one bit. Had I really come all this way just for the sake of a hundred photographs? What was it the captain had said? That I could do whatever I liked as long as I came back with the pictures, and preferably alive? But what use were these pictures, anyway? You couldn't see much behind the walls except for maybe some construction equipment, and all the buildings were nearly finished. Truly pathetic...

I had two options left. Either I could sit here and wait for something interesting to happen — like a jet plane full of VIPs crash-landing on the hill, for example — or I could... No, that option was a bad idea. If I was still here when the sun came up, I'd most likely be spotted, and my chances of surviving would then be slim to none. Cardinal had recommended I time my actions carefully so as to operate exclusively during the hours of darkness, and there was a reason for that.

"Maybe Master could stop accepting these boring missions in the future?" Rambo piped up again, gulping down the last of his candy bar.

"Aw, screw it!" I yelled, waving my hands. "I know what we'll do. We've completed the mission, sure, but going home with this little intel? It's embarrassing! So, if the mission's boring... we'll just have to spice it up! I didn't come to this world to go on nature walks! Come on, let's blast this operation into space!"

"With gunpowder?" Rambo's eyes lit up.

A predatory grin spread across my face. "A tonne of it! Let's go hunt some patrols!"

"With *pleasure*!" the imp cried, pulling his knife from his belt.

"Hang on, not this time," I held up a hand to stop him. I looked around and spotted a dead tree nearby. I went over and tore off a thick, heavy branch — a makeshift club. "*This* is your weapon for the evening," I grinned again.

"Is Master demoting me?" the imp squeaked, looking crestfallen.

"No, no, of course not! But we're in the business of taking prisoners tonight, not making corpses."

We found our first victims easily. Three soldiers were sitting and warming themselves around a fire. On my command, the two imps perched in the trees above them extinguished the flames using the most... well, *natural* method they could think of. This sudden deluge not only quenched the fire, but also fell on the soldiers themselves.

They looked up, briefly astonished that such torrential rain could suddenly fall in the middle of winter, and then started leaping to their feet. A hefty rock flew out of the darkness and hit one square in the head. Another found himself on the round end of a wooden club, while the imps tore the last one apart with their bare hands. They could have knocked him out like the others, but he'd laid eyes on Rambo, and we couldn't risk having witnesses.

We attacked one patrol after another, taking them down so fast that they barely had time to blink. In a heavily mined and monitored area like this, no one was expecting to be ambushed. They all assumed sneaking in this close would be impossible... but they were wrong.

Once our prisoners were all securely tied up and blindfolded, a flock of imps airlifted them to the snowmobile and dumped them next to it in a pile.

We'd gathered twenty prisoners, and we were out of time. Roll call would begin in the base any minute, and the second the patrolling soldiers failed to respond, a squad would be sent out to investigate.

"Dammit! This is *still* boring," I cursed, shaking my head. Rambo touched down next to me with a heavy sigh. "But don't you worry! The fun's about to start!" I flashed the rest of the imps a wide smile. "You remember where we put those big metal spheres? The ones called landmines?"

"Yes, Master!" they chimed in chorus.

"Uhh," one of the bigger (though clearly not smarter) imps scratched its head.

"Show this guy, okay?" I pointed at the blank-faced imp. "Anyway, your task is this: take one of those mines and throw it," I scanned the base and spotted a building I liked the look of — "over there, into that big chimney! I think it's a furnace. Let them freeze! And furnaces can sometimes explode in extreme cold anyway, so it's the perfect crime."

"And then?" an imp asked.

"Then, I want you all to fly away back to your own plane!" I declared. "And you'll receive your payment in full."

"Easy!" the little creatures cheered.

"What about us?" Rambo piped up.

"We're going for a quick jog," I said. "A *very* quick one."

"You mean... we're not going to watch?" the imp said, looking affronted.

"What do you take me for?" I spluttered, affronted by the suggestion. "Of *course* we're going to watch! And then, we jog!"

I knew I was taking a risk, but I just *had* to make a little mischief. I could have picked a more strategically important target, such as the munitions depot or the canteen, but the furnace was beautifully sneaky. It would take the enemy a while to identify the *real* source of the explosion...

... and by the time they realised the truth, me and Rambo would be long gone.

If the blast happened to kill someone important — an officer, say — the chase would begin immediately, and they might even send out helicopters. That would make our escape even harder... But no, I wasn't ready to engage them on that scale yet. I was still too weak. I needed energy, and I needed gold.

* * *

*New Imperial base*
*Sometime later*

Two important people were making their way across the base. The colonel (who was in charge of the place) was walking with the lieutenant colonel, discussing the just-completed visit of an extremely senior committee from the capital.

"Well, aren't *you* full of surprises, Varvarel!" the lieutenant colonel smiled. "I haven't seen the general that happy in a long time. And still, he was complaining about having to come out here, how it's the middle of nowhere, how it's always freezing cold and the forest is full of bears!" he chuckled. "But you managed to cheer him up. I think the bathhouse really did the trick. You know he has the gift of fire, of course, so for him to feel it, you have to heat the steam room to at least two hundred degrees! But you did it!" the lieutenant colonel was beaming by now. "You'll be getting a thank-you note as soon as he gets back to the city, mark my words!"

"Well, thank *you* for giving me the heads-up," the colonel patted the lieutenant on the shoulder.

"That was the only reason we got this bathhouse built in time. Look at that steam pouring from the chimney! I ordered that artefact-powered boiler specifically so we could heat the whole place just right! And then there were the massage rooms, the bar..."

"I agree, you did a wonderful job. And on what scale! The general wasn't the only one in there. The whole committee were sitting in there, too! Every one of them!"

"Well, what do you think they are, aliens?" the colonel frowned. "The committee are human, too. They want a good steam just like the rest of us!"

"Anyway, let's go and check on the general. I bet he's still lounging around, having the time of his life in there," the lieutenant chuckled.

As soon as he took his next step, the bath-house exploded.

When the echoes finally died away, the base was deathly silent, every pair of eyes fixed on the destroyed bathhouse. In fact, it had not been de-stroyed so much as pulverised into tiny specks of rubble.

The lieutenant corporal's cigar fell from his open mouth and rolled away into the crater left by the blast. The man instantly snapped to his senses.

"The general!" the man squeaked. "*How could this happen?*"

"All personnel! On the double!" the colonel roared. "The general might still be alive! All hands on deck, immediately!

As soon as the first soldiers stepped into the rubble, another explosion shook the earth. Then came another, and another... The explosions boomed for several minutes, until finally, nothing was left of the bathhouse but a small cluster of craters. There wasn't the slightest chance that any of the important people trapped inside had survived. Nonetheless, the moment the explosions stopped, a soldier ran up to the colonel with a bucket of water.

"What should I put out, sir?" the soldier asked. When everything was burning, it was hard to choose what to douse first.

"The ashes of my career," the colonel murmured, eyes wide. "Maybe lay some flowers, too."

END OF BOOK ONE

Want to be the first to know about our latest LitRPG, sci fi and fantasy titles from your favorite authors?

Subscribe to our **New Releases** newsletter:
http://eepurl.com/b7niIL

Thank you for reading *Me and My Demons!*

If you like what you've read, check out other sci-fi, fantasy and LitRPG novels published by Magic Dome Books:

**NEW RELEASES!**

**The One Who Changes the Future**
A Dystopian Portal Progression Fantasy Series
by Boris Romanovsky

**How I Built a Magic Empire**
A Portal Progression Fantasy Series
by Konstantin Zubov

**The Afflicted**
A LitRPG Apocalypse Adventure Series
by Konstantin Zubov

**An Ideal World for a Sociopath**
A LitRPG Apocalypse Adventure Series
by Oleg Sapphire

**Banned**
A LitRPG Apocalypse Adventure Series
by Michael Atamanov

**The Dark Summoner**
A LitRPG Apocalypse Adventure Series
by Andrei Tkachev

**Nanomachines**
A Progression Fantasy Adventure Series
by Nikolai Novikov

**The Other Side**
A Progression Fantasy Adventure Series
by Rodion Korablev

**The Last Paladin**
An Action & Adventure Progression Fantasy
by Roman Savarovsky

**Living Ice**
A Portal Progression Fantasy Series
by Dmitry Sheleg

**The Healer's Way**
A Portal Progression Fantasy Series
by Oleg Sapphire & Alexey Kovtunov

**The Selected**
A LitRPG Action Adventure Series
by Vasily Mahanenko & Yuri Vinokuroff

**The Last Portal Jumper**
A LitRPG Progression Fantasy Series
by Konstantin Zubov

**The Dark Healer**
A Historical Progression Fantasy Series
by Alex Toxic & Nadya Lee

**The Strongest Student**
A Portal Progression Action Fantasy Series
by Andrei Tkachev

**A Shelter in Spacetime**
A LitRPG Apocalypse Series
by Dmitry Dornichev

**The Coming of God of Death**
A Portal Progression Fantasy Series
by Dmitry Dornichev

**The Order of Architects**
A Portal Progression Fantasy Series
by Oleg Sapphire & Yuri Vinokuroff

**The Village**
A LitRPG Progression Fantasy Series
by Dmitry Dornichev & Alexey Kovtunov

**Law of the Jungle**
A Wuxia Progression Fantasy Adventure Series
by Vasily Mahanenko

**Condemned (Lord Valevsky: Last of the Line)**
A Progression Fantasy LitRPG Series
by Vasily Mahanenko

**Ghost in the System**
An Apocalypse LitRPG Series
by Alexey Kovtunov

**Crossroads of Oblivion**
A Portal Progression Fantasy Adventure Series
by Dem Mikhailov

**More books and series are coming out soon!**

In order to have new books of the series translated faster, we need your help and support! Please consider leaving a review or spread the word by recommending *Me and My Demons* to your friends and posting the link on social media. The more people buy the book, the sooner we'll be able to make new translations available.

Thank you!

Till next time!

www.ingramcontent.com/pod-product-compliance
Lightning Source LLC
LaVergne TN
LVHW020724200726
843506LV00009B/611